DEAD MEN WAG NO TAILS

DEAD MEN WAG
NO TAILS

Sarah Fox

**SEVERN
HOUSE**

First world edition published in Great Britain and the USA in 2025
by Severn House, an imprint of Canongate Books Ltd,
14 High Street, Edinburgh EH1 1TE.

severnhouse.com

Cover and jacket design by Piers Tilbury

British Library Cataloguing-in-Publication Data
A CIP catalogue record for this title is available from the British Library.

ISBN-13: 978-1-4483-1231-3 (cased)
ISBN-13: 978-1-4483-1232-0 (e-book)

All Severn House titles are printed on acid-free paper.

Typeset by Palimpsest Book Production Ltd., Falkirk,
Stirlingshire, Scotland.
Printed and bound in Great Britain by TJ Books,
Padstow, Cornwall.

Praise for Sarah Fox

"Filled with romance, murder, and magic"
Booklist on *Murder Most Owl*

"Cozy fans will find plenty to like"
Publishers Weekly on *Claret and Present Danger*

"[The] charming atmosphere, solid plotting, and several enticing recipes are sure to please cozy fans"
Publishers Weekly on *The Malt in Our Stars*

"Fox offers plenty of plausible suspects and a thrilling confrontation with the killer, along with a dash of decorous romance"
Publishers Weekly on *An Ale of Two Cities*

"Readers will cheer this brisk, literate addition to the world of small-town cozies"
Kirkus Reviews on *Wine and Punishment*

"Fox capably combines a smart, relatable heroine; plenty of clever red herrings; and the well-realized orchestra setting. Multiple kinds of appeal for cozy lovers"
Booklist on *Dead Ringer*

About the author

Sarah Fox was born and raised in Vancouver, British Columbia, where she developed a love for mysteries at a young age. When not writing novels, she is often reading her way through a stack of books or spending time outdoors with her English springer spaniel.

www.authorsarahfox.com

In loving memory of Nazzy

ONE

'Avast, ye scallywags! Prepare to walk the plank!'

A sword flashed in front of my face as if to punctuate the threat.

I jumped back, disconcerted by the proximity of the blade to my nose.

'Settle down, Jasper,' my aunt admonished the pirate who stood blocking my way. 'You're going to scare Georgie off before the festival even begins.'

The pirate lowered his sword and pushed his eyepatch up to his forehead, revealing the second of his two brown eyes, both of which sparkled with mischief. 'Just getting into character, Olivia,' he said with a grin.

He swept a lock of his graying brown hair off the fair skin of his forehead and stepped aside so my aunt and I could pass through the front door of the Twilight Inn, a beautiful Victorian mansion with its exterior painted cream and light gray. After stepping into the foyer, I paused to take in my surroundings. The hardwood floors gleamed, as did the wooden banister on the impressive, curving staircase that led to the next floor. A chandelier hung above us, the light from the August sun shining in through a transom window to hit the dozens of crystals, sending rainbows dancing on the papered walls.

'If you'll excuse me, ladies,' Jasper said, sheathing his sword, 'Catherine has set out an impressive spread of finger foods, and this scurvy dog has a hankering for some grub.'

Pulling his patch down over his eye again, Jasper disappeared into the dining room to our right. From my spot in the foyer, I could see a large table laden with a wide variety of food. If the smells teasing my nose were anything to go by, the snacks would be delicious.

'We weren't supposed to come in costume, were we?' I whispered to my aunt.

'No, we're fine,' she assured me. 'That's just Jasper for you. He never passes up an opportunity to pretend he's a kid again.'

Olivia had mentioned Jasper Hogan on our way to the meeting

at the Twilight Inn. She'd known him for decades – ever since she and her late husband moved to Twilight Cove – and as a history and pirate buff, he was the most enthusiastic supporter of the town's annual Dead Eye Days, named for Dead Eye Dawson, an eighteenth-century pirate believed by some to have plagued the shores of the Pacific Northwest back before the town of Twilight Cove existed.

I noted that several people had gathered in the parlor to our left, chatting quietly. None of them appeared to be in costume, although one man had what looked like a deep-red pirate coat draped over one arm. A tall woman with chestnut-brown hair and blue eyes was speaking with that man, but she excused herself and approached Auntie O and me with a warm smile on her face.

'Olivia, thank you for coming,' she said to my aunt. Then she turned her smile on me. 'And you must be Georgie.'

'Georgie Johansen,' I confirmed as I shook the woman's hand.

'I'm Catherine Adams,' she said.

'Catherine and her husband own the inn,' Auntie O added.

Catherine smiled. 'Our labor of love. You found the dog run all right?'

It was my turn to smile. 'Yes, thank you. Flossie and Fancy were happy to meet your German shepherd.'

When Catherine had phoned Olivia to ask us to attend the meeting of festival volunteers, she'd assured my aunt that we could bring my two English springer spaniels along with us. While much of the inn's property was unfenced, there was a large dog run located off the back of the owners' private quarters.

'I'm sure Loki's happy to have company.' Catherine inclined her head to our left. 'Please, come and have a bite to eat before the meeting starts.'

She led the way into the dining room, where Jasper was piling finger foods on a small plate. The table was longer than I'd realized. It probably could have seated twenty people easily. Another crystal chandelier hung from the teal-painted ceiling, which was bordered by white crown molding. The walls had dark wood wainscotting below teal-and-white wallpaper, and floor-to-ceiling windows at one end of the room let in plenty of daylight.

'You've done such a beautiful job with the place,' Auntie O commented as she picked up a plate from the stack at one end of the table.

'Thank you, Olivia.' Catherine looked around the dining room with a proud smile on her face. 'There were times when I wondered if we'd survive the renovations, but I'm pleased with how everything turned out.' She tugged her cell phone out of the pocket of her tailored gray pants and checked the time. 'Please, enjoy a snack. I need to run and get some papers before the meeting starts, but I'll be back shortly.'

As she slipped her phone back into her pocket, she hurried off down the hallway that led toward the back of the sprawling house. I didn't quite know what to expect of Dead Eye Days, this being the first time I would experience the festival. Auntie O and I had volunteered to help out with some of the preparations, but I didn't yet know what duties I'd be tasked with.

I grabbed a plate and made my way around the table, trying to decide what tasty treats I wanted to sample.

'Good thing the inn is fully booked,' Jasper said between bites of food. He stood on the far side of the table, his back to an impressive tiled fireplace that currently held an unlit log. 'Catherine and Roger need all the money they can get to pay for the work they did to this place.'

'Roger is Catherine's husband,' Auntie O explained for my benefit. 'They knew they needed to do some major renovations.'

'Some parts of the house were ready to fall down around them,' Jasper added.

Olivia picked up the story again. 'But the work ended up being far more extensive than they expected.'

'They found structural and electrical issues.' Jasper selected another finger sandwich and placed it on his already full plate. 'But everything's been taken care of now.'

'I haven't seen much of the inn yet,' I said, 'but so far everything looks amazing.'

Auntie O set an éclair on her plate. 'I'm glad they maintained the original charm and beauty of the house. It's more than a hundred and thirty years old.'

'Cyrus McDougall was the original owner,' Jasper said. 'He was a gold prospector who struck it rich near Baker City. After that, he moved his family here to Twilight Cove, which was just a small fishing village at the time.'

'At least you got that bit of history right,' someone said from behind me.

I turned to see a man in his late twenties standing in the archway that led to the foyer. He had tousled dark hair and brown eyes that were currently fixed on Jasper with disapproval.

'Ah, Flynn,' Jasper said, unfazed. 'Still as rigid in your beliefs as ever, I see.'

Flynn crossed his arms over his chest. 'If, by rigid, you mean I rely on facts rather than fantasy, then yes.'

Jasper set down his plate long enough to fill a glass from the punch bowl at the end of the table. 'You should try relaxing, Flynn,' he advised. 'It makes life more fun.'

That remark only deepened Flynn's frown.

Jasper grabbed his plate and raised his glass to us. 'Drink up, me hearties!'

He carried his food and glass of punch past Flynn and across the foyer to the parlor.

'Flynn,' Auntie O said brightly, and I knew she was trying to dispel the gloomy atmosphere that had settled over the room, 'this is my niece, Georgie. Georgie, Flynn Smith-Wu.'

Flynn's frown finally disappeared, replaced by a smile that transformed his face from dour to friendly and attractive. 'Nice to meet you, Georgie. I hear you're new to town.'

'I just moved here this summer,' I said.

Aunt Olivia put an arm around my shoulders. 'Though she did live here for a year in her teens.'

A group of four people entered the inn through the front door and Catherine greeted them in the foyer.

Then she called out, 'I think everyone's here now. Please bring your snacks into the parlor and we'll get the meeting started.'

Auntie O led the way out of the dining room, and Flynn fell into step with me as I crossed the foyer.

He leaned in to speak quietly to me. 'I see Catherine managed to rope you into volunteering for the farce that is Dead Eye Days.'

'I'm happy to volunteer,' I said with some confusion. 'Why do you call it a farce?'

'There were no pirates on these shores,' he replied. 'Sir Francis Drake might have sailed past this stretch of the coast while he was a privateer for Queen Elizabeth, but that's the extent of our town's real pirate history.'

Catherine overheard his last words. 'Now, now, Flynn. We all know your stance on the matter, but we want to have our fun. Annaleigh is in the conservatory.'

Looking a tad sheepish, Flynn backed out of the parlor and disappeared down the hall.

'Annaleigh?' I whispered to Olivia.

'The oldest of Catherine's two daughters,' my aunt explained. 'She and Flynn are dating.'

'Speaking of dating,' Leona Powell said, catching Olivia's statement, 'have you got your eye on any of Twilight Cove's eligible young bachelors, Georgie?'

Heat rushed to my cheeks and I didn't know what to say.

Thankfully, Catherine came to my rescue by clapping her hands and calling the meeting to order. I sank down into one of the available chairs set up to face Catherine, who stood in front of another gorgeous fireplace.

Auntie O sat down next to me. Sensing my embarrassment, she gave my hand a pat before turning her attention to Catherine.

Leona Powell was a sixty-something woman with short gray hair and gray eyes. She matched my height of five feet, nine inches, but personality-wise we were complete opposites. She was outgoing and outspoken, while I was far more of an introvert. Leona was a friend of Olivia's and a member of the Gins and Needles group my aunt belonged to. The women in that club got together twice a month to work on sewing or knitting projects while enjoying cocktails and gossip.

I'd met Leona once previously and she'd questioned me about my love life then too. While I did have a romantic interest in a certain good-looking man who lived in Twilight Cove, that wasn't a subject I was ready to talk about with anyone other than my aunt and Tessa Ortiz, my closest friend. To be honest, I hadn't talked about it with them much either, so it came as a great relief to me when Leona's attention shifted elsewhere.

When Catherine had everyone's attention, she gave us a quick rundown of the various events that would be happening during the three-day pirate festival. Then she started assigning tasks to those who didn't already have one.

'Chuck and Deena will be running the beer garden at the park each evening,' she said. 'Chuck, I know you had some questions about lighting. Lance is going to help you out and make sure everything is safe and up to code.'

The man I assumed was Chuck nodded at another man with graying dark hair and gray stubble on his jaw.

'I thought you were retiring, Lance, you old fogey,' Leona called out to the latter man.

He laughed. 'I'm semi-retired, Leona. And I'm three years younger than you.'

'I don't claim to be a spring chicken,' she said. 'But it's a good thing you haven't hung up your electrician's belt for good. With too much time on your hands, you'd be nothing but a troublemaker.'

'Takes one to know one,' Lance said with a grin, his gray eyes full of humor.

After some chuckles from around the room, Catherine got the meeting back on track.

'We're adding some face-in-the-hole boards this year,' Catherine said. 'We'll have a few of them set up at various places in the downtown area so people can take fun photos. Roger will be constructing them and Tessa Ortiz and my daughter Rayelle will be painting them.'

A young woman with a strong resemblance to Catherine gave a slight smile of acknowledgment. She sat off to the side of the room, with what looked like a sketchbook open on her lap. When she turned her head slightly, a silver stud in her nose caught the light coming in through one of the many windows. I noticed she had several piercings in each ear as well.

'Now,' Catherine continued, 'if anyone needs costume alterations or repairs, Tessa is the one to talk to.'

I glanced around for Tessa. I didn't spot her and the reason for that soon became clear.

'She couldn't make it to today's meeting,' Catherine added, 'but she'll be here tomorrow.'

Catherine handed out some assignments then, including my task of putting together gift baskets for a raffle. Auntie O volunteered to sell tickets for the raffle and to field any questions that might arise from the vendors who would be selling their wares at the town's beachfront park during the festival. Then the meeting wound down.

The attendees were getting to their feet when Jasper stepped in front of the fireplace and raised his sword into the air. 'Ahoy! Don't be so quick to abandon ship. I have something to tell you.'

Everyone sat down again and a few people exchanged glances, as if apprehensive about what might come next.

Jasper sheathed his sword and looked around at the waiting crowd, his patch pushed up on to his forehead again.

'Get on with it,' Lance encouraged.

A few people murmured their agreement.

'At this year's Dead Eye Days, I'll be making a special announcement,' Jasper said.

'You're announcing that you'll make an announcement?' Leona asked with a laugh.

Jasper ignored her. 'All I can tell you at this point is that it relates to Dead Eye Dawson and his buried treasure.'

A snort came from the direction of the foyer. I glanced that way to see Flynn standing in the parlor's doorway, arms crossed over his chest and an unimpressed expression on his face. 'The treasure that doesn't exist?'

'Oh, it exists,' Jasper countered.

'Only in wild and childish imaginations,' Flynn muttered.

Jasper's face flushed. 'It exists and I plan to prove it. Just you wait, Flynn.'

'Don't tell me Dead Eye's ghost has been talking to you,' Leona said.

That garnered some chuckles from around the room.

Jasper's face turned a deeper shade of red and I suddenly felt sorry for him.

'Who needs a ghost,' Jasper shot back, 'when you've got a map?'

The room fell silent as everyone stared at Jasper.

When he stayed quiet, Leona spoke up again. 'What map?'

Jasper lifted his chin. 'Dead Eye Dawson's long-lost treasure map.'

TWO

Everyone began talking at once. Some seemed to think Jasper was kidding about having the map, while others appeared to be intrigued and called out to Jasper to tell them more. Flynn, however, let out a scornful huff and stormed out the front door. He didn't slam it shut behind him, but he closed it a little harder than necessary.

At the front of the room, Jasper appeared flustered.

Auntie O jumped up and hurried over to him, and I followed on her heels.

'Are you all right, Jasper?' my aunt asked.

Worry flashed in his eyes before a scowl took over his face. 'They tricked me into making my announcement early.'

'So where is this treasure?' Lance called out.

'Like I'm going to tell you that,' Jasper said, a smug smile replacing his scowl. 'I might not be the first to have laid eyes on the map, but I'm quite certain I'm the only one who knows how to read it properly.'

'Are you sure this map is the real thing?' Catherine asked.

'The paper was tested and it's genuinely from the eighteenth century,' Jasper replied. 'While further tests would provide more confirmation of its authenticity, they can be expensive and I don't think they're necessary. I'll have all the proof I need once I have the treasure in my hands.'

Several people tried to pelt Jasper with more questions, but he refused to say anything more on the subject.

'I'm afraid you'll have to wait until the festival for more answers,' he said. 'Until then, I be wishin' ye a fair wind!' With a salute, he strode out the front door of the inn.

Everyone else stayed around to chatter about Jasper's announcement. While a couple of people seemed to have caught treasure fever, most viewed Jasper's claims with heavy skepticism. Having just met Jasper, I didn't know if he was prone to telling tall tales or not. As exciting as it would be to have real pirate treasure buried somewhere nearby, I wasn't ready to grab a shovel and start digging in random locations around town. The story about Dead Eye Dawson and his treasure was a good one, but I suspected it was nothing more than a story.

After a few minutes of listening to the various conversations going on around the room, Aunt Olivia and I took our leave.

'For a small seaside town, Twilight Cove sure has plenty of excitement,' I remarked on our way to the front door.

'And we do love our pirate tales,' Auntie O said as I opened the door for her. 'The whole town will probably end up with treasure fever now.'

'Do you think Jasper will really find pirate gold?' I asked.

'He can't find what isn't there,' a male voice said from behind us.

We turned to see an unfamiliar man coming down the steps. He was probably a bit older than my thirty-two years. His tousled hair was such a dark shade of brown that it was nearly black, and his eyes were an icy shade of blue.

'I don't believe we've met,' Auntie O said to him.

He offered her his hand. 'Ajax Wolfgang, writer and guest at the Twilight Inn.'

Olivia shook his hand and tipped her head my way. 'My niece Georgie here's a writer too.'

Ajax appraised me with his blue eyes. 'Copywriter?'

'Screenwriter,' I corrected, trying not to show that I was bristling at his obvious disdain.

'Good luck with that.' There was a smug note to his voice now. 'Not many make it past the aspiring stage.'

'No luck needed,' Auntie O said, her tone no longer quite so friendly. 'She's already very successful.'

Ajax smiled, though it looked more like a grimace. 'Nice to meet you both.'

It would have been difficult to sound less sincere.

He was about to stride past us when Auntie O addressed him again. 'I take it you don't believe in Dead Eye Dawson's treasure.'

He turned back long enough to smirk and say, 'I gave up believing in myths and legends right around age ten. That old fool probably still believes in Santa Claus.'

With that, he took off down the street with long strides.

Olivia glared after him. 'What an arrogant so-and-so! He assumed you couldn't possibly be a successful writer. And why? Because you're a woman?'

'Most likely.' I put a hand on her arm. 'Don't worry about it, Auntie O.'

It wasn't the first time I'd encountered someone like Ajax Wolfgang who looked down his nose at fellow writers, especially the female ones, and it wouldn't be the last.

My aunt let out an irritated huff and her ire faded away. She rarely got riled up, and I knew that the only reason Ajax had managed to get under her skin was because he'd attempted to insult me.

I changed the subject as we followed a paved path that led around the side of the inn. 'There seems to be a division in town when it comes to Dead Eye Dawson and his pirate treasure.'

Olivia nodded her agreement. 'There are some who strongly believe it exists, some who strongly believe it's nothing but a story, and there are plenty of people in the middle who are skeptical of the legend but would still love to get their hands on some treasure.'

'What about you?' I asked as we rounded the back corner of the inn. 'Do you believe Dead Eye Dawson was ever in the area?'

'I guess you'd say I'm one of the people in the middle,' she replied. 'The likelihood of finding pirate treasure in our town is slim, but it sure is fun to dream about, and I always get a kick out of Dead Eye Days. Plus, the festival draws in lots of tourists, and that's good for the town.'

As soon as the dog run came into view, my focus shifted away from thoughts of pirate treasure and zeroed in on my two English springer spaniels, Flossie and Fancy, and their new friend, Loki. All three dogs came running when they saw us approaching. I slipped through the gate, making sure that Loki didn't escape. I knew that Flossie and Fancy wouldn't run off if they got out of the dog run without their leashes on, but I didn't know what the German shepherd would do.

The dogs acted like I was a celebrity they'd waited all their lives to meet. I laughed as they wagged their tails and wiggled their bodies with excitement. Once I'd given them all plenty of attention, I snapped leashes on to Flossie's and Fancy's collars and managed to get out the gate without Loki following. Then the spaniels had to spend a moment greeting Aunt Olivia before we could get on our way.

'Hopefully, Dean will have my truck ready by now,' Auntie O said as we reached the street.

We set off along the sidewalk, heading for the local auto repair shop. We'd driven into town in Olivia's old truck since it needed a tune-up. After leaving the vehicle with local mechanic Dean Haskell, we'd walked over to the Twilight Inn. I didn't mind the exercise and neither did the dogs. It was a gorgeous summer day – wonderfully warm without being too hot and with a cloudless blue sky overhead.

I was, however, worried about my aunt. She'd broken her ankle just over two months ago and had only recently removed her boot and started walking without crutches again. I offered to go pick up the truck and drive it back to her so she wouldn't have to walk any farther, but she refused.

'Walking is good for me,' she said. 'And I'll have plenty of time to rest once I'm home.'

I didn't argue. I knew she wouldn't change her mind. She did agree to stop for a rest at the ice cream parlor, though, much to the delight of my dogs. Aunt Olivia and I each got two scoops of chocolate ice cream in a waffle cone, and we treated the excited spaniels to pup cups, which were filled with lactose-free vanilla ice cream. We sat on a shaded bench outside the shop while we enjoyed our treats.

Flossie and Fancy got to work immediately devouring their ice cream. Auntie O and I licked at our cones at a more leisurely pace. Across the street was the town's main beach, giving us a good view of the ocean. I spotted a man dressed as a pirate, standing next to a car in the beach parking lot. Thanks to his costume, he was easy to recognize as Jasper Hogan. He was arguing with a petite, dark-haired woman who appeared to be in her mid-fifties, like Jasper.

'Is that another skeptic?' I asked my aunt, directing her attention toward the woman with Jasper.

Olivia's forehead furrowed as she watched the two arguing. 'That's Elsie Suárez. She and Jasper have been dating for about a year now. I've never seen them argue before.'

We couldn't hear anything they were saying, but it was clear that they were disagreeing about something. As we watched, Elsie shook her head in exasperation and stormed away from Jasper. She climbed into a red sedan and slammed the door before starting the engine and driving away. Jasper watched her go and then walked off.

'Maybe Elsie's not a fan of Jasper's pirate fever,' I speculated.

'Could be,' Aunt Olivia said.

She slipped the last bit of her waffle cone – with no ice cream left – to Fancy and I did the same for Flossie.

'Jasper does have a tendency to get fixated on things,' she continued. 'With the map in his possession, he's probably living and breathing pirates and treasure these days.'

We got up from the bench and started walking up the hill, away from the ocean.

'Jasper will probably start looking for the treasure right away,' I said. 'I don't know him, but from what I've witnessed, I can't picture him waiting very long.'

'No, I'm sure he'll be out there searching tomorrow, if not today,' Auntie O agreed. 'The question is, will he find anything?'

'I'm not sure what to believe about the history of pirates along the coast of Twilight Cove,' I admitted, 'but I'm still curious to know if he'll find real pirate loot or not.'

Aunt Olivia smiled. 'It's hard to remain untouched by treasure fever. I'm curious myself. But it probably won't be long before we know if Dead Eye Dawson's treasure is real or just the stuff of a good story.'

THREE

Dean Haskell had Aunt Olivia's truck ready and waiting when we arrived at the auto repair shop. He gave each dog an enthusiastic greeting, which made him an immediate friend of theirs, and then he led the way into his office, where my aunt paid the bill.

'She might be old, but she's still in good shape,' Dean said as he handed the keys to Auntie O. 'I wish I could say the same about myself.'

'Come on now, Dean,' Olivia chided. 'You don't look a day over fifty-five.'

Dean laughed and rubbed a hand over his short gray beard. It matched the color of his hair, which he wore long enough to pull back into a short ponytail. A streak of grease stained the fair skin of his forehead, which – like the rest of his face – sported several creases.

'We both know that's not true,' he said. 'My sixty-fifth birthday is coming up next year, and I'm thinking of retiring.' He massaged his right hand with his left. 'The arthritis in my hands is giving me trouble. I'm calling it quits for today and heading home for that very reason.'

'Won't you go crazy if you retire?' Aunt Olivia asked.

'I've wondered the same thing,' he admitted. 'And that's the only reason I haven't already turned in my tools and coveralls.' He nodded toward a young woman who was bent over the open hood of a dark blue minivan. 'Daphne is interested in taking over the business. Maybe I'll hand the reins over to her and help out a few hours a week. Just enough to keep me from getting bored.'

'I'm glad Daphne is willing to take over for you,' Aunt Olivia said. 'That means we won't have to worry about entrusting our vehicles to total strangers once you've retired.'

'You definitely don't need to worry with Daphne on the job,' Dean assured her.

On that note, Olivia thanked him and climbed into the driver's seat of her truck. I leaned the passenger seat forward so the dogs could jump up into the back seat. Once they were settled, I joined my aunt in the front of the cab.

We were about to turn out on to the street when Auntie O stopped the truck and rolled down her window. Jasper, still in his pirate costume, was striding along the sidewalk toward us.

'Are you all right, Jasper?' my aunt asked.

He stopped by her window. 'Fine, fine,' he said, brushing off her question, his gaze shifting to the auto repair shop. 'Is Dean working today?'

'He was,' Auntie O replied, 'but he's leaving early.'

'Darn,' Jasper muttered, looking distracted.

'Is there something wrong with your car?' Olivia asked.

'I've got to run,' he said, as if he hadn't heard the question. 'See you later, Olivia.'

Jasper turned and walked briskly back down the street.

With a shake of her head, my aunt rolled up her window. 'Absent-minded as always.' As she pulled out on to the street, she directed a question at me. 'What are your plans for the rest of the day?'

'I need to spend a few hours writing.' I was about halfway through my latest screenplay, a thriller that I hoped would be made into a TV movie. 'Other than that, just looking after the animals.'

Fancy gave a 'woo-woo' from the back seat.

I smiled and amended my statement. 'And taking Flossie and Fancy for a walk.' I tugged my phone out of the pocket of my shorts and woke it up. No new messages.

Auntie O glanced my way before returning her eyes to the road. 'Have you heard from Callum?'

'Not since yesterday,' I said, trying my best to sound nonchalant.

'I'm sure you'll hear from him before the end of the day.'

I tucked my phone away. 'I'm not worried.'

Callum was the farm manager Olivia had hired to work at her animal sanctuary back in the spring, a few weeks before I'd arrived in town. He and I had barely had a chance to strike up the beginning of a romance before I'd gone back to Los Angeles so I could pack up my apartment and get ready to move to Twilight Cove permanently. About three weeks after I returned to the Oregon coast, Callum had left on a trip of his own.

He was a retired major league baseball player and had received a call from a former teammate, one who was just a rookie when Callum was playing his final seasons in the major leagues. He'd been a mentor to the younger player, Javi Fuentes-Otero. Javi was a rising star, but recently he'd fallen into a slump hitting-wise and was really struggling. He'd asked Callum to fly to Toronto and see if he could help him turn things around. Although Callum had hesitated, not wanting to leave all the farm work to me and Aunt Olivia, we'd both urged him to go. We knew he'd feel guilty if he wasn't there to support his friend.

While I believed that Callum loved working at the animal sanctuary, and while I didn't doubt that he had feelings for me, I did wonder if returning to the world of baseball would make him realize he missed it so much that he wouldn't want to return to life in Twilight Cove.

OK, so maybe I was a bit worried.

So often, I'd grown attached to people only to move away or have those people disappear from my life. I'd changed schools frequently growing up, leaving friends behind. I'd lost my mom at a young age and all my grandparents by the time I finished college. On the rare occasions that I'd ventured into the dating world, I ended up being ghosted or dumped by text message early on in the relationship. I wanted to protect my heart, so it frightened me how quickly I'd started falling for Callum. Even though we'd spent a mere few weeks together, I knew my heart would crack if he decided he didn't want to stay in Twilight Cove any longer.

When we got back to the farm, I checked my phone once more, but it still had no new messages for me. I set the device well out of reach as I settled at the table in the farmhouse kitchen to spend a few hours on my screenplay. Callum was supposed to return in a few days. He'd been so good about messaging me several times each day while he was away, so part of me wondered if today's silence had to do with him considering if he really wanted to return.

Enough, I silently scolded myself.

All thoughts of Callum and pirate treasure would have to wait.

I had a script to write.

* * *

That evening, Auntie O and I worked together to feed all of the sanctuary's animals. We had chickens and ducks, goats and donkeys, alpacas and horses. Until recently, we'd also had pigs, but Olivia had found a new home for them at a farm about an hour away from Twilight Cove, where they were being well loved and well cared for by a couple and their three children. The newest additions to the sanctuary were two adorable Nigora goats named Sid and Lilybelle. Sid was black and Lilybelle was white.

Thanks to Callum, I knew that a Nigora goat was a cross between a Nigerian Dwarf goat and an Angora, and they were known for their good milk production and their quality fleece. Like the other goats we had on the farm, Sid and Lilybelle were sweet and friendly, but they also had a mischievous side.

I lingered in the goat pen, giving the newcomers lots of attention. They seemed to be settling in well at the sanctuary, but I wanted to make absolutely sure that they felt safe, loved and at home.

Flossie and Fancy kept me company the entire time. When I walked out of the barn with my chores complete, the dogs trotted ahead of me. After a few paces, they sat down and looked back toward the barn. Flossie gave a short bark and Fancy let out a 'woo'. I followed their gazes up to the peak of the roof. A beautiful great horned owl sat perched there.

'Evening, Euclid,' I called out.

The owl ruffled his feathers and took off toward the woodland that stood between the back of the farm and the ocean.

Some people might have considered me nutty if I said the owl was a friend of mine, but that's what he was. I'd adopted Flossie and Fancy after their previous human, Dorothy, had been murdered back in June, an event that had shaken the peaceful town of Twilight Cove to its core. Although I'd initially dismissed the rumors about Dorothy being a witch, I no longer felt so certain that there was no truth to that story. While Dorothy may or may not have had magical powers, her dogs certainly did. Flossie could open any lock with a touch of her paw, and Fancy could camouflage herself and glow with blue light at will. Euclid had been a friend of Dorothy's as well, though he still lived in the wild. Now I counted myself lucky enough to call him a friend. While I didn't yet know if Euclid had any special powers, he certainly had an uncanny intelligence and had come to my aid while I was in a bind back when I first arrived in Twilight Cove.

I hadn't yet told anyone about the animals' abilities. Whether I'd ever share that information with Aunt Olivia or Callum, I hadn't yet decided. I hated keeping secrets from them, but I also didn't want them thinking I was crazy if the animals declined to give a demonstration of their powers in front of anyone other than me. Whatever my decision would be, it was one for another day. For now, I tried not to dwell on the subject, although it always hung there in the back of my mind.

Aunt Olivia came out of the barn then, so the dogs and I waited until she caught up to us.

'I think I'll pop back into town this evening,' she said as we walked together. 'I want to check in with Jasper and make sure he's OK. That argument with Flynn seemed to leave him flustered.'

'Do you want me to come with you?' I offered.

'Only if you want to,' Auntie O said. 'I'd love your company, but I don't want to keep you from anything.'

'We'll come along for the ride, won't we, girls?' I said to Flossie and Fancy.

Flossie wagged her tail and woofed, while Fancy tipped her head back and let out a long 'woo' of agreement. My aunt and I laughed.

'That's settled, then,' Olivia said. 'I'll wash up and change and then meet you in the driveway.'

With that decided, she struck off in the direction of the converted carriage house, while the dogs and I continued on to the yellow-and-white farmhouse. After breaking her ankle, Olivia had moved into the carriage house, where she had a bathroom and bedroom on the ground floor. That was meant to be a temporary arrangement while she recovered, but when I'd decided to move to Twilight Cove, she'd insisted that I live in the farmhouse while she stayed in her new quarters. She preferred the coziness of the smaller dwelling, having found the farmhouse big and empty on her own. The house was big for me too, but I had the dogs to keep me company, and Aunt Olivia unwaveringly maintained that she wanted to remain in the carriage house. I, in turn, had vowed to pay rent, something that my aunt didn't want to accept. Eventually, however, I'd worn her down after pointing out – several times – that she could put the money toward the running of the sanctuary.

Once at the farmhouse, I took a quick shower and changed into clean clothes. I spent a few minutes taming the frizz out of my short wavy hair, and then I emerged from the bathroom. I expected Flossie and Fancy to be waiting for me in the hall, but they were nowhere in sight. A woof from Flossie let me know that they were in my bedroom. I peeked into the room and saw them sitting by my closet.

'What's going on, girls? We don't want to keep Auntie O waiting.'

Flossie, who had black-and-white fur in contrast to her sister's brown-and-white coat, pressed her nose to the closed closet door. Fancy remained sitting but pointed her nose to the ceiling and let out a long 'woo'.

The spaniels had trained me well, so I opened the closet door.

'What are you looking for?' I asked.

Both dogs wiggled their way into the closet, nosing at one of the cubbyholes where I kept sweaters and accessories. I finally realized what they were after. I leaned past the dogs and retrieved the two bandannas I'd recently purchased for them at the Pet Palace, their favorite store.

'The pirate festival hasn't started yet, but I'm guessing you think you should show off your new togs anyway.'

Fancy replied with an 'a-woo' while Flossie wagged her tail and bounced around in a circle, both of them radiating excitement.

'All right. Message received,' I said with a laugh.

The dogs sat patiently while I fastened the bandannas around their necks. They were black with a white skull and crossbones, like a Jolly Roger flag.

I stepped back to admire the dogs. 'You're adorable.'

They thumped their tails, their brown eyes bright.

I glanced down at my T-shirt and denim shorts. 'But now I feel underdressed.'

With a woof, Flossie scampered back into the closet and pressed her nose to the garment bag that held my pirate costume.

Laughing, I tugged her out of the closet and shut the door. 'I'm saving my costume for the actual festival.'

Flossie and Fancy didn't waste any more time trying to convince me. They bounded out the bedroom door and clattered down the stairs to the main floor before I'd even made it out into the hall. I caught up to them at the back door, where they waited with tails wagging. As soon as I opened the door, they burst outside, raced down the porch steps and galloped across the yard to greet Aunt Olivia as she emerged from the carriage house.

My aunt gave the spaniels lots of attention and complimented their new bandannas. Then we all bundled into my car.

'Whereabouts does Jasper live?' I asked my aunt as I turned the car on to Larkspur Lane.

'Sunset Heights,' she replied. 'It's a newer neighborhood on the far side of town. Take Ocean Drive until we hit Hemlock Street.'

It didn't take long to reach Ocean Drive, the road that hugged the coastline. Flossie and Fancy sat in the back seat, watching out the windows as we whizzed along. We passed Main Street, but I slowed down before we reached Hemlock Street.

On our right, Twilight Park sat between the road and the beach. It was a broad expanse of green grass with a picnic area, a small playground and a gazebo. At the moment, more than a dozen people in pirate costume were gathered around the white octagonal structure.

'Let's stop here for a minute,' Auntie O said. 'I'd love to get a sneak peek at everyone's costumes.'

I pulled into the lot at the far end of the park and found a free spot for my car. I'd only just shut off the engine when a blur of movement caught my eye a split second before Captain Jack Sparrow sprawled across the hood of my car.

FOUR

'Son of a biscuit eater!' The pirate heaved himself off the front of my car and staggered around.

Flossie and Fancy barked and danced about in the back seat. I told them to wait in the car as I climbed out.

'These boots are too big!' Captain Sparrow lamented.

A pirate queen strode over our way, her black boots shiny and her hat at a jaunty angle on her head. 'Utter bilge! It's not the boots; it's all that grog you've been chugging.'

Laughter rang through the air as more people dressed as pirates came over our way.

'All right,' Catherine Adams called out. She was one of only a few people wearing modern-day clothes. 'I think you've got your characters down pat, but I still want to do a run-through of all the scenes we've got planned.'

Captain Jack removed his hat and gave me an unsteady bow. 'Apologies for putting me grubby hands on your carriage.'

'Apology accepted, Captain,' I said with a smile.

Aunt Olivia climbed out of the car, laughing as the pirate staggered off with his mates, all of them heading in the direction of the gazebo.

'I think we got our sneak peek,' I said.

Auntie O was still smiling. 'If that's just a teaser, then I definitely want to be here to see the full performances.'

'Same here,' I agreed.

Although Flossie and Fancy were well trained, I snapped leashes on to their collars before letting them out of the car. That gave me peace of mind with all the people around and the traffic going by on Twilight Cove's busiest road.

As we crossed the park toward the gazebo, I spotted a familiar face among the costumed pirates. My friend Tessa Ortiz noticed me at almost the same moment. She smiled and waved as she broke away from the other pirates to come and greet us. She said hello to Aunt Olivia and me, and then crouched down to give each dog a hug and a kiss on the top of the head. Flossie and Fancy rewarded her with tail wags and kisses on her cheek.

'I didn't know you were one of the actors,' I said as Tessa straightened up and the dogs sat down between my aunt and me.

'I'm not,' Tessa replied, 'but I'm doing some painting, and I couldn't help myself.' She looked down at her outfit of a red-and-black striped skirt, black boots, a white peasant blouse and a black-and-red corset. 'I love costumes, and even though the festival doesn't start until next weekend, I knew I wouldn't be out of place dressed like this tonight.'

'You look great,' I told her, and Fancy gave a yip of agreement.

'Thank you.' Tessa twirled once so her skirt flared out around her.

Flossie copied her and we all laughed.

'How is the painting going?' Aunt Olivia asked Tessa once we'd calmed down.

'Come and have a look.' Tessa led us over to the far side of the gazebo, a short distance away from where the actors were now gathered, listening to instructions from Catherine.

When we rounded the small structure, I saw several face-in-the-hole boards standing on the grass with painting supplies strewn about around them. Designs had been sketched on to the boards, but so far only one had paint on it. That one looked like a ship, and the holes where people could put their faces were made to look like portholes.

'I thought Rayelle Adams was helping with the painting,' Aunt Olivia said.

'She is,' Tessa said, 'but she's also acting in one of the scenes, so she has to rehearse as well. Though I haven't seen her yet.' My friend glanced over at the group of actors, but then returned her attention to us as she picked up a paintbrush. 'Did you hear about the treasure map?'

'We were at the meeting when Jasper made the announcement,' I said.

'It caused quite a stir,' Auntie O added.

'Do you think it's authentic?' Tessa asked, her brown eyes alight with excitement.

'Jasper thinks it is,' Olivia replied.

I voiced a thought that had been on my mind for the past couple of hours. 'He never said where he got it.'

Tessa started painting white sails on the pirate ship. 'Maybe he bought it from Giles Gilroy.'

'He owns the local antiques shop,' my aunt added for my sake. 'But it wasn't very long ago that Jasper told me he'd never buy antiques from Giles.'

'Why's that?' I asked.

'He wouldn't say.'

'Maybe Jasper found it somewhere,' I suggested.

'Could be,' Tessa agreed.

Auntie O and I spent a few more minutes chatting with Tessa while she painted.

'We should probably head to Jasper's place before it gets any later,' Olivia said eventually.

After sharing some parting words with Tessa, we returned to my car with the dogs. I drove a little farther along Ocean Drive before turning on to Hemlock Street. From there, Aunt Olivia guided me through a series of turns that took us into a residential neighborhood at the edge of town. A sign at the entrance to the neighborhood welcomed us to Sunset Heights.

'When were these homes built?' I asked as we followed a curving road lined with a mix of ranchers and two-story homes.

'About twelve years ago.'

'No wonder I don't remember this neighborhood.' I'd lived with Auntie O for a year in my teens while my dad was overseas, but that was about fifteen years ago, and I hadn't returned to Twilight

Cove until recently. 'The houses are nice, but I prefer the character of the older neighborhoods.'

'I feel the same,' my aunt said.

She instructed me to turn right at the next intersection, so I slowed down to do so. It was growing dark now and I almost missed the flash of movement off to my left. A woman dressed in a pirate costume ran across the front lawns of the houses, a purple sash flowing out behind her. She soon disappeared into deep shadows.

I made the turn and spotted another pedestrian. This person wore a black sweatshirt with the hood up. They walked quickly, going in the opposite direction from us. I never got a look at their face, but when I glanced in the rearview mirror, I noticed a white logo on the back of the sweatshirt.

Returning my attention to the road ahead of me, I followed Aunt Olivia's next instructions and soon pulled up to the curb in front of a rancher with an attached garage. Light glowed in one of the windows, and a blue sedan sat in the driveway.

'Looks like Jasper's home,' Aunt Olivia said as she undid her seatbelt. 'That's his car in the driveway.'

This time, I didn't bother with the dogs' leashes. Once out of the car, I breathed in the fresh evening air. Even though the sun had disappeared from the sky, it was still warm out, and the sound of crickets and frogs reached my ears. Otherwise, the neighborhood was quiet, with no cars driving by.

'There's something else that worries me about this map,' Aunt Olivia said as we walked up the driveway. 'Somebody could be trying to make Jasper look like a fool.'

'You mean it might be a hoax?'

'It's a possibility,' she said with a sigh. 'I hope he acquired the map from a trustworthy source, but sometimes he lets his excitement get the best of him.'

I voiced one of the many thoughts that had been swirling around in my mind since Jasper's announcement. 'If the map is real and someone else had it in their possession, why wouldn't they have searched for the treasure themselves before selling the map?'

'Remember what Jasper said at the inn? He believes he's the only one who knows how to read the map.'

That had slipped my mind. 'How do you think that's possible? Could the map be coded or something?'

Auntie O shrugged. 'I haven't a clue.'

'I guess there's only one way to find out if there really is treasure still to be found.'

My aunt nodded as she started up the few concrete steps leading to the front door. 'Let Jasper dig and see what happens.'

When we reached the front door, Aunt Olivia rang the bell. I listened for the sound of approaching footsteps but heard nothing. Beside me, Flossie whined quietly.

My aunt rang the bell again. When that still got no response, she knocked on the door.

'That's odd,' she said after waiting several seconds. 'Maybe he's in the backyard?'

Flossie whined again and then bounded down the steps and took off around the side of the house.

'Flossie!' I called out.

Fancy took off after her sister.

I hurried down the steps and ran after the spaniels. There was no fence on Jasper's property, so I jogged right around the house. I found Flossie and Fancy sitting by the back door, waiting for me.

'What are you up to?' I asked as I approached them.

Fancy tipped her head back and bayed.

The sound sent a prickle of unease dancing along my spine.

As Fancy fell quiet, I realized that the back door stood ajar.

Dread settled in my chest like a lead weight. For some reason, the open door struck me as ominous. Maybe Flossie had unlocked it, but I didn't think so. I'd never seen her actually open a closed door, and the round knob would have been difficult for her to turn even if she'd tried.

Aunt Olivia came around the back corner of the house. 'Any sign of him?'

'No,' I replied, 'but the back door is open.'

Olivia reached my side. When her gaze landed on the door, I could tell she felt as uneasy as I did.

She rapped on the door frame and called through the opening, 'Jasper! Are you home? It's Olivia and my niece, Georgie.'

Nothing but silence came back at us.

Fancy whined and Flossie pushed her nose against the door. It swung open wider.

Before I could tell the spaniels to stay outside, they rushed into the house.

'Flossie! Fancy!' I called.

Fancy bayed again, the sound both eerie and mournful.

I exchanged a glance with my aunt. Then, in unspoken agreement, we entered the house, with me taking the lead.

The back door led into the kitchen. Across the room, a doorway opened to a hallway that stretched toward the front of the house. The dogs sat waiting for us in the kitchen, but once we were inside, they hurried into the hall.

I hesitated, a sense of foreboding hanging heavily in the air around me. 'Maybe we should wait outside and call the police,' I whispered to Auntie O. 'What if there are robbers in the house?'

The mere thought terrified me, especially since Flossie and Fancy had disappeared from sight.

'But what if Jasper's been hurt and needs immediate help?' my aunt whispered back. She produced her phone from her pocket. 'I'll be ready to call for help in an instant.'

That made me feel marginally better, but I still considered grabbing a frying pan or other potential weapon. Jasper didn't have any pans or other heavy objects sitting out in the open, though, so I scratched that plan.

Flossie woofed somewhere deeper in the house. I realized that she and Fancy would have been making far more of a fuss if they'd found someone with nefarious intentions in the house.

I headed in the direction of the sound, turning down a left-hand branch of the hallway. A door stood open at the end of the short corridor. I could see Fancy sitting just inside the room, her brown-and-white back to us.

'That's Jasper's study,' Auntie O whispered from behind me.

'Shiver me timbers!' a voice yelled from inside the room.

My heart nearly leapt out of my body.

There was a loud kissing sound, followed by maniacal laughter.

I was about to turn tail and run out of the house when a loud squawk made me pause.

I pressed one hand to my chest and put the other to the wall for support as I turned toward my aunt. 'Is that . . . a parrot?'

The surprise that had widened Olivia's eyes faded away. 'I forgot about Gizmo. He's an African grey.'

My thumping heart slowed. 'Sounds like he's caught Jasper's pirate fever.'

An 'a-woo' came from Fancy, and the parrot immediately copied the sound.

Shaking off the last of my surprise, I continued along the hall. When I reached the study's threshold, Fancy stood up and turned around to face me, letting out a sad whine.

The first thing I noticed upon stepping into the room was a giant birdcage with Gizmo the parrot sitting on one of the many perches. Then I took in the sight of a wall of shelves displaying books and a variety of small antiques and artifacts.

My gaze danced over those items in mere seconds before landing on Flossie. She stood across the spacious room, looking at something on the other side of the large desk that sat on a Persian rug.

Some of my apprehension had dispersed in the wake of Gizmo's outburst, but now it returned full force.

'Jasper?' I said, my voice sounding too loud in the quiet that had settled over the room.

Gizmo ruffled his feathers as I took a few more steps into the room.

'Oh no. Oh no,' the parrot said, shifting restlessly on his perch.

Flossie moved aside and I rounded the desk.

I drew in a sharp breath as horror hit me like a wrecking ball.

Jasper lay sprawled on his back, with a blade that appeared to be attached to a pistol sticking into his chest.

My aunt let out a cry of shock from over my shoulder.

'Auntie O,' I said, my voice surprising me with its steadiness, 'make that call.'

Her face pale, she nodded and put the phone to her ear.

I dropped to my knees at Jasper's side and touched my fingers to his neck.

Just as I'd feared, he had no pulse.

FIVE

A siren wailed in the distance, quickly drawing closer.
My aunt lowered the phone from her ear, looking confused. 'Is that emergency vehicle coming here?'

She put her phone back to her ear before I could respond. I didn't know the answer to her question, but the siren was definitely getting louder with every passing second.

While my aunt spoke to the emergency operator, I returned my full attention to Jasper. His skin was still warm, so he hadn't been without a pulse for long, but I wasn't sure if I should try to perform chest compressions when there was a blade sticking out of him, perilously close to his heart.

'Yes, I'll go now,' Olivia said into the phone. Then she addressed me, 'That's the police on their way here. I'll go out to meet them.'

She hurried out of the study. I almost called after her, wanting her to ask the emergency operator if I should try to administer any form of first-aid, but then the siren cut off right near the house. Hopefully, the officers would be on the scene within seconds.

I climbed to my feet, realizing that I'd missed kneeling in Jasper's blood by a mere inch or two. I backed away from him and glanced over my shoulder, looking for Flossie and Fancy. They stood on either side of the open door. They sniffed at the air, and I realized that there was a faint odor, one that I couldn't place. The harder I tried to focus on the scent, the fainter it seemed to get.

Flossie whined and moved around the desk toward the black leather swivel chair. For a second, I could see only the white tip of her tail, but then she popped up, resting her front paws on the surface of the desk. She pressed her nose to a book lying open on the blotter. Then she looked at me expectantly.

I hurried around the desk. The book appeared to be a journal or diary. The words 'Old Birch Road' had been written in blue ink, but the open pages were otherwise empty.

Voices sounded from near the front of the house, quickly followed by hurried footsteps. I darted out from behind the desk and patted my leg so the dogs would follow me. We gathered together at the side of the door just as two police officers strode in. They quickly took charge of the scene, converging on Jasper and asking us a few quick questions. Two other officers arrived in short order, one of them Officer Brody Williams, whom I'd met previously. They escorted Olivia, me and the dogs outside. As I left the study, I averted my eyes from Jasper and tried to detect the faint smell again. I had no luck.

Out in the backyard, the police officers separated Olivia and me.

'I'm sorry this has happened to you again,' Brody Williams said as I sank down on to a low stone wall at the back of Jasper's yard.

I'd first met Brody back in June after I'd found the body of Dorothy, the woman Flossie and Fancy had lived with before.

I drew in a deep breath and let it out slowly, trying to calm myself so I could think clearly.

'Earlier today, Jasper claimed to have found Dead Eye Dawson's treasure map,' I said. 'Do you think someone was trying to steal it?'

Over on the patio, my aunt was speaking with another officer. Although I could tell she was trying to maintain her composure, she was using a tissue to wipe tears off her face. My heart ached for her. It was bad enough for me to see Jasper like that when I barely knew him. Olivia had been friends with him for decades.

Thankfully, Flossie had stayed by Olivia's side while Fancy stuck with me. I was grateful for Fancy's company, and I knew my aunt felt the same way about Flossie's presence. As she spoke to the other officer, she kept a hand on the black-and-white spaniel's head.

'At this point, we don't know what happened,' Brody said.

'But it was murder.' I didn't see how there could be any other explanation.

'It certainly looks that way.'

'How did you know to come to Jasper's house?' I asked. 'By the time Aunt Olivia called nine-one-one, we could already hear a siren.'

'A neighbor called to report a gunshot.'

'Coming from Jasper's house?'

'Or in the vicinity,' Brody said.

'That must have happened right before we arrived. We didn't hear anything.' I tried to focus on how I could help the police with their investigation. 'There were a couple of people out and about in the neighborhood when we were on our way here.'

Brody was interested to hear that. I told him about the woman dressed as a pirate and the person in the hoodie. I wished I could provide him with more details about one or both of the individuals, but I couldn't remember much. Although I knew there'd been a white logo on the back of the hoodie, all I could tell Brody was that the logo had consisted of several curving lines. I'd been too far away to observe any further details.

Brody asked me a series of questions and I provided him with a witness statement. While we talked, paramedics and other police officers arrived on the scene. Among the other officers was Isaac Stratton, the chief of the Twilight Cove Police Department. He paused to speak with my aunt before pulling protective covers over his shoes and entering the house.

Soon after, my aunt and I were allowed to go home. Brody walked us around the house and down the driveway. I gave my aunt a hug before she could climb into the car.

'I'm so sorry about your friend, Auntie O,' I whispered as I held her.

She returned the hug and patted my back. 'Thank you, sweetie.'

I released her and we got in the car with the dogs. It took some maneuvering to get around all the emergency vehicles and the small crowd of curious neighbors who had gathered on the dark street, but eventually I was able to pick up speed and drive freely.

Back at the farm, I offered to keep Auntie O company, but she said she would go to bed and try to sleep. I suspected she wouldn't have much luck with that, but I gave her another hug and told her to phone me at any hour if she wanted me to come over to be with her.

The dogs and I waited until my aunt disappeared inside before we headed into the farmhouse. In the kitchen, I sank into the nearest chair. Flossie and Fancy came up on either side of me and rested their chins on my lap.

'I can't believe this happened,' I said as I stroked the glossy fur on their heads. 'Could someone really have killed Jasper for a silly treasure map? It might not even be real.'

Fancy whined and I sighed.

'I guess we won't know anything concrete for a while. Let's just hope the police find whoever did this.'

I got to my feet, deciding to head for bed and at least try to get some sleep.

'I wonder what will happen to Gizmo,' I said, thinking of the parrot as I climbed the stairs to the second floor.

The spaniels clambered up ahead of me, offering no insight into the parrot's future.

I made a mental note to contact the police in the morning to check on the bird. There was no longer anything Olivia and I could do to help Jasper, but, if needed, we could provide a safe haven for his beloved parrot.

I met up with Auntie O in the barn the next morning. Anyone who didn't know her likely wouldn't have noticed that anything was wrong, but I could tell she wasn't quite her normal self. There were dark circles beneath her blue eyes, which weren't as bright and cheery as usual, and she lacked her usual energy.

'Did you get any sleep?' I asked as we led the alpacas out to the pasture.

'A little,' she replied. 'I spent a lot of time thinking about Jasper, hoping he didn't suffer too much.'

I closed the gate to the pasture once all the alpacas were safely through. 'I wish you hadn't seen him like that.'

'It's certainly not the way I want to remember him.'

We stayed by the fence to watch the alpacas for a few minutes. The youngest, Violet, was born at the sanctuary back in June. She was a healthy and spunky young alpaca with white fleece and big, beautiful eyes. At the moment, she was cavorting about the pasture while the older alpacas grazed peacefully. Violet's mother, Daisy, occasionally looked up to keep an eye on her daughter, but otherwise she stayed focused on munching the grass.

'I also spent a lot of time thinking about Gizmo,' Aunt Olivia said after a moment. 'I talked to Elsie first thing this morning to ask about him. She said she can't look after him, so the police are planning to hand him over to a shelter.'

I rested my forearms on the top of the fence. 'I was planning to call Chief Stratton to ask if we could bring Gizmo here until we know what Jasper wanted to happen with him.'

I wondered if the poor bird had any real grasp of what had transpired in front of him the night before. For his sake, I hoped not.

'I had the same thought,' my aunt said. 'I left a message for Isaac after I spoke with Elsie. Hopefully, he'll get back to me soon.'

'Do you think the pirate festival will be canceled because of the murder?' I asked.

'I hope not,' Auntie O replied, 'because that's the last thing Jasper would have wanted. He loved the festival.'

'Then I hope it goes on as planned too.' I pushed off from the fence. 'I'm supposed to meet Tessa for breakfast, and then we were going to head over to the Twilight Inn to help out with the Dead Eye Days preparations, but I can cancel if you want company.'

'I'll be fine,' she assured me. 'You stick with your plans and leave the dogs with me. They can keep me company while I make some phone calls to Jasper's other friends. After that, I'll probably do some baking.'

We turned and headed toward the barn.

'Call me if you need anything,' I said.

Auntie O put an arm around me and gave me a squeeze as we

walked side by side. 'I'm so glad you decided to move here to Twilight Cove, Georgie.'

I smiled despite the cloud of sadness hanging over us. 'Me too, Auntie O.'

SIX

T he Moonstruck Diner, located on Main Street, was one of my favorite hangouts when I briefly lived in Twilight Cove as a teenager. Now that I'd moved back to the seaside town, the retro diner had once again become one of my top choices for a place to meet my friend for a bite to eat. With the black-and-white checkerboard floor and the turquoise-and-chrome color scheme, walking into the diner was like stepping into the 1950s.

By the time I arrived at the diner, the breakfast rush was winding down, but the place was still more than half full. Tessa waved to me from our favorite booth at the back of the restaurant, and I hurried to join her after saying a quick hello to Jackie, the owner.

Over a breakfast of huevos rancheros, I told my friend about the terrible scene Olivia and I had stumbled upon at Jasper's house the night before. Tessa already knew about the murder – news and gossip often spread at supersonic speed in Twilight Cove – but she hadn't yet heard that my aunt and I were the ones to find Jasper's body. I told her that part of the story in a hushed voice to make sure no one overheard us. I didn't want to get peppered with questions from random townsfolk, especially when I was trying to eat. Tessa and I had to agree to put the subject aside until we were finished with our food; otherwise, our appetites would have been ruined.

After we'd finished breakfast, we climbed into our individual cars and drove over to the Twilight Inn, where Tessa would be dealing with costume alterations and I would be helping with the gift baskets for the raffle. We found parking spots down the street from the inn and walked toward the stately Victorian together.

'Are you going to be all right?' Tessa asked. 'Everyone's probably going to be talking about Jasper's murder.'

'I'll be fine,' I assured her. I'd prepared myself on the drive over to the inn and now felt ready to face whatever questions might come my way.

As we turned on to the paved pathway that led up to the Victorian, I pulled out my phone and checked for messages. I'd received one new text, but it was from Auntie O rather than Callum.

'An officer's going to drop Jasper's parrot off at the sanctuary later this morning,' I told Tessa after I'd read the message. 'That's a relief. We were worried about Gizmo.'

'He'll be in the best hands with you and Olivia.' Tessa sent a sidelong glance my way. 'When's Callum coming back?'

'In a few days.' I bit my bottom lip, wondering if I should say anything else.

Tessa picked up on my indecision and stopped short at the base of the inn's front steps. 'What's going on, Georgie? Are the two of you having problems?'

'No,' I said quickly. 'Except . . . I haven't heard from him for more than twenty-four hours. It's silly of me to expect regular contact, but up until yesterday he texted every day. Now I'm wondering . . .' I trailed off, embarrassed by my insecurities.

Tessa's eyes grew wide. 'You think he might be ghosting you?'

'No,' I said without any doubt. 'He wouldn't do that.'

Callum was too kind to ghost anyone. If he knew that he wanted to break off our still-new relationship, he would tell me. I just worried that he was taking time to decide whether he wanted to return to Twilight Cove or not, or how to break the news to me that he planned to leave the animal sanctuary for good.

I shared that worry with Tessa.

Her brown eyes were kind and understanding. 'Have you asked him if he's thinking of going back to the baseball world permanently?'

'I'm way too chicken for that,' I admitted. 'And I don't want to pester him about not getting back to me. But I did text him last night to say I was looking forward to seeing him soon. Was that too much?'

'Not even close to too much.' Tessa hooked her arm through mine and we climbed the steps to the inn's front porch. 'But he didn't respond to that?'

My phone buzzed in the pocket of my shorts. I tugged it out. 'He did just now.' I couldn't help but smile as I read the text.

'Is it shareable?' Tessa asked with a mischievous smile.

I rolled my eyes. 'Of course it is.' I angled my phone so she could read the message for herself.

Same. Can't wait, he'd written.

'That's good news,' Tessa said.

I paused on the front porch to send back a smiley face and the words, *How are things in Toronto?*

I watched for the telltale three dots to inform me that he was composing a reply right away, but they didn't appear.

I tucked my phone away again. I didn't want to be glued to it, desperate for any little message from him, even if it did worry me how much I missed him. We'd known each other for less than three months, and in that time we'd been apart for a few weeks.

Tessa opened the front door of the inn, and I followed her inside, deciding to put thoughts of Callum aside for the time being, no matter how hard that might be. I wanted to be fully present for my volunteer duties.

Catherine greeted us in the foyer and led us into the parlor, where two folding tables had been set up. One held a sewing machine while the other was laden with several gift baskets waiting to be wrapped with cellophane. Catherine's daughter Rayelle held a clipboard as she inspected the contents of each basket. Two women and two men were also in the parlor, lounging on the sofa and chairs. They wore modern-day clothing but held various pieces of pirate costumes. I recognized Esther Yoon, a member of Auntie O's Gins and Needles group, and Dean Haskell, the mechanic who'd tuned up Olivia's truck the day before. Electrician Lance Earley was also present.

Catherine introduced me to the other woman, Fae Hawthorn, who wore a maxi dress and lots of beads and bangles. She had a fair complexion, and her curly red hair was streaked with gray and piled on top of her head in a messy topknot.

'Fae owns the gift shop on Main Street,' Catherine said. 'The Treasure Trove.'

Fae got up from her chair to clasp my hand. 'I also sell crystals and other metaphysical supplies. And I offer tarot readings.'

I wasn't quite sure what to say about that, so I stuck with, 'Nice to meet you.'

'You knew Dorothy Shale,' she said to me as Catherine talked with Tessa about the sewing work that needed to be done.

'Only briefly, but I've adopted her two dogs, Flossie and Fancy.'

'Oh, yes,' Fae said with a nod. 'They're such sweethearts. I'm glad they've got a good home. Dorothy was a friend of mine. I miss her dearly.'

'I'm sorry you lost your friend,' I said. 'She was a good woman.'
Tears shone in Fae's eyes, but she smiled. 'She was.'

I realized that Fae might be able to satisfy my curiosity about
the spaniels' origins. 'Do you know where Dorothy got her dogs?'
I asked, keeping my voice casual, even though my heart rate ticked
up in anticipation of a potentially enlightening answer. Ever since
I'd become aware of Flossie's and Fancy's unusual abilities, I'd
wondered if they'd been born that way or if they'd come into their
powers in some other fashion.

'She found them roaming through the forest, up in the hills where
she sometimes foraged for food,' Fae replied.

Catherine called her over to the other table, so Fae took the pieces
of her costume to Tessa to be altered. I hoped I'd have another
chance to speak with Fae, to see if she could give me a more exact
location so I could go there and check it out. For what, I wasn't
sure. Magic tingles in the air?

I knew it was highly likely that I'd never know how Flossie and
Fancy had ended up with their unusual abilities, but I couldn't help
wanting to try to find answers to at least some of the questions that
had been floating around in the back of my mind for weeks now.

I'd have to make an attempt to get more details from Fae another
time, though. Rayelle declared that all of the gift baskets contained
everything they were supposed to, so her mother showed me the
boxes of cellophane and ribbons she had on hand for wrapping
them. Rayelle and I tackled that job while Catherine hurried off to
attend to the inn's guests.

As I grabbed some cellophane and a length of red ribbon, the
conversation in the room unsurprisingly turned to the topic of
Jasper's murder. Everyone seemed shaken by the terrible event and
shocked that murder had once again cast a dark cloud over our
town. I admitted that Aunt Olivia and I had found Jasper's body,
and I accepted the flood of sympathy that came my way. I didn't
give any details of what I'd seen the night before. I didn't know
how much information the police wanted out in the community, so
I decided it would be better to share only the very basics of what
had transpired.

'How was he killed?' Dean asked as he helped himself to a cup
of coffee from a tray on a side table.

I wasn't sure how to respond to that question. I definitely didn't
want to mention the murder weapon, which I thought was an antique

of some sort. It was up to the police to decide if they wanted the public to know about it.

'Let's not get into any details,' Tessa said quickly as she paused in her sewing. 'I don't think I can handle hearing anything more.'

I sent her a quick, grateful smile, knowing she'd said that to save me from feeling pressured to share more than what felt comfortable.

Rayelle seemed to appreciate Tessa's request as well. Her face, fair to begin with, had gone ghostly white as we chatted, but her cheeks regained a tinge of pink as the conversation shifted from the gruesome scene Olivia and I had discovered to other aspects of the murder.

'I talked to Elsie earlier this morning,' Esther said. 'She told me the police haven't been able to find Jasper's treasure map.'

'That's probably why he was killed.' Tessa snipped a thread with a pair of scissors and then handed a repaired purple corset to Fae. 'Somebody wanted to get their hands on that map.'

'I doubt it even exists,' Lance said.

'Then why would anyone kill Jasper?' Esther asked. 'He was a sweet man. I can't imagine him having any enemies.'

'Somebody thought his story about the map was true,' Dean theorized. 'The killer probably demanded that Jasper hand it over, but he couldn't do that since there is no map.'

'Then the killer murdered him out of anger?' Fae asked.

Dean shrugged. 'Or so that Jasper couldn't report the attempted robbery to the police.'

'But what if there really is a map?' Rayelle spoke up as she finished tying a bow on one of the wrapped gift baskets. 'The killer must have it now.'

'So if anyone's caught digging for treasure, they might well be the murderer,' I said.

We all glanced at each other, as if expecting someone to suddenly jump up and make a mad dash out of the inn to go in search of treasure.

Nobody moved.

I went back to wrapping gift baskets. 'I'm curious to know where Jasper got the map.'

'If he got it from Giles Gilroy, it's probably a fake,' Dean said.

Rayelle looked up from the basket she was setting on a large piece of cellophane. 'Why do you say that?'

Dean took a swig of coffee before responding. 'I don't trust the guy, that's all.'

'He could have bought it online,' Rayelle said quietly before pulling the cellophane up around the basket with plenty of crinkly noises.

'Can you get a real treasure map online?' Fae asked, sounding skeptical.

Rayelle grabbed a red ribbon. 'You can buy pretty much anything online, if you know where to look.'

'Wherever he got it, and whether it's real or not, I think one thing is certain,' Dean said, looking grim. 'That map got Jasper killed.'

SEVEN

R ayelle dropped the ribbon she was holding. The cellophane she'd pulled up around the basket she was working on slowly drifted back down to lie on the table.

'Are you all right?' I asked her.

She'd gone awfully pale again.

'I'm not feeling well. Sorry.' She hurried out of the room.

The others had changed topics and were now chatting about the various scenes that would be acted out during Dead Eye Days. I finished wrapping the last of the baskets, and by that time Tessa was done mending and altering the costumes.

She and I left the inn together, and on our way down the front steps we encountered Flynn Smith-Wu, who was on his way inside.

'Morning, Flynn,' Tessa greeted. 'Here to see Annaleigh?'

'We're going out for lunch,' he said with a nod.

'Have you met my friend Georgie?' Tessa asked. 'She just moved to Twilight Cove recently.'

'We met here yesterday,' I said, giving him a smile.

He nodded. 'Olivia's niece.'

'That's right,' I confirmed.

'It's terrible about Jasper,' Tessa said. 'You've heard the news, right?'

Flynn's expression darkened. 'I've got to go,' he mumbled, already turning away from us.

He took the steps two at a time and disappeared into the inn.

'He seemed really upset about Jasper's treasure map announcement yesterday,' I said as Tessa and I walked along the front path. 'And that was an odd reaction just now.'

'Flynn is such a stickler for facts and historical accuracy, and he tends to let things get under his skin.'

'Is he a historian of some sort?' I asked, wondering about the source of his strong feelings.

'He teaches history at the high school, and it's more than a job to him. History is his passion.'

As we turned on to the sidewalk, I glanced back at the inn. 'You don't suppose . . .'

'What?' Tessa asked.

'Could Flynn have been so upset about Jasper's announcement that he confronted him?'

Tessa's eyes widened. 'You mean, could Flynn have killed Jasper?'

I shrugged. 'I don't know the guy. How well do you know him?'

'I wouldn't say we're friends, but we've been colleagues for a few years.' Tessa taught English and drama at the local high school. 'As long as he's not up in arms about something to do with history, he's easy to get along with.' She frowned, clearly troubled. 'I sure hope he's not the killer.' She shook her head. 'No, I can't see it.'

Despite that claim, I could tell that she was still unsettled. I wondered if there was some part of her that *could* imagine Flynn killing Jasper in a flash of rage.

Before driving back to the farm, I responded to a text message from Aunt Olivia asking where I thought Gizmo should reside while at the sanctuary. I told her to put his cage in the farmhouse. Although I'd never lived with a parrot, I knew they could be quite noisy at times, sometimes letting out loud shrieks, so I figured it would be better to have him in the larger dwelling, rather than in the close quarters of the carriage house. That way, I could set him up on the main floor, at the northern end of the house, well away from my upstairs bedroom.

When I got back to the sanctuary, Flossie and Fancy ran to greet me as soon as I climbed out of my car. After ruffling their fur and giving them each a hug, the dogs led me into the farmhouse, where I found my aunt in the sitting area attached to the kitchen, setting up Gizmo's large cage, which stood more than five feet tall. The African grey parrot watched the proceedings from his travel cage, which was currently sitting on a side table.

'Release the kraken!' Gizmo shouted as we entered the house.

'Hello, Gizmo,' I said to the bird. 'Welcome to your new home.'
'Hello, hello, hello!' he said back. 'Flipping malarkey!'
Auntie O and I laughed. Flossie gave a woof and Fancy let out
a 'woo'.
That seemed to encourage the parrot. He hopped around his cage,
saying, 'Davy Jones's locker. Yes, yes, you're going to Davy Jones's
locker.'
Then he sang a short melody that I didn't recognize.
'He's been singing that over and over,' my aunt said.
'Do you recognize the tune?' I asked as Gizmo sang the notes
again.
'It doesn't ring a bell for me, but I fear it'll be stuck in my head
for the rest of the day now.'
I helped Auntie O set up the large cage and then we transferred
Gizmo into it. I provided him with fresh water, and Aunt Olivia left
to head into town to meet up with some friends who'd also known
Jasper. I hoped their company would provide my aunt with some
comfort.
When I sat down at the kitchen table to work on my latest
screenplay, I quickly realized that I'd have to move elsewhere. I
was used to writing with peace and quiet around me, but Gizmo
kept chattering away. As much as I wanted to spend the day keeping
him company, I needed to put in a few hours of work.
I ended up moving out on to the back porch with my laptop. It
was quiet enough out there that I could concentrate, but I was also
close enough to hear if Gizmo got agitated or upset.
Thankfully, that didn't happen. He quieted down once the dogs
and I were out of the house, and I hoped that meant he was settling
in as well as could be expected. I decided I would do some research
later, so I'd know how to best care for Gizmo. While I didn't know
much about parrots, I did know they were intelligent animals, and
Gizmo would likely need interaction and enrichment activities to
keep him happy and calm.
A few hours later, I'd made good progress on my script. Although
I'd taken a couple of short breaks to check on Gizmo, I hadn't eaten
any lunch and my stomach growled in protest. Settling at the kitchen
table this time, I ate an apple, responded to a couple of emails and
then decided it was time to stretch my legs. Flossie and Fancy
seemed to agree with me. Before I'd even stood up from my chair,
they were already at the back door, their tails wagging.

I told Gizmo we wouldn't be long and then we set out for a walk through the woods and down to the secluded section of beach that, while public, I thought of as our own. I'd visited the spot many times since moving to Twilight Cove and I'd never seen another person there.

The small beach was bordered on both sides by cliffs that jutted out into the sea. With the forest behind us and the ocean before us, it felt as if we were in our own little world, a safe haven from the busyness of daily life.

I strolled back and forth along the shoreline a couple of times, while Flossie and Fancy splashed in the shallows, chased seagulls and swam out a short distance to retrieve a stick I threw for them. The dogs finally emerged from the water and shook themselves, sending sparkly water droplets in every direction. Some of the spray hit me, but I didn't mind, especially since the afternoon sun was beating down on us.

With the dogs soaking wet but happy, we made the trek back to the farm. As we walked past the barn, I heard the sound of a vehicle driving on to the property. At first, I thought it was Auntie O returning home, but then I realized that it didn't sound like her truck.

Beside me, Fancy gave a woof followed by a long 'woo-woo'. Then she and Flossie streaked off ahead of me.

I almost called them back, worried that they'd get in the way of the moving vehicle, even though they were careful about such things. The engine shut off before I could say anything, so I figured there was no danger. Whoever had arrived on the farm, it was clearly someone the spaniels knew and liked.

A few more steps took me past the shed that had been blocking my view of the driveway. I stopped short when I saw the blue truck parked near the farmhouse. The driver's door opened and Callum climbed out of the cab. The dogs went crazy, bouncing around him with excitement and Fancy talking up a storm.

My heart soared and I was tempted to run for Callum like the dogs had, but I managed to exercise restraint. I couldn't, however, stop a big smile from taking shape on my face.

When Callum looked up from greeting the dogs and met my gaze, the slow grin that appeared on his face warmed me from the inside.

Although I didn't run, I still managed to cover the distance between us in a matter of seconds. Callum helped by meeting me part way. That meant I didn't have time to hesitate or wonder whether his feelings for me had changed in recent days. As soon as he was close enough, Callum pulled me into his arms and held me close. He drew in a deep breath, as if trying to breathe me in. I closed my eyes, relishing the fact that he was there with me.

When he pulled back, he took hold of my hands.

'Did I ever miss you,' he said.

I smiled at that. 'Really?'

His forehead furrowed. 'You doubted that?'

'Not exactly. I just . . . I mean . . .' I sighed and gathered my thoughts so I could speak coherently and put to rest the concern now showing in his green eyes. 'I wondered if you'd realize how much you missed the baseball world and wouldn't want to come back.'

Callum put both hands to my face and looked me straight in the eyes. 'Georgie, this is where I want to be. I love baseball, but I'm ready for this new chapter in my life. OK?'

The sincerity behind his words scattered my doubts and worries into the summer breeze. Instead of answering with words, I kissed him. One of his hands slipped around to my back and pulled me closer as he deepened the kiss. We didn't pull apart until Fancy let out a happy but impatient 'woo-woo'. Even then, we stayed so close that our foreheads nearly touched.

'Did I mention that I missed you?' Callum asked, his slow grin making a comeback.

I smiled and rested a hand on his chest. 'Even if you hadn't, I would have got that impression.'

'I'm happy to impress it upon you even more,' he said.

His stomach rumbled, and I took a step back from him, still smiling.

'I'm going to hold you to that,' I said, 'but it sounds like you could do with a meal first.'

'And a shower.'

'You go shower while I fix us something to eat.' My smile faded. 'There's a lot to catch up on.'

'Is something wrong?' he asked, concerned again.

'Nothing to do with me or the sanctuary,' I assured him. 'There's just lots to tell you.'

'Then I'll get a move on.' He opened the driver's door of his truck, but then stopped and stood there, regarding me.

'What?' I asked, his scrutiny making me feel a tad shy.

He grinned again. 'I'm glad to be home.'

After the worrying I'd done in his absence, those words were like music to my ears.

EIGHT

By the time Callum joined me in the farmhouse kitchen, I'd thawed and heated some spaghetti sauce that I'd made the previous week. The pasta was nearly cooked, and I'd tossed together a salad of greens, tomatoes and cucumber, all fresh from my aunt's vegetable garden. It hadn't been long since my late lunch, but that meal had consisted of only an apple, so I was more than ready to eat again.

When Callum arrived, Gizmo startled him by squawking out some pirate speak, and I laughed at the surprise on his face. As I dished out the pasta, I explained how Gizmo had come into our care, growing more subdued as I relayed the worst of the details.

We sat down at the table and Callum reached across to take my hand.

'I'm sorry you went through that,' he said, running his thumb over my knuckles. 'It couldn't have been easy to see Jasper like that. Are you sure you're OK?'

'I had a couple of bad dreams last night,' I confessed. 'But otherwise, I'm all right. I'm more worried about Auntie O. Jasper was a friend of hers.'

'Does she have any idea who would have wanted to hurt him?' Callum asked as we started in on our meal.

'I think she and just about everyone else agree that the murder had to do with the treasure map. But who the killer could be, we don't know.' I told him about Flynn's irritation with Jasper. 'I also saw Jasper arguing with his girlfriend, Elsie Suárez, before he was killed.' I paused to take a sip of water. 'But that doesn't mean things were bad enough between them to lead to murder. Someone probably wanted the map so they could find the treasure.'

'Pirate treasure,' Callum said with a shake of his head. 'Sounds a bit far-fetched to me.'

'To me too, but stranger things have happened.' I glanced at the dogs, who were lying next to the table, watching us eat with wistful expressions, even though they'd just scarfed their own dinners. Not for the first time, I wished I could tell Callum about the dogs' unusual abilities. I definitely wasn't ready for that yet, though. Would I ever be?

I shoved that question to the back of my mind and refocused on the gorgeous man across the table from me. His wavy blond hair was still damp from his shower, and his blue T-shirt hugged his body just enough to show off his muscles.

As much as I wanted to drink in the sight of him, I forced myself not to stare.

'How are the animals?' Callum asked as I enjoyed a forkful of spaghetti.

'They're all doing well.' I spent the next while filling him in on all the cute moments he'd missed with the spaniels and the farm animals.

Callum laughed at a story I told him about the donkeys, and the sound had a familiar and pleasant effect on my stomach. Even though I'd missed him and had looked forward to his return, having him back home felt even better than I'd expected.

'So how come you're home already?' I asked as we finished up our meal. 'Not that I'm complaining, but I wasn't expecting you for another couple of days.'

Callum twirled the last few strands of spaghetti around his fork. 'Javi was doing better and didn't need me going on the road with him and the team. Besides, I was getting antsy to come home.'

That brought a smile to my face.

'I'm sorry I didn't text you much over the past couple of days,' he continued. 'I misplaced my charger and my phone died. Once I found the charger, I was scrambling to get an earlier flight last-minute. I didn't mention that I was coming back today because I thought I'd surprise you.'

'It was a great surprise,' I assured him.

He reached for my hand again and gave it a squeeze. 'Speaking of Javi . . .' He released my hand and pushed his chair back. 'He sent you a present. I left it on the porch.'

He got up from the table and disappeared out the back door, returning a second later with a rectangular-shaped present wrapped in paper with white and blue stripes. I accepted the package from Callum as he sat back down at the table.

'Javi doesn't even know me,' I said, surprised by the gift.

'He said he feels like he does.' Callum's grin was a tad sheepish. 'I guess I talked about you a lot.'

A warm glow lit inside of me. Maybe Callum's feelings for me were just as strong as the ones I had for him. That thought left me feeling like I was floating up off my chair.

I started peeling one end of the present open. 'What is it?'

'I have no idea,' Callum said. 'And to be honest, I'm a little apprehensive.'

I stopped unwrapping the gift. 'Why?' Now I was wary too.

'Javi can be a bit of a joker sometimes.'

'So something might jump out at me when I open this?' I guessed.

Callum winced. 'It's more likely something that's supposed to embarrass me.'

'OK, now I'm more curious than worried.'

I tore the paper away to reveal a rectangular white box. I lifted the lid and pulled away some white tissue paper to reveal a folded garment in a beautiful shade of blue. I removed the item from the box and held it up so it would unfold itself.

A smile spread across my face when I saw the team name and logo on the front. 'A Toronto Blue Jays jersey!'

I'd never owned a team jersey of any sort before. I hadn't watched much in the way of sports until I met Callum. Over the summer, he'd converted me into a baseball fan. While Callum liked to cheer for his home-state team, the Colorado Rockies, we also cheered for the Toronto Blue Jays, since that was the team he played for during the last years of his career.

'Oh, man,' Callum said, when he saw the back of the jersey.

Wondering what caused that reaction, I turned the jersey around and my smile grew even brighter. On the back was the number thirty-three and the name McQuade, for Callum McQuade.

'It's *your* jersey!' My smile was probably outshining the sun now.

Callum groaned and rubbed a hand down his face. 'You don't have to wear it.'

'Are you kidding me?' I jumped up from my chair and pulled the jersey on. I buttoned it up and then spun around to show it off from all sides. 'How do I look?'

Callum got up and came around the table. 'You look amazing.'
He kissed me. 'But you really don't have to wear it.'

I searched his eyes, trying to decipher the reason why he kept
saying that. 'You don't want me to?'

'I do, but only if you're OK with it.'

'I'm more than OK with it,' I said. 'After all, I'm pretty sure I'm
one of your biggest fans.'

He put his arms around me and pulled me closer. 'Not my
number-one fan?'

The way his green eyes looked into mine sent my heart thundering.

'It might be hard to beat out your parents,' I said, 'but I'm willing
to give it a shot.'

'I like the sound of that.'

He kissed me, and we might have stayed that way all evening if
Gizmo hadn't suddenly shouted, 'Shiver me timbers!'

We laughed as we broke apart, and the dogs bounced and danced
around us.

After cleaning up the kitchen, we moved to the living room at
the front of the house and settled in on the couch to watch Javi play
in that evening's game. He still wasn't at his best, batting-wise, but
he was definitely doing better than before Callum had gone out to
Toronto to help him.

'He'll get there' Callum said after Javi struck out. 'He'll find his
rhythm. Once you lose it, you get in your head.'

'And then things just get worse?' I guessed.

'Exactly. But he's getting his confidence back and the rest will
follow.'

Later, when Javi got a base hit, we cheered as if he'd hit a
homerun, Fancy joining in. After we'd calmed down, my phone
buzzed on the coffee table. I picked it up and saw that I'd received
a text message from Tessa.

*I saw Giles Gilroy hitting on Elsie Suárez. She seemed upset,
and no wonder! Jasper hasn't even been dead for twenty-four hours!*

As I finished reading that message, she sent another.

*Maybe Giles killed Jasper to get him out of the way because he
has a thing for Elsie?*

I showed the texts to Callum and asked if he knew Giles, but he
didn't. That's what I'd expected. Callum hadn't yet spent a lot of
time around town.

No idea, I texted back. *I've never met Giles.*

We should change that, Tessa wrote next. *Want to meet up in town tomorrow?*

Definitely, I wrote in response.

We decided on a time and place, and then I went back to watching the ball game.

'Are you investigating Jasper's murder?' Callum asked.

I saw concern in his eyes and knew he was thinking about the time a few months earlier when I'd tangled with a murderer.

'I'm not planning on it,' I said. 'I'm sure the police will catch the culprit. I'm curious about Giles now, but I have plenty of other things to focus on.'

'Like?' he asked with a glint of humor in his eyes.

I pretended to ponder the question. 'Like my writing. Getting Gizmo settled in. The dogs. The sanctuary animals. Volunteering at Dead Eye Days.'

'Anything else?'

I leaned closer to him, so our shoulders were touching, and he slid an arm around me. 'And maybe a certain guy with blond hair and green eyes.'

'I hope you're not talking about Conrad Rigsby,' he said, referring to the guy who lived across the street.

I rested my head on his shoulder. 'I'm pretty sure his eyes are blue.'

'Can't say I've noticed.'

I raised my head. 'You don't notice eyes?'

'I definitely notice your eyes, Georgie Johansen.'

I shifted on the couch so I could swing my legs over his lap and be at a better angle to kiss him. We got distracted from the baseball game, but we did manage to resurface to see the end when the Blue Jays won.

A short while later, I said goodnight to Callum on the back porch, and the dogs and I watched him walk off into the night, heading toward his cabin located beyond the barn.

Yes, I thought to myself as I watched the darkness swallow him up. *I have much better things to focus on than murder.*

NINE

The next morning, I stopped by the carriage house to check in on Aunt Olivia before I headed out to the barn. I knocked on the front door of the cute two-story, yellow-and-white building. When my aunt opened the door moments later, the smile on my face slipped away.

'Auntie O, have you been crying?' I asked.

'Just a little.' She tried to force a smile. 'I was looking through some old pictures from times spent with Jasper. It was probably too soon for that.'

I hugged her. 'I'm so sorry.'

She gave me a squeeze and drew in a deep breath. Then she released me and stood straighter. 'I'll be out to help with the animals in a few minutes.'

'You don't have to if you don't feel up to it,' I assured her. 'Callum got back yesterday.'

'I saw his truck.' She searched my face. 'Things are good between the two of you?'

'Things are great,' I assured her. 'And we can look after all the farm chores today.'

'I want to work,' she insisted. 'It'll do me good. The animals always cheer me up.'

'Is there anything I can do to help?' I asked.

'Just having you around does my spirits good, Georgie. Once the police catch whoever killed Jasper, at least I'll know that the quest to get justice for him is well underway.'

Auntie O needed to put on sunscreen and her work boots before heading out, so I walked over to the barn on my own. I couldn't help but wonder if the police had any suspects yet. Murder investigations could drag on for years or even remain unsolved forever. I hoped that wouldn't be the case with Jasper's murder. I wanted my aunt to have the closure she needed. Plus, everyone in Twilight Cove would feel safer once the killer was behind bars.

I'd told Callum I had no plans to investigate the murder. That was true the night before, and it still was now. I could, however, feel a waver in my resolve. I already had two suspects in mind:

Flynn Smith-Wu and Elsie Suárez. Did the police have either of those individuals on their radar? They most likely would have considered Elsie as a potential suspect since she'd been dating the victim. But Flynn? And now Tessa had raised the possibility of a third suspect in Giles Gilroy. If I were completely honest with myself, I was curious to find out more about the antiques dealer and his potential motives for murder.

I shook my head as I reached the barn, the spaniels trotting along at my heels.

You're not a detective, I reminded myself.

Maybe not, but I was curious. Too curious for my own good? Possibly, but that didn't stop thoughts of suspects from spinning around in my head.

Perhaps it wouldn't hurt to find out more about the people in Jasper's life. Maybe I could learn something and pass it on to the police to help them in their investigation. Like the friction between Flynn and Jasper. If the police didn't know about that, it might be helpful to tell them.

No, I decided. Better to stay focused on a safer mystery like the one surrounding Flossie's and Fancy's origins. At least in that case, I knew where to start looking for clues.

After taking care of the sanctuary's animals, the dogs and I got in my car and drove to the center of town. I had wondered if I should leave the spaniels at home, but Tessa had assured me by text message that there was a safe place they could wait while we were in the antiques shop.

Sure enough, when we met Tessa at the store, there was a small vestibule inside the first of two doors, with a sign saying that dogs were welcome to wait in that area. There were even a couple of metal hoops I could attach the leashes to. I knew Flossie and Fancy weren't likely to take off on to the street if the door was opened, but I hooked them up to the hoops anyway.

Tessa held the second door open for me and we entered the main part of the store. The scent of old wood and leather greeted us as the floorboards creaked beneath our feet. The shop was quite large, but it was crammed full of antiques of all sorts. As I did an initial sweep of the store with my eyes, I spotted everything from antique furniture to neon signs.

'I love this place,' Tessa said to me in a low voice as we began browsing. 'You never know what treasures you might uncover.'

'Speaking of treasure,' I whispered, 'do you think there's any chance that Mr Gilroy would tell us if he sold the map to Jasper?' Tessa shrugged. 'It's worth asking.'

As if on cue, a white man with slicked-back graying brown hair emerged from a doorway behind the sales counter. He wore a suit without the jacket and appeared to be in his late fifties. I figured he was probably Giles Gilroy.

The man smiled at us, but the expression struck me as a tad unctuous.

'Good morning, ladies,' he greeted from behind the counter. 'Tessa, I don't think I've had the pleasure of meeting your friend before.'

'I'm Georgie Johansen,' I said.

'Olivia van Oosten's niece,' Tessa added.

He nodded. 'Of course. I heard you'd moved to town. Is there anything I can help you ladies with?'

'We're just browsing, thanks, Mr Gilroy,' Tessa said, confirming the man's identity. 'Although you know I'm always interested in any vintage clothing you have in stock.'

'Call me Giles,' he said with another flash of that same smile. 'And I did have something come in a few days ago that you might like.' He came out from behind the counter and led the way to a far corner of the shop.

There, displayed on a mannequin, was a black-and-silver flapper dress.

Tessa's eyes lit up at the sight of it. 'Oh, this is beautiful. What do you think, Georgie?'

'It's gorgeous,' I said in agreement. 'And it would look amazing on you.'

It also looked as if it would fit her. Tessa had a slender build and was a few inches shorter than my height of five feet nine inches. She fingered the price tag and winced.

'It's the real deal,' Giles said. 'I got it from a woman who had photos of her grandmother wearing it in 1924. She gave me a copy of one of the photos. I'll go grab it.' He hurried back behind the counter.

'I really love it,' Tessa confessed to me in a whisper. 'But can I justify buying it?'

'Would you wear it on special occasions or keep it as a costume?' I asked.

'A costume, I suppose. I'd love to dress up as a flapper girl for Halloween, and the local museum is planning a 1920s-themed fundraising party.' She touched the fabric gently, a wistful look in her brown eyes. 'It seems to be in really good shape.'

Tessa had always had an interest in fashion and sewing, ever since I'd known her as a teenager. She often sewed her own clothes, and she also made costumes for the school plays she put on with her drama students at the local high school. And, of course, she was volunteering her sewing skills for the people who needed costumes for Dead Eye Days.

I checked the price tag. The dress wasn't cheap, but the price didn't strike me as unreasonable. Not that I knew anything about vintage clothing.

'What do you think?' Tessa asked as Giles came back our way.

'If you love it and can afford it, go for it,' I suggested. 'But if you have any doubts, you can always take time to think about it.'

We cut off our conversation as Giles reached us. He showed us the promised photograph and chatted with Tessa about the dress for a while longer. Within minutes, Tessa had made up her mind. I could see it in her eyes before she said, 'I'll take it.'

Giles smiled, and once again I thought the expression was a tad slimy. I didn't think he was taking advantage of Tessa, though, because she knew her stuff when it came to vintage clothing.

'Wonderful,' he said. 'I'll put it in a garment bag for you.'

As he carefully removed the dress from the mannequin, I began browsing the shop again.

Tessa followed Giles over to the sales counter. Once he had the dress carefully encased in a plastic garment bag, he rang up the sale.

'I guess you've heard about what happened to Jasper,' Tessa said to Giles.

I was glad I had my back to them, because a smile touched my lips before I was able to hide it. Tessa was about to do some sleuthing. I was certain of it.

'It's pretty much all anyone's talking about,' Giles said. 'Upsetting news.'

I wondered how upset he really was, considering that he'd already made a move on Jasper's girlfriend.

'Everyone's curious about how Jasper got the treasure map,' Tessa continued. 'Did he buy it from you, by any chance?'

Pretending to admire a large porcelain pitcher, I angled my body so I could watch Giles out of the corner of my eye. He hesitated briefly before answering Tessa's question.

'Even if he did, I wouldn't be able to share that information with you. My clients expect and appreciate that I keep my dealings with them confidential.'

'But anyone can see if someone comes in the store and buys something,' I pointed out.

'Of course, but there are more rare items that I don't place for sale in my store. I have several clients for whom I broker private deals.'

The phone on the sales counter rang, so Giles excused himself after Tessa and I assured him that we had everything we needed.

Tessa draped the garment bag carefully over one arm and we retrieved the dogs from the vestibule before stepping out on to the street where the summer sunshine was already making the day a warm one. On the nearby street corner, electrician Lance Earley stood chatting with mechanic Dean Haskell, each with a take-out cup from the local coffee shop in hand.

'Morning,' they both greeted as we walked their way.

Before we could say anything in response, Giles called out from behind us, 'Ms Johansen!'

I turned back to see the antiques dealer hurrying our way.

'My contact information,' he explained as he handed me a business card. 'I know your aunt has several nice antiques. Please let her know that I'd be happy to come out to the farm and give her an appraisal if she's ever interested in selling anything.'

I slipped the card into my pocket. 'Thank you. I'll pass on the message.'

'Have a nice day,' Giles said to me and Tessa. Then he nodded at Lance and Dean. 'Gentlemen.'

He turned and hurried back into his shop.

Lance and Dean watched him go.

'I wouldn't trust that man as far as I could throw him,' Lance said. 'Best to keep him away from your aunt and her antiques.'

'He wants to appraise them for less than they're worth so he can offer to buy them for a song,' Dean added.

'That sounds unethical,' Tessa said.

'It is,' Lance assured her.

Tessa glanced back toward the antiques store. 'He does have some nice things in his shop, though.'

'Sure, but how does he get all of it?' Lance didn't seem to be expecting an answer. 'Just be careful around him,' he cautioned.

'We will,' I said.

Tessa and I left them to their coffee and continued on our way along the street with the dogs.

'I bet Giles Gilroy did sell the treasure map to Jasper,' I whispered to Tessa.

'Agreed,' she said with a nod.

'He has some potentially unethical practices,' I continued, 'and he's been cozying up to Elsie Suárez, practically before Jasper's body has gone cold. But is he a murderer?'

'That,' Tessa said, 'is the million-dollar question.'

TEN

Tessa and I made the coffee shop, Déjà Brew, our next stop. We sat at one of the outdoor tables, in the shade of the awning, enjoying our ice-cold drinks. The barista had kindly provided a bowl of cold water for the dogs, and they lapped it up gratefully before lying at our feet.

'What are you thinking?' Tessa asked me after we'd enjoyed a few sips of our drinks. 'It's got to do with Giles Gilroy, right?'

'Are you reading my mind?' I asked with a smile.

'More your face and eyes,' she said, smiling back at me. 'We might not have seen each other for fifteen years, but I still know you.'

That statement – very much true – set off a glow of happiness in my chest.

'I *was* thinking about Giles,' I confirmed. 'And Elsie and Flynn. Basically, all of my suspects.'

Excitement lit up Tessa's eyes. 'Does this mean we're on the case?'

'I'm not sure,' I hedged.

She regarded me from across the small table. 'Don't you want to be?'

I took a moment to consider the question. 'Yes,' I said eventually. 'For Auntie O's sake. Jasper's death has hit her hard.'

Tessa's happy energy faded away. 'Poor Olivia. We'll keep trying to figure this out. I know the local and state police are investigating, but maybe we can ferret out some information that they can't. There might be things people are more likely to tell us than the cops.'

'But we need to be careful,' I cautioned, remembering all too clearly how I'd nearly become a killer's next victim back in June.

'Always,' Tessa agreed. 'Let's think of our list of suspects and reconvene in a couple of days.'

'Maybe we should have an actual list, rather than just a mental one,' I suggested.

'I'll make one right now.' Tessa whipped out her phone and opened a notes app.

I did the same with my phone.

Consulting with each other, we listed Giles, Elsie and Flynn as our current suspects, along with their possible motives. After we put our phones away, two women sat down at the other bistro table, well within earshot, so from there on out we kept our conversation away from the topic of murder.

Once we finished our drinks, we went our separate ways. Tessa had errands to run, and I had another mystery to tackle. I'd walked past Fae's gift shop, the Treasure Trove, a few times since moving to Twilight Cove, but I'd never been inside. When I reached the teal storefront with its purple door, I stopped to look in one of the large windows. The display showcased local interest books, a pretty tea set, scented candles, a deck of tarot cards and what resembled a crystal ball in shape and form but was made of something black, possibly obsidian.

I was still studying the items when Fae appeared on the other side of the display. She smiled and waved at me through the window before hurrying toward the door. She opened it and poked her head outside.

'Georgie! Are you coming in?'

'I was thinking about it,' I said, 'but I've got the dogs with me.'

'Don't worry about that.' Fae beckoned me closer as she stepped through the door. 'Dorothy used to bring them along when she visited my shop.' She rested her hands on her knees and addressed the dogs. 'You're always well behaved, aren't you?'

The spaniels wagged their tails and happily received pats on the head.

Fae straightened and held the door open for us. 'Come on in.'

The dogs and I followed her inside. The atmosphere shifted

noticeably as soon as I crossed the threshold. The air was pleasantly cool, and calming instrumental music played quietly in the background. Displays of scented candles sent out a light and pleasant perfume, and somehow the outside world seemed far away. Maybe it was my imagination, but stepping into the shop was almost like getting a comforting hug.

'Did Dorothy visit your shop often?' I asked as the door drifted shut behind me.

'She didn't come to town much,' Fae said, confirming what I knew about Dorothy, 'but when she did, she dropped in to say hello or have a cup of tea. Sometimes she'd buy a crystal or two.'

'She gave me a crystal,' I said before I could think better of it. 'An amethyst. For my headaches.'

Fae nodded with a sad smile. 'Dorothy was kind like that.' She moved behind the sales counter, her maxi skirt swishing around her ankles. As she opened a cardboard box that sat beside the cash register, she said, 'It's been a couple of months since she passed, so you might need to recharge the crystal.'

'Recharge it?' I had visions of electrical sparks flying out of the amethyst.

'Under the full moon,' Fae explained. 'The next one is three nights from now. Just set the crystal outside or on a windowsill where the moonlight will hit it. By the next morning, it'll be recharged.'

It was true that the crystal hadn't seemed quite as effective of late, but I had figured that was simply the power of suggestion wearing off. Even though I knew what Fancy and Flossie could do, I wasn't quite ready to accept every claim of magic and mysticism. I was more open-minded than I had been previously, however. It was hard not to be after seeing the spaniels' powers in action.

'I'll try that, thanks,' I said, because I figured why not give it a shot.

I looked down at Flossie and Fancy. They sat by my feet, looking up at me with their brown eyes. I wished I could know what they were thinking. Were they laughing inside because I was willing to try something so far-fetched? Or were they thinking that I was finally catching on to the fact that there was far more to the universe than I'd ever before realized?

'What can I help you with today?' Fae asked as she started unpacking candles from the box on the counter. 'Are you in need of more crystals?' She left the box and moved over to a display of crystals of varying sizes and colors.

'Not today, thank you,' I declined. 'I wanted to talk to you about something you mentioned the other day. You said you thought Dorothy found the dogs roaming through the woods in a place where she liked to forage.'

'That's right.' She smiled at the spaniels. 'They were just pups at the time. Dorothy thought maybe someone had abandoned them there in the forest.' Fae shook her head, her smile gone now. 'I can't wrap my head around some people's cruelty.'

'I know what you mean,' I said.

She returned to unpacking candles from the box and setting them on the counter. 'What was it you wanted to ask me?'

'Do you know more specifically where Dorothy liked to forage?'

Her face lit up. 'Are you into foraging too?'

'No. At least, not yet.' Aside from picking wild berries, I'd never considered going out in the woods to look for food.

'I have a book in stock on local edible plants,' Fae said, 'but that's just something to keep in mind.' She ducked behind the counter. 'Now, where are those maps?' she muttered.

One of the candles she'd just unpacked rolled toward the edge of the counter. I lunged forward, hoping to catch it before it fell. I drew back with a jerk when the candle suddenly changed direction and rolled back toward the other candles, coming to a stop next to the pile.

Startled, I looked at Flossie, who was staring hard at the candles. She blinked and then turned her gaze to me. Then she tipped her head to one side before wandering off to sniff at a display of crystal balls on a nearby shelf.

My heart thudded in my chest. Had Flossie really changed the candle's direction with her mind?

'Aha!'

Fae's exclamation made me jump.

She resurfaced with a folded paper map in hand. After moving the box to the floor, she spread the map out on the countertop and grabbed a red marker from a penholder on the far side of the cash register.

'I know everyone likes to do things on their phones these days,' she said as she uncapped the pen, 'but I can't help but still love paper maps.' She circled an area in red ink. 'This is Witch's Peak.

It was one of Dorothy's favorite spots for foraging. We went there together once or twice. The best way to get there is to follow Larkspur Lane up to this unpaved road.' She traced the route with the pen. 'The road ends at a big clearing right about here.' She placed an X on the map. 'Then if you hike up the hill, you'll reach a spot with a great view of town, right down to the ocean. In and around that area, you can find everything from pineapple weed to wild bergamot. It was somewhere in there that Dorothy came across these beauties.' She smiled over the counter at the spaniels again.

Flossie and Fancy wagged their tails, their eyes bright.

'Thank you, Fae,' I said.

She folded the map and handed it to me. 'My pleasure.'

'How much do I owe you for the map?' I asked.

She waved off the question. 'I give those away for free.'

I thanked her again, but she'd been so helpful that I wanted to buy something from her shop. I told her I'd spend a few minutes browsing, and she set about shelving the candles while I wandered around the store.

Near the back, I found a display of non-fiction books on a rotating wire rack. One book caught my eye immediately. It was called *Pirates of the Pacific Coast of South America*. It wasn't so much the Jolly Roger flag on the cover that caught my attention, but rather the author's name: Ajax Wolfgang.

I picked up the book and flipped it over to read the back cover, but I looked up when Fancy gave a quiet whine. She and Flossie stood by a door leading into another room, sniffing the air. A beaded curtain covered the otherwise open doorway.

'What's wrong?' I asked.

They sniffed the air again and then sat down next to the doorway.

Fae appeared with a smile on her face. 'Can I help you with anything?'

I held up the book. 'I see you mostly have books on local subjects or by authors from this area. Ajax Wolfgang isn't from around here, is he?'

'He's from California, I believe, but he's going on tour to promote his latest book when it comes out next month, and Twilight Cove is going to be one of his stops. I thought it made sense to have a couple of his other books in stock while he's here.'

I returned the book to the rack. 'He's already in town.'

'Yes, I've spoken to him briefly. Maybe he's doing some research.'

The bell above the door jingled as someone entered the shop.

Fae excused herself and headed to the front of the store to greet the new customer. Flossie and Fancy followed her so they could do the same.

While they did that, I wandered into another section of the shop and picked out a candle that smelled like apple pie. As I did so, I couldn't stop thinking about the candle that had nearly rolled off the counter. I'd never witnessed Flossie display that particular ability before, but I hadn't known her all that long. While part of my brain wanted to come up with a more rational explanation for what I'd witnessed, in my heart I knew that Flossie had changed the candle's direction. I was relieved that Fae hadn't witnessed the incident. She was an open-minded woman, but I didn't want her or anyone else knowing about the spaniels' unusual abilities.

Fae and the other customer – a gray-haired woman in a tie-dyed skirt – were chatting about moon phases and planetary alignments, but they paused their conversation while Fae rang up my purchase. The dogs and I left the shop soon after, and I waved to Fae through the front window. Then we struck off along the street with the map and candle safely tucked in my cloth shopping bag.

I was excited to have a path to follow, one that might lead me to some clues about Flossie's and Fancy's origins. Maybe it was a long shot, but at least it was a place to start.

ELEVEN

As the dogs and I made our way back toward my car, parked one street away, I spotted Catherine Adams inside the bookstore, putting a poster up in the window. I smiled at Catherine through the glass and paused to admire the poster. It featured a pirate ship flying the Jolly Roger, and it announced that Dead Eye Days would be taking place the following weekend. The design was bright, colorful and eye-catching.

Catherine came out of the shop and joined me by the window.

'I take it the festival is going ahead?' I said to her.

'The organizing committee had an emergency meeting shortly after I saw you yesterday,' she replied. 'We decided to stick to our plans, since that's what Jasper would have wanted.'

'My aunt said the same thing.'

Catherine wiped a tear from her eye. 'He will be sorely missed.' She took a steadying breath and then smiled at the poster with pride. 'Rayelle designed that.'

'Wow,' I said, impressed. 'She's very talented.'

Catherine beamed. 'I might be biased, but I agree wholeheartedly.'

Rayelle came out of the neighboring store, which had a poster in the window as well.

'She's studying both graphic design and business at college,' Catherine continued as her daughter headed our way. 'She wants to take over the inn when her father and I decide to retire. Thank goodness. For a while there, she desperately wanted to be a tattoo artist. All I could picture was my daughter hanging out with bikers and gangsters.'

Rayelle overheard that last statement and rolled her eyes. 'I wanted to open my tattoo shop here in Twilight Cove, and it's not like we have a lot of bikers and gangsters.' She offered me a weak smile. 'The problem is, I don't think I'd have enough customers of any sort. Besides, I've discovered I love designing book covers even more than tattoos. I can do that and work at the inn, so I get the best of both worlds.'

'And I don't have to suffer through constant nightmares about my daughter and biker gangs,' Catherine said in a stage whisper.

'Mom.' Rayelle shook her head.

'Whatever your career path, the posters are gorgeous,' I said.

'Thank you.' Rayelle gave me another faint smile before moving along to the next business on the street, a stack of the posters and a roll of tape in hand.

I could have sworn I'd seen her blinking away tears as she turned away from me. I definitely noticed that she had dark rings under her eyes, as if she hadn't slept well, and a subdued air about her. Even when she tried to smile, the expression seemed weighed down by sadness and something else I couldn't quite identify.

Catherine watched her daughter disappear into the next shop, a mixture of worry and sorrow on her face.

'She's taken Jasper's death hard,' Catherine said. 'She's known him since she was a baby. Jasper used to play pirates with Rayelle and her sister for hours on end.' A sad smile appeared on Catherine's face. 'Jasper was really just a big kid himself.'

'I didn't know Jasper,' I said, 'but it seems he'll be missed by many.'

Catherine nodded. 'His death is a terrible loss to the community.'

An idea struck me as I watched Rayelle taping up a poster on the inside of the window of the antiques shop. Aunt Olivia and I were planning on holding a fundraiser at the farm in October, right around Halloween. Ticketholders would take a spooky walk through the fields and woods on the farm, with actors playing the parts of ghosts and other scary creatures. We would need posters to advertise the event. Maybe Rayelle would be willing to volunteer her artistic skills to design one for us.

I decided not to raise the subject with her right then. I'd consult with Aunt Olivia first and give Rayelle time to recover from the shock of Jasper's death.

After saying goodbye to Catherine and waving to Rayelle, I climbed into my car with the dogs and we headed back to the farmhouse. Even though I was itching to follow the route that Fae had outlined on the map for me, I would have to leave that for another day. Earlier that morning, I'd received notes from the producer I was working with on one of my latest screenplays. The network we sold the script to wanted some rewrites done, and they wanted to see the new version within a week. That meant I needed to get cracking. Besides, the sun was now high in the sky and the day was too warm to take the dogs hiking.

Back at the farmhouse, I spent a few minutes chatting with Gizmo before settling in on the shady back porch to write. As much as I wanted to study the map, I left it in the kitchen so it would be out of sight. I didn't want any distractions while I was supposed to be working. Fortunately, I'm a self-disciplined writer – most of the time, at least – so I was able to spend several hours focused solely on the story about a woman whose life spins out of control when she realizes that someone – whose identity she doesn't yet know – is aware of all the details of her deepest, darkest secret.

By the time I wrapped up my work day, I was satisfied with what I'd accomplished. After taking care of the evening farm chores, Callum and I drove into town with the dogs so we could indulge in ice cream cones and pup cups from the ice cream parlor. We took our treats across the street to the beach, where Callum and I sat on a log to enjoy the view and the soothing sound of the waves breaking gently upon the shore.

Flossie and Fancy made short work of the vanilla ice cream in their pup cups. Still licking their lips, they bounded off to play in the shallows. Callum and I took a little longer to finish off our desserts, but when we did, we strolled slowly through the sand while the dogs followed us from a short distance away, still splashing about in the water.

Callum wore swim trunks and a T-shirt, while I wore a shirt and shorts over my two-piece swimsuit. I had towels in the tote bag I carried over my shoulder, and we planned to take an evening swim when we reached a quieter spot farther along the cove. It would be the perfect way to end a summer's day.

Halfway to our destination, I noticed a woman standing alone by the shoreline, watching the frothy waves roll in toward her.

'Elsie?' I said when we got close to her.

She turned at the sound of her name, blinking away tears.

I felt bad for interrupting her solitude, but since I'd already done so, I reminded her who I was and introduced her to Callum.

'I'm so sorry about Jasper,' I said once the introductions were complete.

Callum added his condolences as well.

Elsie gave us a grateful but watery smile. 'Thank you.' She directed her next words solely at me. 'You and Olivia found Jasper when . . .' She couldn't bring herself to finish the sentence.

'We did,' I confirmed gently.

'I can't even imagine,' she said. 'It must have been terrible.' She fished a rumpled tissue from her pocket and dabbed at her eyes.

My heart ached for her, even though her name was on the suspect list Tessa and I had written up. Standing there with her, witnessing her tears, I couldn't see her as anything other than a bereaved woman deserving of kindness and sympathy.

'How is Olivia doing?' Elsie asked. 'She and Jasper were friends for a long time.'

'She's upset, of course,' I said. 'But she's doing OK.'

'Please tell her that she's in my thoughts,' Elsie requested.

'I will,' I assured her. 'I know you're in her thoughts as well.'

Callum and I parted ways with her then, leaving her to go back to watching the ebb and flow of the ocean.

'It's so sad,' I said quietly to Callum. 'Jasper's death seems so senseless, and it's hit his friends, including Aunt Olivia, hard.'

Callum took my hand as we walked through the sand. 'The police will catch the killer soon. That might help Elsie and Olivia get some closure.'

'I hope so.' I glanced at Callum and then focused on my feet as they sank into the wet sand with each step.

'Is something else on your mind?' Callum asked.

I raised my eyes to find him studying my face. 'I'm just not sure how you'll react when I tell you something.'

He squeezed my hand and drew to a stop. I faced him and he took hold of my other hand as well.

'Georgie, I don't want you ever to worry about telling me what's on your mind.'

I gave his hands a grateful squeeze. 'It's just that the other night I told you I had no plans to look into Jasper's murder. And at the time, that was the truth.'

Callum knew what was coming. 'But things have changed.'

'Tessa and I talked things over, and we want to put our heads together and see if we can come up with anything that might help the police. We aren't going to do anything major,' I rushed to add. 'Mostly, we want to find out more about the relationships various people had with Jasper. That sort of thing.'

'And you thought I might not like that?'

I shrugged. 'You seemed worried when you asked me last night if I was going to investigate.'

He pulled me closer and wrapped his arms around me. 'I only worry because I don't want anything bad to happen to you,' he said, speaking quietly near my ear. 'I can't forget what you went through back in June. It terrified me then, and now . . .' He pulled back enough that I could see one corner of his mouth turn upward. 'Let's just say my feelings have only grown stronger as time has passed.'

Tingles of happiness danced along my skin as I rested my hands on his chest. 'I feel the same way. About not being able to forget, and about the growing feelings.'

He kissed me briefly. 'I'm very glad to hear that last part.'

'So you're not exasperated?' I asked to be sure.

'How could I be? You're driven by a desire to help.'

'Unstoppable curiosity might play into it too,' I confessed.

'OK, there's that,' he agreed with a grin before growing more serious again. 'But a lot of it is about you wanting to help. To help Olivia get closure, to help Jasper get justice. That's admirable, not exasperating. All I ask is that you do everything you can to keep yourself safe. And if I can help in any way, even if it's just to act as a sounding board, let me know.'

I smiled and kissed him. 'That I can do.'

We'd reached the far end of the cove and had the area to ourselves. Callum and I stripped down to our swimsuits and joined the dogs in the water, much to their delight. Flossie and Fancy swam literal circles around us as we floated and paddled around in the cool water.

The sun was starting to sink lower in the sky when we emerged from the water and toweled off. We had to dry off a second time after the dogs shook water all over us. Then we began the trek back along the beach to the parking lot where we'd left Callum's truck. When we reached the lot, I saw Elsie for the second time that evening. She stood near the driver's side of a red sedan. Ajax Wolfgang was with her and they appeared to be deep in conversation.

As I watched, Ajax tried to put an arm around Elsie. She deftly slipped out of his reach and opened the driver's door of the sedan. After giving him a weak smile, she climbed into the car and shut the door. Ajax stood watching as she pulled out of her parking spot and drove away.

From what I'd seen and heard lately, Elsie was a very popular woman. I couldn't help but wonder if that had always been the case or if the sudden demand for her attention was somehow related to Jasper's death and the missing treasure map.

TWELVE

I woke up the next morning with a sense of excited anticipation humming through my veins. Today was the day I planned to go hiking to the spot Fae had pointed out on the map. Even though I knew I likely wouldn't gain any insight into the origins of the dogs and their unique abilities, I still wanted to see for myself where Dorothy had found them – or where they had found Dorothy. Judging by what Fae had said about the amazing view, that alone was reason enough to make the trip up into the hills. If I came across something that revealed more about the spaniels, that would be a bonus.

I started the day by helping out with the farm chores, as was the norm for me ever since I'd arrived in Twilight Cove. Once Aunt Olivia's broken ankle had healed, she'd assured me that she and Callum could take care of all the farm work, with occasional help from our teenage volunteer, Roxy Russo. Since I'd insisted on paying rent, my aunt didn't want me thinking I needed to do anything more to earn my keep. I, in turn, had insisted that I wanted to be involved in caring for the animals. It was physical but rewarding work, and I would have missed it if I'd left it all to Auntie O, Callum and Roxy.

Grooming the donkeys was my favorite task, so caring for them was my main job, but I also helped out with the other animals as needed. After lingering to chat with the freshly groomed donkeys, I joined Roxy by the horse pasture. She'd finished grooming the two ponies and Sundance, a sorrel Quarter Horse, and now sat on the fence.

'How's Sundance doing today?' I asked as I leaned my forearms on the top rail.

'Feisty,' Roxy replied with a smile on her face.

Sure enough, Sundance cantered around the pasture while the ponies stuck to one corner, half watching their friend as they grazed. Flossie and Fancy trotted over as Sundance galloped past. Fancy gave an excited yip and both dogs broke into a run, charging up and down the fence line. Sundance copied them, bucking with excitement. When she reared up on her hind legs, Flossie did the same.

Roxy and I laughed as the antics continued. Eventually, Sundance and the dogs wound down. The horse came over to get a pat from Roxy while the spaniels flopped down in the grass, their tongues lolling out.

'Goofball,' Roxy said affectionately as she stroked Sundance's nose.

'Are you looking forward to your trip?' I asked.

Roxy squished her lips together and shrugged. 'I guess.'

The fifteen-year-old wasn't one for sharing her feelings easily, so I tried to read her face for what she wasn't saying. After spending a good deal of time with her over the summer, I was getting better at that.

She would be leaving the next day to go visit her dad in California before the school year started. She'd had very limited contact with her father over the past several years but, apparently, he was making an effort to reconnect with her now.

I sensed that she was both excited and apprehensive about the trip. I worried that her dad might end up letting her down, which would only damage her self-esteem. On the other hand, if she ended up with a positive relationship with him, that could be great for her. All I could do was hope that things worked out and be there for her when she returned, no matter what happened in California.

Feeling a surge of affection for the teenager, I gave her a hug.

'Hey!' she protested as she teetered on the fence.

She tried to scowl at me when I released her, but I could see in her eyes that she wasn't really upset.

'Will we see you this evening?' I asked as she hopped down from the fence.

She shrugged. 'Maybe.'

She crouched down to give Flossie and Fancy each a pat on the head. Then, with a wave, she walked off, her volunteering done for the day.

Soon after, the dogs and I returned to the farmhouse. I wanted to head out on our hike before the day got too warm. I told Auntie O and Callum that I was taking the dogs hiking up in the hills, and I texted Callum a photo of the map Fae had given me so he'd know exactly where I intended to go, just in case we ended up getting lost. As much as I hated keeping things back from Callum and my aunt, I told them that I'd chosen that particular destination because Dorothy had come across the dogs there. That was true, of course, but I held back the fact that I was also hoping there might be something there to explain how Flossie could undo locks with a touch of her paw and how Fancy could camouflage herself and glow with a blue light.

Callum wanted to join us, but he had to make a trip to the local farm supply store and fix one of the stall doors in the barn. I would have loved his company, but it was for the best that he couldn't come along on the hike. Maybe one day I wouldn't have to keep any secrets from him, but even though I felt that our relationship held a lot of promise, it was still in its early stages.

I filled a backpack with bottled water, a collapsible water dish for the dogs, some food, a fire-starter kit, a flashlight, neon orange ribbons and an emergency blanket. I couldn't tell from the map how rugged the terrain would be or how long it would take us to reach our destination, and I wanted to be prepared in case we ran into trouble along the way.

As I got ready, Gizmo sang what seemed to be his favorite tune. I still didn't recognize it, but I now knew the musical phrase by heart.

Aunt Olivia was going to do some baking in the farmhouse kitchen while I was away, so she could keep Gizmo company. So far, we hadn't received any news about Jasper's will and what arrangements he'd made for Gizmo's care in the future, if any. Elsie had promised to fill my aunt in as soon as she had any news in that regard, but so far only Jasper's lawyer was privy to the contents of his will.

Before heading out, I took a closer look at the map, not wanting to miss the turnoff that would get us as close to our destination by car as possible. With my finger, I traced the red line that Fae had drawn. I stopped my finger at the spot where the route branched off from Larkspur Lane. I did a double take when I saw the name on the map: Old Birch Road.

Those were the same words I'd seen written in Jasper's journal. I stared across the kitchen, thinking. Maybe the note in Jasper's journal had nothing to do with his death. On the other hand, what if it was a clue? Another long shot, but I was going that way anyhow, so maybe once I'd visited the area, I would know if the note held any significance with respect to the murder.

After I folded the map and grabbed the dogs' leashes, we set off on our journey. The first part of the trip was easy. The farm was located on Larkspur Lane, and that was the road I had to follow up into the gentle hills. We drove past several other farms, but it didn't take long before the fields and pastures were replaced by forest on both sides of the road. Not long after, Larkspur Lane came to an end, the paved road giving way to a dirt-packed area large enough to easily turn a vehicle around. Instead of doing that, I parked the car and climbed out, the dogs scrambling after me.

Leaving the door open, I looked around, searching for a sign near the start of what was little more than a dirt track leading into the forest. I peered into the bushes and other undergrowth, but there was no sign to be found. I was certain I'd reached the right turnoff, but if not for the label on the map, I never would have known that the dirt track was called Old Birch Road.

I turned in a slow circle, taking in my surroundings. I couldn't see anything but the forest, Larkspur Lane and the start of the dirt road. There was nothing sinister about the place and nothing to indicate that Jasper or anyone else had been in the area recently. I walked a few feet along the dirt road, checking for tire tracks. I could see hints of tire imprints here and there, but I had no clue how long ago the tracks had been made. It hadn't rained for a few weeks, and the top layer of dirt was bone dry and crumbly.

Flossie and Fancy sniffed around as I studied the area. They appeared unconcerned and didn't draw my attention in any particular direction. So far, my search for clues related to either mystery was a complete flop, but our trip had just begun.

I called to the dogs, and we were about to get back in the car when Flossie stopped, looked upward and gave a woof. I followed her line of sight to the top of a nearby tree. A great horned owl sat perched on a branch, watching us.

'Hi, Euclid,' I said with a smile, knowing I wasn't mistaken about the owl's identity. 'I'm glad you're joining us.'

Fancy let out a 'woo-woo' of agreement and she, Flossie and I piled back into my car. Driving slowly so we wouldn't get bounced around too much, I followed Old Birch Road as it wound its way through the forest and up into the hills. In some places, the road was so overgrown that I slowed the car to a crawl and cringed, expecting to hear branches scraping at the paint. Fortunately, that happened only once, and briefly at that. It didn't sound as though the branch had caused too much damage.

Eventually, the road came to an end at a grassy clearing. I parked and let the dogs out of the car before I retrieved my backpack. I took a moment to inspect the side of my vehicle but couldn't find any scratches. Relieved, I pulled the straps of my backpack over my shoulders and set off after Flossie and Fancy. They'd already found a narrow path on the far side of the clearing and were trotting along it, their noses to the ground and their tails wagging.

As I entered the forest, the sunlight flickered above me and to my right. I glanced up to see Euclid gliding down to land on a tree branch. He accompanied us on our hike. Sometimes he'd disappear from sight, but he'd always be there waiting for us farther along.

I enjoyed the stroll through the woods. The morning was warm, but not too hot, especially in the shade of the forest. Birds twittered in the trees around us, twigs crunched under my feet, and the dogs' tails occasionally rustled the bushes pressing in on either side of the trail, but otherwise there was nothing but peace and quiet around us.

After several minutes of walking, Flossie and Fancy led me around a bend in the path and the trail opened out into another clear area, this one far larger than the last. We found ourselves standing near the top of a grassy hillside. Down below, a swathe of forest sat between us and the town of Twilight Cove. Beyond that, the blue ocean sparkled in a haze of sunlight.

'Beautiful,' I said, taking a moment to enjoy the view and catch my breath after the steady, uphill climb.

Then I turned around to look for the dogs. They were above me, cresting the top of the grassy hill. Euclid sat perched on a tree at the edge of the forest, near the spaniels.

'Wait for me!' I called out.

Flossie and Fancy paused, looking back and wagging their tails. When I caught up to them, they started trotting off ahead of me again. Euclid, too, took off, leading us along. When I reached the top of the hill, the land dipped downward before sloping upward again. Just beyond the dip was the edge of the forest. There was no clear path among the trees, but the undergrowth wasn't too thick, so we were able to make our way along without too much trouble.

As the dogs and I walked and Euclid glided from tree to tree, I took out my neon orange ribbons and tied them to branches, marking our trail. The animals would probably be able to find our way back, but I felt better knowing I had some added insurance in that regard.

The slope ahead of us grew steeper and I was starting to feel short of breath when we crested the next hill. The sound of gurgling water reached my ears moments before we broke free of the tree-line to see a stream rushing along before us.

The dogs sat down and looked up at me, as if waiting for me to do or say something.

'What is it?' I asked.

Their tails swished against the ground.

They exchanged a look and then returned their gazes to me.

'Is this the place where you first met Dorothy?'

Fancy threw her head back and let out a long 'a-woo'. Then she and Flossie jumped to their feet and bounded over to the stream. I followed more slowly, taking in the area around us. By the time I reached the stream's edge, the dogs were lapping up the water with gusto.

The sun sat high in the sky now, and it felt good to remove my backpack and let it drop to the ground. Once Flossie and Fancy had their fill of water, they waded into the middle of the stream. Fancy seemed content with sniffing at the occasional rock that stuck up above the surface, but Flossie kept dunking her face in and blowing bubbles out through her nose as the water rushed around her.

The stream was too tempting to resist, so I kicked off my hiking boots and pulled off my socks. Then I sat down on the bank and eased my feet into the cool water. A refreshing chill ran up from my feet and through my entire body, accompanied by a pleasant tingling sensation. The chill dissipated quickly, but the tingles lingered.

'It's a beautiful place,' I said to the dogs.

They were too busy with their own activities to pay me much attention. I kept talking anyway.

'How did you get here as puppies?' I hated to even think about them or any other animals being abandoned, but I knew it happened all the time. I wondered if the low-key tingles I could still feel had any sort of magical origin. 'Does this place have anything to do with your special abilities?'

Flossie raised her head, rivulets of water running off her face. She looked right at me for a second and then dunked her head into the stream again, back to blowing bubbles.

I laughed. 'You're a goofball.'

Flossie wagged her tail and started nipping at the water gurgling over a rock, as if trying to catch it as it rushed by.

Eventually, the spaniels waded out of the water, shook themselves off, and lay down on the bank. I pulled my feet out of the stream, wanting to give them time to dry before putting my socks and boots back on. My feet were ice cold now, but I felt completely refreshed, even energized.

I lay back and watched a couple of puffy white clouds drift across the blue sky. I had no more answers than I'd started out with earlier that morning, but I felt a deep contentment. The dogs snoozed peacefully by my side, apparently just as content and relaxed as me.

Once my feet were dry and the sun was starting to feel a bit too warm on my skin, I pulled my socks and hiking boots back on.

'Should we look around a little more or head home?' I asked the spaniels.

Their ears perked up and they jumped to their feet, suddenly on alert.

My state of lazy relaxation disappeared in an instant. 'What is it, girls?' I asked, apprehension prickling up my spine.

I looked around, but couldn't see or hear anything out of the ordinary.

I hurried to tie my boots, but the dogs didn't wait.

With a woof from Flossie, the spaniels took off and raced into the forest.

THIRTEEN

'Flossie! Fancy!'

I scrambled to finish tying my boots and then jumped to my feet. I remembered at the last second to grab my backpack before running after the dogs.

The forest seemed to swallow me up and I stumbled to a stop. The world had gone quiet. Not even a bird chirped in the trees.

Panic swelled in my chest. Had I lost the dogs?

I called their names again.

This time, I heard an answering bark off in the distance.

Then the sunlight filtering through the treetops flickered, drawing my attention upward. Euclid landed on a tree branch above my head. He gazed down at me with his yellow eyes and then swooped off the branch, flying deeper into the forest.

I ran after Euclid.

Flossie barked again, the sound closer now.

I pushed my way through some undergrowth and slipped and slid down a steep slope. At the bottom, Flossie and Fancy waited for me, tails wagging. Flossie was looking my way, but Fancy was staring into the space beneath a rock that jutted out near the bottom of a cliff face.

Above me, Euclid circled his way up through the leafy canopy and disappeared into the sky.

'You gave me a fright, running off like that,' I said to the spaniels.

Fancy dropped to her stomach, still looking beneath the rocky outcrop. Flossie circled around behind me and nudged the back of my leg.

'All right, I get the message.'

After dropping my backpack, I got down on my hands and knees and peered into the space beneath the jutting rock. It seemed to stretch far back, like a low-ceilinged cave.

'I can't see a thing,' I said. 'It's too dark.'

I grabbed my backpack and retrieved my flashlight. I flicked it on, but nothing happened.

I groaned and tossed the flashlight back into my pack. 'I can't believe I forgot to check the batteries.' I fished around in the pack for my phone, planning to use the flashlight app.

Fancy crawled forward on her belly until she'd almost disappeared beneath the outcrop. Then she began to emit a blue light, like bioluminescence.

I smiled and gave up my search. 'But who needs a flashlight or phone when Fancy's here, right?'

Flossie swished her tail against the hardpacked ground, and I sensed she was agreeing with me.

I peered into the cave again. This time, Fancy's glow lit up the space, allowing me to see that the low cave stretched back about ten feet.

My breath caught in my throat when I spotted a little ball of fur huddled against the back wall. Fancy's light reflected off two eyes, making them glow yellow-green.

The little ball of fur let out a tiny mew.

'A kitten!' I whispered, not wanting to scare it.

I reached out my hand, but the kitten cowered against the back wall of the cave, so I pulled my arm back to my side.

'Here, kitty,' I said quietly.

The tiny cat let out another mew, but didn't move from its spot at the back of the cave.

'We're here to help, sweetie.'

Flossie's nose pressed against my elbow as Fancy crawled farther into the cave. I ducked out into the open air to give her more room. I heard a scuffling sound and another mew. When I peered back into the cave, I saw that Fancy had managed to turn herself around and was crawling my way, holding the kitten in her mouth by the scruff of its neck.

When Fancy had crawled free of the outcrop, she stood up, her blue glow fading away, and gently set the kitten in my waiting hands. The adorable creature was mostly smoky gray, but with white paws, a white marking on its chest and two white patches on either side of its nose.

'You poor thing,' I said to the kitten as I cradled it against my stomach. 'How did you get here?'

The cat mewed again, and the plaintive sound almost broke my heart.

'Where there's one kitten, there could be others. And maybe the mother is around too.' I looked at the spaniels. 'What do you think?'

Flossie and Fancy glanced at each other and then fixed their gazes back on me. They didn't appear concerned that there could be other cats around in need of assistance. I decided to make a quick search of the surrounding area anyway.

Holding the kitten against my chest, I got to my feet and slung my backpack over my shoulder. I walked in a circle, several times, widening my search area with each round. The dogs accompanied me, sniffing here and there, but in a casual way, not as if they were following any particular scent.

After several minutes of searching, I called it quits.

'I don't know how you ended up here on your own,' I said to the kitten, who'd stayed snuggled against my chest during the entire search, 'but you're safe now and you're going to be well taken care of. I can promise you that.'

Checking the time on my phone, I found that it was already past noon. My stomach gave a rumble of complaint, but I ignored it. Even though I had some food in my backpack, I wanted to get the kitten back to town as soon as possible. Lunch could wait.

Fortunately, the dogs led me back to the stream without any problem. They also led me back to Old Birch Road, without any need for my orange ribbons. I kept a careful hold on the kitten with one hand while I collected each ribbon on our way past. Then I stuffed them in my pocket when we reached my car.

I opened the door and Flossie and Fancy clambered into the back seat. I took a moment to consider what I should do with the kitten. In the end, I fetched a sweatshirt from the trunk of the car and formed it into a nest on the passenger seat. I hoped the kitten wouldn't get too adventurous and try to climb all over the car while I was driving. At the moment, that didn't seem like it would be the case. The little creature lay down in the makeshift bed and mewed but made no move to explore the vehicle.

'I'm going to take you to the vet clinic,' I told the kitten. 'The doctor will check you out and make sure you're OK.'

That garnered another adorable mew from the kitten, along with an 'a-woo' from Fancy.

I cracked open the window and set the car in motion, driving carefully down the bumpy dirt road. When we were about halfway along the forest track, Euclid swooped down from the sky and landed on a tree branch just ahead of us. I braked carefully, not wanting to dislodge the kitten from the passenger seat. Keeping an eye on the little creature to make sure it wouldn't escape the car, I climbed out with the dogs and shut the door.

Up on the tree branch, Euclid ruffled his feathers. The dogs looked up at the owl and then trotted over his way. When they reached the spot below Euclid's branch, they sniffed around on the ground. I walked toward them. When I reached the spaniels, they touched their noses to a patch of dirt at the side of the road and then looked up at me.

The sunlight glinted off something silver. I crouched down and picked up a pen that lay in the dirt, partially concealed by the undergrowth that was encroaching on the road. It was a maroon pen with a silver clip. As I straightened up, I turned the pen around in my fingers and noticed the letters 'SMK' on the barrel, written in silver script.

'Is this important?' I asked the dogs.

Flossie gave a woof while Fancy wagged her tail.

All three of us looked up at Euclid. The great horned owl shook out his wings and then took off into the sky.

'All right, we'll take this home with us,' I said, closing my fingers around the pen.

Flossie and Fancy seemed satisfied with that and trotted ahead of me to the car.

Once I was back in the driver's seat, I set the pen in one of the cup holders.

The kitten had fallen asleep, snuggled into my sweatshirt. My heart almost cracked from the cuteness overload. No more delays, I decided. I wanted to get the sweet cat to the vet clinic as soon as possible, in case it was in need of any medical care.

I navigated the rest of Old Birch Road without any further stops, and once I turned on to Larkspur Lane, I increased our speed. Bypassing the animal sanctuary, I continued towards town. On the way to the vet clinic, I pondered the letters SMK. I couldn't think of anyone I knew locally with those initials or of any businesses in town that might have those letters in its name.

Of course, the pen might not hold any significance. After all, I had no idea how long it had been lying there on the edge of the forest road. Nevertheless, I'd learned to trust Euclid and the spaniels. They'd wanted me to find that pen. Now I just had to figure out why.

FOURTEEN

I left the little kitten – a girl, I now knew – in the care of the local veterinarian, Dr Mahika Sharma. I felt a tug at my heart when I handed the sweet little thing over, but I knew the clinic was the best place for her. Dr Sharma promised to update me on the kitten's condition once she'd been examined and treated for any medical issues she might have.

When I returned to the animal sanctuary, I found Auntie O in the farmhouse kitchen, setting a batch of blueberry muffins on a wire rack to cool. Gizmo greeted the dogs and me with a command to walk the plank, followed by a maniacal cackle that left my aunt and me laughing.

While Gizmo continued to chatter in the background and the dogs lapped up fresh water from their dish on the floor, I told Aunt Olivia about the kitten we'd found.

'I don't understand how people can abandon animals,' I said once I'd finished the tale.

My aunt rested a hand on my arm. 'It's unfathomable, but that's why I started the sanctuary, so animals that are abandoned or otherwise in need will have a safe haven.'

I hugged her. 'And I'm so glad that the animals here have you to love and care for them.'

She gave me a squeeze in return. 'Now they've got you too, and we're all better off because of that.'

Auntie O left the farmhouse a short while later, leaving some muffins behind for me. I ate two of them right away, finally silencing the grumbling in my stomach.

It was too hot to work out on the porch that afternoon, so I took my laptop into the living room, where the sound of Gizmo's singing and chattering was slightly dampened. I'd made good progress on my script rewrites by the time I received a call from the receptionist at the vet clinic.

The kitten, who was about eight weeks old, was dehydrated but otherwise healthy. The clinic staff would care for her overnight, but if all was well the next day, I could pick her up, unless I wanted the clinic to put her up for adoption. I'd already talked to Aunt Olivia about bringing the kitten to the farm, at least temporarily, so I assured the receptionist that I'd swing by the clinic the next day.

After helping out with the farm chores that evening, I returned to the house to feed Gizmo. Then the dogs and I waited on the back porch until Callum drove his truck over from his cabin beyond the barn. Flossie, Fancy and I joined him in the truck, and he drove us to Twilight Cove's sports field. We'd arranged to meet up with Tessa and a few others so Callum could teach beginners like me how to play baseball and help more experienced players improve their skills.

There was a mixed fun league in neighboring towns, but Twilight Cove hadn't had a team for several years. Callum had decided it was time to change that. It was too late to join the league this year, but he wanted to get a jumpstart on forming a team for next spring. I'd made no promises about joining an actual team, but I was looking forward to learning to play the sport.

We arrived at the field half an hour before we'd arranged to meet the others. When I confessed my fear of having an audience when I tried to hit a ball for the first time (I'd only ever played T-ball and that was well over two decades ago), Callum had promised me some one-on-one time to help build my confidence. I didn't know how much success he'd have with that, but I wasn't about to turn down a chance to spend time alone with him. We'd been apart so much over the summer that I now wanted to make up for lost time whenever possible.

Part of me worried about how fast my feelings for him were growing, but I was trying not to get stressed over it. That was easier said than done for an overthinker like me, but I was giving it my best shot, and I was determined to simply enjoy the evening without worrying about keeping my heart safe or what the future might hold.

When we climbed out of the truck, a couple of kids were kicking a soccer ball around at the far end of the park, but the baseball diamond was empty. Flossie and Fancy explored the area with their noses while I helped Callum unload his pitching machine from the back of the truck. The contraption weighed nearly a hundred pounds but fortunately had wheels, so once we had it on the ground, Callum easily moved it on to the field.

Finished exploring, the dogs lay down on the grass in front of the nearby bleachers while Callum loaded the pitching machine with balls. Once that was done, he fished a bat out of his bag of gear and passed it to me.

'That's a good one to start with,' he said.

I tested the weight of the bat in my hands as I warily eyed the machine. 'How fast will the balls come out of that thing?'

Callum grinned. 'Up to a hundred miles per hour.' He laughed when my eyes widened. 'Don't worry.' He set a batter's helmet on my head. 'We're going to start with it on the lowest setting.'

'One mile per hour?' I asked, hopeful.

'Not quite.'

I decided I didn't want any further details.

'We'll work on your swing before we turn the machine on,' he said.

I liked the sound of that, but I wasn't about to take my eyes off the contraption he'd set up by the pitcher's mound. 'Are you sure it's not going to go rogue and start throwing balls at us before we're ready?'

Callum grinned again and dangled a set of keys from his fingers. 'It won't turn on without these, so we're good.'

He stashed the keys in his pocket and I breathed a sigh of relief. He didn't fail to notice.

'Why are you so nervous?' he asked.

'Because I don't want a broken face,' I said, although that was only the partial truth. I was also a little afraid of being so hopeless at the sport that I'd have to sit on the sidelines next spring while all my friends played on the team. I didn't want to feel left out, and I knew that baseball was a big part of Callum's life. If I was hopeless at the sport, would that make it harder for me to fit into his life?

'I won't let that happen,' Callum assured me.

His utter confidence in that regard helped to ease my worries about getting a baseball to the face. Somewhat, anyway.

'All right,' he said, standing a few feet away from home plate, where I'd stationed myself. 'Let me see your stance.'

I did my best to mimic the players I'd seen on television over the past few weeks.

He moved in to correct me.

'Shoulders down a bit.' He guided them into place. 'And this elbow like this.' He moved my arm, his touch gentle. 'Get your feet farther apart.'

I did as he instructed.

He stepped back to scrutinize my new stance. 'Looking good.'

'Really?' The word popped out of my mouth, heavily laced with skepticism.

'Believe in yourself, Georgie. That's half the battle.'

'I should have worn the jersey Javi sent me,' I said, holding my stance. 'Then I could channel some McQuade magic.'

Callum stood before me. 'You've got McQuade magic right here. Isn't that better?'

'Infinitely, but I'm still wearing the jersey next time.' I had second thoughts. 'Except it's so nice that I don't want to get it dirty.'

He nodded, looking serious except for the twinkle in his eyes. 'When you're sliding into the bases.'

'OK, so maybe that's unlikely,' I conceded as I lowered the bat and relaxed my stance.

'Don't be so sure.' He stepped closer to me. 'But let's stay focused. There are three parts to the swing. The load, the stride and the swing itself.'

He took the bat from me and demonstrated each part separately before putting them together.

I'd watched online videos of him playing baseball, but that was nothing like seeing him in action in person. Even just swinging at the air, no ball in play, he took my breath away. There really was magic in his movement. It didn't hurt that he also looked so good that I got butterflies in my chest.

He demonstrated another swing and then handed the bat to me. 'Your turn.'

We went through the three components, one at a time, with him correcting my movements.

'Now put it all together,' he said after a few minutes.

I did so, trying to remember all of his instructions.

Despite my efforts, I managed to forget a few things. Callum reminded me and gave me some other pointers as well. Then he had me swing the bat several more times.

'That's great!' he finally declared. 'Nice work, Georgie.'

I let the bat dangle from my hand. 'If only the game were played without a ball, then I'd be set for the big leagues.'

Callum grinned and fished the keys for the pitching machine from his pocket. 'Just wait,' he said. 'Once you feel the satisfaction of hitting the ball to the outfield, you'll be hooked.'

I'm already hooked on something, I almost said.

My cheeks flushed. I couldn't believe those words nearly came out of my mouth. It was way too soon to be saying things like that to him, even if the statement was frighteningly true.

Callum turned on the machine and I backed away from home plate.

'Where are you going?' Callum asked, amused.

'I don't want to stand in front of that thing.'

'That's kind of the point, Georgie.' He crossed from the pitching mound to home plate. 'Come on.'

I eyed the machine with suspicion. 'When's the first ball coming out?'

He held up a small remote. 'Not until I tell it to.'

I relaxed, slightly, and joined him by the plate.

'Do you want me to help you with the first few?' he offered.

'Does the sun set in the west?'

He chuckled and moved behind me so my back was against his chest. He reached around and settled his hands on the bat, with mine in between.

'Don't white-knuckle it,' he said, speaking right near my ear.

I tried to relax my hold, but his proximity was more than a little distracting.

'That's better,' he encouraged when I no longer had a death grip on the bat. 'We're just going to look at the first pitch.'

'You mean watch it go by without swinging?'

'Exactly.'

I relaxed a little more. 'That I can do.'

His low rumble of laughter reverberated through my back to my chest and made my stomach swoop.

'Ready?' he asked.

'As I'll ever be.'

Callum took one hand off the bat to hit a button on the remote, but soon his hand was securely next to mine again.

A rattling sound came from the machine and then it shot a ball our way. To my relief, it didn't fly as fast as I thought it might.

'We're getting the next one,' Callum said. 'Remember: load, stride, swing.'

'Load, stride, swing,' I repeated.

The machine rattled again and spat out another ball.

We swung the bat and hit the ball with a satisfying crack, sending it flying just past second base.

'Nice!' Callum said.

'Do you think the fun league allows batters to have a plus one?' I asked in jest. 'Because if so, I'm ready.'

The machine pitched the next ball. Again, with Callum's guidance, the bat made contact.

'I'm always happy to be your plus one, Georgie,' Callum said quietly into my ear, sending tingles over my skin. 'But I'm pretty sure that'll be a no from the league.'

Together, we hit another ball.

Then, to my dismay, Callum released the bat and stepped away from me.

'Where are you going?' I leaned back as the next ball came sailing by. I didn't even try to hit it.

'The training wheels are off.'

'But I really like my training wheels,' I protested.

'Focus, Georgie,' he said, though I could hear amusement in his voice.

I sighed and followed his advice.

'Load, stride, swing,' he reminded me as a ball rattled in the machine.

I did my best to put everything I'd learned to work.

I swung the bat.

And missed the ball.

'Don't worry about it,' Callum said.

I missed the next one as well.

'Don't overthink things, Georgie.'

'That's what I do best,' I said, only half joking.

'It's just you and the ball.'

I let the next one fly past me. Then I let out a breath and cleared my head of all distractions.

The machine gave its telltale rattle and pitched a ball.

I swung the bat and . . .

Crack!

I watched in astonishment as the ball flew over the pitching machine, hitting the ground near the baseline.

'Did you see that?' I ignored the next ball, still astounded by the fact that I'd actually hit one.

Over on the sidelines, Fancy bayed and Flossie woofed.

Callum tugged me away from home plate and into his arms. 'I saw it.' He stroked a thumb across my cheek. 'I see you, Georgie.'

I closed my eyes as his lips touched mine.

The machine kept pitching balls, but we ignored them.

I dropped the bat and tipped the helmet off my head as our kiss deepened.

'Practice hasn't even started and you two are already at first base,' a familiar voice called out.

My cheeks hot, I took a step back from Callum.

Tessa was walking our way from the parking lot, a mischievous smile on her face.

Despite the interruption – and the teasing – I was glad to see her.

Another car pulled in next to hers. Cindy Yoon, owner of the spaniels' favorite store, the Pet Palace, climbed out of the vehicle along with her brother, Nicholas, and her girlfriend, Genesis.

'Brody has to work tonight,' Tessa said when she got closer. 'But he's hoping he can be here next week.'

I wasn't surprised that Brody was still on duty. Even though the state police would be heading the murder investigation, there would no doubt be plenty of work for the local officers as well.

Cindy, Genesis and Nicholas joined us at the baseball diamond, and we all exchanged greetings.

I smiled when I saw Roxy heading our way on foot. Her steps grew hesitant when she got close, but when I waved her over, she picked up her pace.

Roxy was a big baseball fan. Although she wasn't old enough to join the fun league, Callum and I had encouraged her to join our practices this summer. She didn't have many friends or an easy home life, and I was hoping we could help build her confidence and give her something fun to do outside of volunteering.

She would be going to California the next day, so I was glad she'd showed up this evening. She wore her dark brown hair in a pony tail, and the smattering of freckles across her nose had darkened with the summer sunshine. Roxy, like Genesis and Nicholas, had brought her own baseball glove.

'Are you sure everyone's OK with me being here?' she whispered as we stood on the edge of the group gathered near home plate.

She knew Callum from the farm and Tessa, one of her teachers, but I didn't know if she'd met Cindy, Genesis or Nicholas.

'Of course. Just watch.' I raised my voice and addressed the others. 'Hey, everyone, if you don't already know, this is Roxy.'

I appreciated how enthusiastically the group welcomed her, and I was pleased to see her hesitancy fade away.

Callum gave her ponytail a gentle tug and she stuck her tongue out at him, but I could tell she was pleased with the reception.

We all spent a couple of minutes chatting and catching up. Then Callum clapped his hands, his green eyes alight, and said, 'Let's play some baseball!'

FIFTEEN

The practice session involved as much laughter as it did baseball. Tessa and I were both total beginners at the sport, but the others had at least some experience, and Nicholas and Genesis were both quite good. Callum was completely in his element, and I could tell he loved coaching. He was great at providing instruction as well as encouraging everyone, especially Roxy, and I swore I could see her confidence building already. My hope was that any confidence she gained on the field would translate to the rest of her life.

After we wrapped up for the evening, Tessa drove Roxy home and then met Callum and me at the beach, where we'd taken the dogs to let them play in the water. By the time Tessa joined us, Callum had bought cold drinks at a nearby food truck. We enjoyed the beverages as we took a leisurely stroll along the shoreline and the dogs splashed and galloped through the shallows.

We'd arranged this meeting because Tessa had something she wanted to share with me about Jasper's murder. Fortunately, she'd told me that after practice. Otherwise, I might have burst from the suspense of waiting to hear the new information.

'I had lunch with my cousin Valentina today,' Tessa said after taking a long drink from her glass bottle of lemonade.

Valentina worked at the local police department in a civilian capacity. She had looser lips than was prudent, considering her place of employment, and she loved sharing juicy tidbits of information with Tessa.

'I don't suppose they've caught the killer yet,' I said without much hope.

If someone had been arrested for the crime before Tessa's lunch with her cousin, the whole town would likely know by now.

'Unfortunately, no,' Tessa confirmed. 'But the murder weapon belonged to Jasper.'

'It was an antique knife or something, wasn't it?' Callum asked.

I'd filled him in on everything I'd seen at Jasper's house on the night of the crime.

'It looked like a combination knife and pistol,' I said.

Tessa nodded. 'Apparently, it's an eighteenth-century dagger pistol. Jasper kept written records of all the antiques he owned. Those records and Elsie both confirmed that the dagger pistol belonged to him. Elsie said it was on display in Jasper's study.'

'So, the killer didn't take the murder weapon with them to Jasper's house,' I said, thinking out loud. 'That might suggest that the murder wasn't premeditated. The back door was standing open when Auntie O and I arrived at the house, but Jasper still could have invited the killer in.'

'But he probably didn't,' Tessa said. 'I'm betting the killer left through the back door, without bothering to shut it properly, but the police think the murderer entered through the study window. It was unlocked, and there was a partial shoe print on the sill.'

'An attempted break-in gone wrong?' Callum suggested. 'Maybe Jasper interrupted the thief.'

'Possibly,' Tessa said, 'but there's more.' She paused to take a sip of her drink.

'I can't handle all this suspense, Tessa,' I complained.

She smiled and then, to my relief, continued. 'The killer might have been armed, even though they used the dagger pistol to kill Jasper. You know how a neighbor called to report hearing a gunshot coming from Jasper's house or thereabouts?'

I nodded. Brody had told me that much. 'But Jasper was stabbed, not shot.' And because of that, I hadn't given much thought to the report of a gunshot.

'True,' Tessa agreed. ' But there was a bullet in the wall of the study.'

'Valentina's information is like gold,' I said with appreciation.

'Or pirate treasure,' Callum countered.

'And she knows it,' Tessa said.

'Did the bullet come from the dagger pistol?' I asked.

'No,' she replied. 'And the gun that fired it hasn't been found by the police.'

'OK.' I tried to put all my thoughts together. 'So the murder could have been premeditated. Or the killer took the gun to Jasper's house just in case their plan to steal the map went awry. They climbed in through the window and then were interrupted by Jasper. The killer tried to shoot Jasper but missed . . .'

'Then there was a struggle and the killer lost the gun,' Callum picked up the theory.

I nudged him with my elbow. 'Careful, you'll be catching the sleuthing bug.'

He grinned. 'It does seem to be contagious.'

I tried to get back on track. 'After dropping the gun or losing it to Jasper, the killer then grabbed the closest weapon at hand.'

'The dagger pistol,' Tessa finished with a nod.

'It definitely could have played out that way,' I said. 'And considering the timing and the fact that the intruder broke into the study, I think there's a very good chance that they were after the map.'

'Especially since the map is still missing,' Tessa said. 'That's another tidbit I got from Valentina.'

'Wouldn't Jasper have kept the map in a safe or something?' I wondered out loud.

Tessa shrugged. 'You'd think so, considering how he didn't want anyone else seeing it. But, according to Valentina, there was no map in Jasper's safe when the police searched the house. Maybe Jasper had taken it out to study it. After all, he was planning to dig for the treasure soon.'

'That's a good point,' I said.

'So what does all this tell us?' Callum asked. 'Did the killer go there intending to harm Jasper or did a planned theft escalate to murder when Jasper arrived on the scene?'

'I really don't know,' I admitted. 'But it does seem like the map is at the heart of everything.'

'Unless someone other than the killer took the map.' Callum shook his head as soon as he said the words. 'I guess that doesn't make sense.'

'No,' I said, not so ready to dismiss the possibility. 'I wouldn't say that. If somebody found Jasper dead before Aunt Olivia and I did, they could have seen the map, grabbed it and hightailed it out of there.'

Callum didn't seem convinced. 'Doesn't that seem less likely than the killer taking the map?'

'Yes,' I conceded, 'but it's not something we can rule out entirely.'

'Where does this leave us suspect-wise?' Tessa asked. 'We've got Giles, Elsie and Flynn on our list.'

I thought things over for a moment. 'I don't think the information from Valentina changes our list.'

'I agree,' Tessa said. 'We need to find out who has an alibi and who doesn't.'

'Hopefully, we can do that tomorrow.' As we turned around to stroll back toward the parking lot, I remembered something else I wanted to talk about. 'Do the letters SMK mean anything to either of you?' I explained about the pen I'd found on Old Birch Road, leaving out the fact that the animals had led me to it. Callum and Tessa already knew that I'd seen the road name written in Jasper's journal.

Unfortunately, neither Tessa nor Callum could think of a person or local business with those initials.

'The pen probably has nothing to do with any of this,' I said, knowing there was a good chance that was the case.

'Don't worry,' Tessa said, probably hearing the note of dejection in my voice. 'We've got this, Nancy Drew. Before you know it, Jasper's killer will be behind bars, and Olivia and everyone else who cared for him will at least have some closure.'

I hoped she was right about that.

We didn't have a chance to continue our conversation about suspects. Three women in their forties approached us, practically bubbling over with excitement. They had eyes only for Callum.

'Excuse me,' one of the women said to him. 'Are you Callum McQuade?'

He confirmed his identity and the women's excitement grew.

'We're such big fans!' one of the women enthused. 'Do you mind if we get pictures with you?'

Callum graciously agreed to the request, so I spent the next minute or two snapping photos of them with Callum, using each woman's phone in turn.

After that, they asked for autographs and dug around in their oversized handbags for something he could sign.

Callum, meanwhile, chatted with them in an easy, amiable way that I admired. I definitely didn't have his skill for making small talk with complete strangers.

The dogs were still in the ocean, Flossie nipping at the crests of the gentle waves before they broke against the shore, and Fancy shaking a stick she'd found floating in the water. Tessa and I wandered closer to them, stopping at the water's edge.

'Does this happen a lot?' Tessa asked, inclining her head in the direction of Callum and the women.

He was now signing the back of one woman's T-shirt.

'We haven't been out in public together much yet,' I said, 'but this is already the second time it's happened.'

Tessa sent a sidelong glance my way. 'Are you OK with it?'

'Sure.' After a brief hesitation, I decided to provide a more fulsome and more truthful answer. 'I like that he's so popular. I guess I just feel awkward when it happens because I'm like a fifth wheel and I fade into the background. And it makes me feel like maybe I'm not enough for his world. You know, not shiny or glamorous enough.'

I wondered if I'd said too much, but at the same time it felt good to confess those feelings to my friend.

Tessa hooked her arm through mine. 'Georgie, when it comes to whether or not you're enough for his world, Callum's opinion is the only one that matters. And judging by the way he looks at you – and by the way he was kissing you at the ball park earlier – I'd say he thinks you're exactly right for him.'

I managed a small smile. 'He does like me. He's come right out and said it more than once, and I believe him. I guess there's just a part of me that wonders how long that will last before he gets bored with ordinary Georgie and wants to date a model or a popstar again.'

Tessa gave my arm a squeeze. 'There's so much I want to say to that, but . . .' She glanced over her shoulder. The women were thanking Callum and turning away from him. 'For now, all I'm going to say is he's been there and done that, and now he's with you. That should tell you something.'

'Thank you.' I gave her a hug. 'I'm trying not to be insecure or overthink everything.'

She returned the hug. 'Keep trying.'

Callum joined us then, as did Flossie and Fancy, who both had water streaming off their fur in rivulets.

'And now,' Tessa said, giving the wet dogs each a careful pat on the head. 'I'll leave you two humans to get back to that kiss I interrupted earlier.'

Her mischievous smile was back as she waved at us before hiking up the beach toward her car.

'That sounds like a good plan to me,' Callum said with a grin.

I glanced around, noting that there were still plenty of people out on the beach even though it was growing dark.

'I love the idea,' I said, 'but not so much the location.'

Callum took my hand. 'Then let's get the heck out of here.'

Flossie and Fancy woofed and bayed their agreement before shaking the water out of their fur, giving Callum and me a shower in the process.

When we got back to the farm, Callum and I shared a long kiss goodnight on the farmhouse porch, but after that I was left with the dogs and my thoughts. The dogs were great company. My thoughts, not so much, focused as they were on Jasper's murder and my own insecurities.

SIXTEEN

After feeding the donkeys the next morning, I spent a solid couple of hours working on my screenplay. Even though I was eager to talk to Elsie Suárez and pick up the kitten from the vet clinic, I knew I'd spend the day feeling stressed if I didn't finish rewriting my script before turning my attention to other things.

By the time I stood up from the couch and stretched out my muscles, I'd made all the changes requested by the network with several days to spare. I wanted to read the script through one more time before emailing it to the producer I was working with, but that could wait without causing me anxiety. Besides, a headache was brewing behind my eyes, so a break from staring at the computer screen would do me good.

I had the amethyst Dorothy had given me in the pocket of my shorts. I'd developed a habit of pulling it out and rubbing the smooth stone between my fingers whenever I paused in my writing. For weeks, that had seemed to prevent me from getting headaches, whether that was because of the power of suggestion or because of the amethyst's magic. I recalled what Fae had told me about recharging it. The moon would be full tonight.

Not wanting to forget to take Fae's advice, I ran upstairs and set the amethyst on the windowsill in my bedroom. I still wasn't quite sure if I believed that the moon could make the purple stone more powerful, but I hated suffering through headaches, so I was willing to give the moonlight a chance.

When I returned downstairs, Gizmo was chattering away to Flossie and Fancy as they sat gazing at the parrot.

'Thar she blows!' Gizmo cried. 'Splice the mainbrace!'

Then he started singing his favorite tune again.

I fetched a head of broccoli from the refrigerator and cut off a floret. I offered it to Gizmo and he grabbed it greedily.

'I don't suppose you know any other songs,' I said as the parrot pecked at his snack. 'That one's getting a bit old – if you keep singing it, I might go crazy.'

'Cuckoo!' Gizmo said before going back to eating the broccoli.

I laughed and Fancy joined in with a 'woo'.

'That's right,' I said to the parrot. 'I'm going to go completely cuckoo.'

'Cuckoo!' Gizmo said again. Then he hopped to another perch and repeated the word several times, ending with, 'Ooh, you're cheeky!'

I laughed again. 'Really, Gizmo? Because I think you might be the cheeky one.'

Flossie woofed her agreement, but Gizmo went back to singing that same old tune.

The dogs followed me as I stepped out on to the back porch. I planned to head into town, but first I decided to check in with Aunt Olivia and see if she needed me to pick anything up from the shops.

Flossie and Fancy bounded off ahead of me, somehow knowing my destination before I'd even finished descending the porch steps.

We found Auntie O in the kitchen of the carriage house, taking two trays of cookies out of the oven. A loaf of banana bread already sat cooling on a wire rack.

'You've been busy,' I commented when the dogs and I entered through the open French doors at the back of the carriage house.

'I wanted to get some baking done before it gets too hot outside,' she said.

As she shut off the oven, I told her why I'd stopped by.

'Actually, I was about to head into town myself.' She removed her apron and hung it on a hook on the wall. 'I sold all my raffle tickets and I need to turn the book and money in to Catherine at the inn. I also want to take some of this baking to Elsie and see how she's holding up.'

'Would it be all right if I came with you?' I asked.

'Of course.' Auntie O bent down to fuss over Flossie and Fancy. 'And these girls can come too.'

The spaniels wagged their tails as they gazed up at Olivia.

'Elsie loves dogs,' my aunt continued, 'but she hasn't had one of her own since her Pomeranian passed away last fall.'

We ended up sitting down at the kitchen table to enjoy a cold glass of lemonade while the freshly baked cookies cooled. Then Aunt Olivia packaged some of the cookies up with the loaf of banana bread and we all piled into my car for the trip into the center of town.

Olivia directed me to Elsie's house. It turned out she lived in the same neighborhood as Jasper, but closer to the main entrance of the housing development. When we were a few houses away from our destination, Auntie O pointed to a man crossing a home's front lawn as he headed toward a van parked at the curb.

'It's Lance,' my aunt said as she lowered her window.

I slowed the car to a stop and she called out a greeting.

Lance altered his path and bypassed his van, which had the name of his business written on the side.

'Does he live in this neighborhood too?' I asked.

'No, he lives closer to Main Street,' Auntie O replied. 'He must be here for a job.'

Lance came over to Olivia's side of the car and greeted us with a smile.

'Good news,' he said after we'd exchanged hellos. 'I talked to everyone at the theater and the vote was unanimous to allow you to use our costumes for your fundraiser in the fall.'

'That's fantastic!' Auntie O exclaimed. 'Thank you, Lance, and please pass on our thanks to the others.'

'Will do.' He tipped an imaginary hat at us and turned away. When he reached the side of the road, he stretched out his back and then opened the double doors at the rear of his van.

Another car was approaching from behind, so I started driving again, pulling over when my aunt pointed out Elsie's house. Olivia had called ahead to make sure that Elsie was home, so she knew we were coming and opened the front door before we'd reached the porch.

'What sweet dogs,' Elsie cooed to Flossie and Fancy as she greeted them with lots of pets and attention.

Then she accepted Olivia's baked offerings with thanks and led us to the sunny kitchen at the back of the house.

'How are you doing, Elsie?' my aunt asked once she and I were seated at the kitchen table with Flossie and Fancy lying at our feet.

Elsie set a bowl of water on the floor for the spaniels and they jumped up to get a drink. 'I'm hanging in there. How about you, Olivia? It's so awful that you saw Jasper that way.'

My aunt blinked away tears. 'It's certainly not how I want to remember him, but I'm doing OK too.'

Elsie fetched a pitcher of iced tea from the fridge and three glasses from one of the cupboards. 'I think things will be easier once the killer is behind bars.'

'Has there been any progress in that regard?' I asked as Elsie set the pitcher and glasses on the table.

The information I'd received from Tessa, via Valentina, was probably the most recent, but I figured it was worth asking in case the police had told Elsie something I didn't already know.

She sat down at the table. 'Not as far as I know.' She sighed as she poured iced tea into the glasses. 'If only Jasper had let me see the map. Then I could tell the police where it led and they could watch to see who shows up to dig for the treasure.'

'Are you certain that's why Jasper was killed?' Auntie O asked. 'So someone could get their hands on the map and the pirate treasure?'

'I can't think of any other reason why somebody would harm Jasper.' Elsie passed us each a glass and we thanked her. 'He was such a gentle soul.'

We let a moment pass, those words hanging heavily in the air.

'Jasper seemed convinced of the map's authenticity,' I said after taking a sip of iced tea.

Elsie curled a hand around her glass, but otherwise ignored her drink. 'He was completely convinced. Whoever sold him the map had the paper tested and it was determined to date back to the eighteenth century. The ink wasn't tested, though. Jasper said that would be too expensive and time-consuming. Besides, he figured the best way to test the map's authenticity was to get out and dig up the treasure.'

Which the killer might have done by now.

I kept that thought to myself and tried to fish for more information. 'I heard that a neighbor called nine-one-one on the night Jasper was killed because they heard a gunshot.'

Elsie nodded. 'The police think Jasper interrupted a thief trying to steal the map.'

'I'm glad you weren't there that evening,' Olivia said.

'Except, if I had been, maybe things would have turned out differently.'

My aunt reached across the table to place a hand over Elsie's. 'Most likely, you would have been hurt or killed as well.'

'Were you at the Dead Eye Days rehearsal that evening?' I asked, even though I didn't recall seeing her among the costumed people at the park.

'No, I'm not one of the actors,' she replied. 'I went to bed early that night. I've been feeling so guilty for sleeping peacefully while poor Jasper was being killed.'

'You had no way of knowing,' I said, hoping to ease her guilt if she wasn't the murderer.

Yet, even as I spoke those words, I digested the implication of what she'd said.

If Elsie lived alone, she likely didn't have an alibi for the time of the murder.

She gave me a sad but grateful smile, clearly having no clue what was going on inside my head.

'Did Jasper leave a copy of the treasure map with anyone in case something happened to the original?' I asked.

'No,' Elsie replied with a sigh. 'I'm sure he didn't. He wouldn't even let me peek at the map. He didn't want anyone to see it, original or not.'

'What about the funeral?' Aunt Olivia asked, steering the conversation in a slightly different direction. 'Do you know when that will be?'

Elsie shook her head. 'It all depends on when the police release Jasper's body.' Her eyes grew shiny and she took a moment to compose herself. She sipped at her tea, and when she set the glass down on the table again, the welling tears had subsided. 'I had a visit from Jasper's lawyer this morning. His sister and I will each inherit half of his estate.' She had to blink back a fresh set of tears. 'That was so generous of Jasper, especially since we weren't married or engaged. We hadn't even moved in together. We talked about it, but I wanted to wait until the fall, once my son was settled into college life.'

A tear escaped and she wiped it away with one finger.

Aunt Olivia reached over the table to pat her hand. 'Jasper loved you very much.'

Elsie attempted a smile. 'He was a sweet man. Exasperating at times, but he had a good heart.'

'Exasperating?' I echoed, recalling the argument I'd witnessed between her and Jasper shortly before his death.

'He could get . . . overly enthusiastic about certain things,' Auntie O said. 'Is that what you mean?'

'Yes, that's one way of putting it,' Elsie said. 'Like all this pirate stuff. He lived and breathed it, especially whenever Dead Eye Days rolled around. He'd also get obsessed with other things from time to time.'

'Anything recently?' I asked, hoping I wasn't pressing too hard.

Elsie shrugged. 'There was usually something.' She picked up the pitcher. 'More tea?'

Aunt Olivia and I both declined. I still had half a glass remaining and Auntie O had taken only a couple of sips of her tea.

Elsie seemed eager to change the subject, so she chattered on for several minutes about Dead Eye Days and the fact that she would be doing face painting during the festival.

'Elsie's a talented artist,' Aunt Olivia said to me.

Elsie gave my aunt a humble smile. 'That's kind of you to say. Painting is really just a hobby, but one I enjoy.'

We spent the next several minutes chatting about various mundane happenings around town. When Auntie O and I had finished our tea, we got up to leave, the dogs instantly waking up from napping at our feet.

'I saw that writer, Ajax Wolfgang, with you at the beach the other night,' I said as Elsie walked us toward the door. 'Was he bothering you?'

'It wasn't anything I couldn't handle,' she assured me. 'I think he was hoping to find out if I'd seen the map and knew the treasure's location. I'm sure he's not the only one who's hoping he can get his hands on the loot. He'll probably leave me alone now that he knows I haven't a clue where the treasure's buried.'

'There's something I've been wondering about,' I said to Elsie as Aunt Olivia and I stepped out on to the front porch. 'I couldn't help but notice the words "Old Birch Road" written in Jasper's journal. Do you know why he made that note?'

'Old Birch Road,' Auntie O mused. 'There's nothing up that way.' Elsie shook her head. 'Olivia's right. That's an old road to nowhere. I have no idea why Jasper had that written down. Unless it had something to do with the location of the treasure.'

'We'll probably never know,' Olivia said.

We exchanged goodbyes with Elsie and drove off in my car.

As we made our way through the center of Twilight Cove, I couldn't help but feel that Elsie had lied when I asked her about Old Birch Road.

SEVENTEEN

'Does Jasper's sister live in Twilight Cove?' I asked as I turned my car on to Main Street.

'In England,' Auntie O replied. 'I know her name is Meredith and she's several years older than Jasper, but I've never met her. She has some health issues, so she doesn't travel much. Jasper used to go visit her every couple of years or so.'

'He doesn't have any family here?'

'Not anymore. His parents passed away a few years back. I think he has some distant cousins scattered around the country, but no one he was close to.' My aunt dug a tissue out of her handbag and wiped at her eyes.

Seeing her tears, even though they hadn't quite spilled over on to her cheeks, strengthened my resolve to find a way to help the murder investigation along. I didn't yet have anything concrete enough to share with the police, but I hoped that would change soon.

'I'm glad he had Elsie's companionship over the past year,' Olivia continued. 'He was really quite smitten with her.'

Again, I recalled the argument we'd seen between Jasper and Elsie. Of course, most couples argued at some point. That didn't necessarily mean the relationship was in trouble.

'Does Elsie live alone?' I asked.

'She does. She has a son, but he's been living and working in Portland since he graduated high school in June.' Auntie O sent an astute glance my way. 'Are you checking up on her alibi?'

I winced. 'I hope I wasn't so obvious when we were talking to Elsie.'

'I don't think she had a clue what you were digging for.'

'The significant other is often a suspect,' I pointed out. 'And she does inherit half of Jasper's estate.'

'I can't imagine Elsie killing Jasper,' Aunt Olivia said. 'Then again, I can't imagine anyone killing him, but someone did.'

I decided to change the subject for my aunt's sake and told her my idea about asking Rayelle if she would be interested in helping with posters for the animal sanctuary's fall fundraiser. Auntie O thought it was a great idea, so I added talking to Rayelle to my mental to-do list.

I found a free parking spot and climbed out of the car. The beautiful summer's day showed off Main Street in all its charming, small-town glory. The road ran perpendicular to the shoreline and sloped gently uphill from the ocean. Colorful shops lined the street, and flowers bloomed in window boxes and hanging baskets.

Out on the water, sailboats glided along and motorboats cut across the sparkling, blue-green water. I could smell a hint of salt on the gentle breeze coming off the ocean as I breathed in deeply. Even though I'd lived in Twilight Cove for just one year in my teens and had been back only since June, the seaside town already felt far more like home than any of the many other cities and towns I'd lived in.

As I shifted my focus away from the ocean, my gaze landed on Cursive, the local stationery shop. I hadn't intended to stop there today, but I decided a change of plans was in order.

Aunt Olivia waved at two women seated outside the coffee shop across the street. Dolores and Leona were both members of Auntie O's Gins and Needles group. Dolores, as always, was dressed in a muumuu, this one bright pink.

'I'm going to have a chat with Dolores and Leona while you run your errands,' Aunt Olivia said. 'How about I take the dogs with me?'

'That would be great, thanks,' I said.

The dogs wagged their tails as I handed over their leashes and they trotted happily along with Olivia as she headed for the nearest crosswalk.

'I'll come back for them before I go to the Pet Palace,' I called after my aunt.

The dogs' tails wagged harder at the name of their favorite shop. 'You wouldn't want to miss out on that, would you?' Auntie O said to the spaniels.

Flossie had a big doggy grin on her face as she gazed up at Olivia. Fancy tipped her head back and let out a long 'a-woo'.

I smiled as the dogs crossed the street with my aunt. I loved to see them so happy.

Although I'd planned to get bread from the bakery and pick up a new mystery release from the bookstore, I entered the stationery shop first. I decided to buy a birthday card for my stepmother, but mostly I was on the hunt for information.

Ever since Elsie had mentioned the tests conducted on the paper the map was drawn on, a question had burned in my mind. Two questions, actually. I wondered if the map was a fake, drawn on authentically old paper. I also wondered how easy it was to get one's hands on eighteenth-century paper.

I browsed the shop for a minute or two before picking out a card suitable for my stepmother. I wasn't close with Audrey, the woman my dad had married when I was seventeen, but we had a cordial relationship. She and my dad now lived in New Mexico, and I typically saw them only once or twice per year, but I always made sure to send cards on their birthdays.

With the card in hand, I approached the sales counter, where the store's proprietor was flipping through a catalogue. I knew from visiting the store on a couple of previous occasions that her name was Tina Kwan.

She smiled and set the catalogue aside when I approached her.

'Found everything you need?' she asked.

I set the card on the counter. 'Yes, thanks.'

She began ringing up the small purchase.

'Do you happen to sell any vintage paper?' I asked.

'Are you talking about paper that's been made to look old or paper that actually is old?' Tina asked before telling me the total cost of my card.

I counted out the right amount of cash and handed it over. 'Paper that actually is old.'

'No, I'm afraid not. There's not much call for it here in Twilight Cove, but I can special order certain types of vintage paper. Are you looking for something in particular?'

'No, I'm just asking out of curiosity, really,' I admitted.

A shrewd light showed in Tina's dark brown eyes. 'Are you thinking about the treasure map that everybody's talking about?'

'Guilty as charged,' I said with a slight smile.

Tina slid the birthday card into a small paper bag. 'I had a detective in here asking me similar questions. I guess the cops think Jasper's death is tied to the map, like everyone else does.'

'That's all the police wanted to know? Whether you sold eighteenth-century paper here?'

'When I told her the answer was no, the detective asked if anyone had placed a special order recently. Nobody has. In fact, nobody's ordered eighteenth-century paper through me the whole time I've had this shop, which is going on eight years now.'

'Could it be ordered online?' I asked.

Tina nodded. 'That's what I told the detective. You can find just about anything online. There are companies that specialize in vintage paper of various sorts.'

I took a second to digest all of the information she'd provided so far. 'Did you get the impression that the police think the map is a fake?'

'The detective – she's with the state police – was unforthcoming. The only impression I got was that the police believe the map could have played a role in Jasper's death. But if someone faked the map and sold it to Jasper, why would they bother killing him? Or was the killer someone who didn't know the map was a fake and wanted it for themselves?'

I knew she wasn't really expecting an answer from me, but I shared my thoughts. 'That's a definite possibility, but it could also be that Jasper figured out the map was a fake and was going to expose the person who made it.'

Tina considered that theory. 'I suppose, but it doesn't seem worth killing Jasper over that. The forger could have laughed it off as a joke and given Jasper his money back. The other scenario is probably the right one. Unless, of course, the map is the real deal.'

Another customer came into the shop, so I just nodded and thanked Tina before leaving. With respect to the forger-as-the-killer theory, I agreed that it didn't seem worth murdering Jasper over a fake treasure map, but people had killed for far less. Maybe the culprit no longer had the money Jasper had paid for the map, or maybe the forger didn't want their reputation damaged.

I didn't know for certain if Giles Gilroy had sold Jasper the map, but if he did, maybe he'd also made the map, if it really was a fake. If Giles had forged the map, there was definitely a chance that he wouldn't want his reputation damaged. Who in the antiques world would trust him once it became known that he'd faked a map and sold it? Even if he tried to laugh it off as a joke, clients and customers might not buy into that explanation.

It was all so complicated, but whether or not Giles had forged the map, he was still a suspect. I recalled that Jasper had said he believed he was the only person who could read the map. Maybe it included some sort of code. If that was the case, Giles could have sold the map in the hope that Jasper would crack the code. Then, after killing Jasper, Giles took off with both the map and any sort of clues or key that Jasper had written down.

Of course, that was all speculation. I really needed to find out if Giles had an alibi for the time of the murder. I had to do the same for Flynn. I was pretty sure Elsie didn't have an alibi. She seemed genuinely saddened by Jasper's death, but that didn't mean I could strike her off the suspect list. Her tears could have been for show, and I couldn't forget her reluctance to talk about Jasper's recent obsessions, other than the pirate one. I felt certain she was hiding something. Whether that secret was a murderous one, I didn't know.

I hurried through my trip to the bakery and even managed to keep my visit to the bookstore under ten minutes. I could easily while away a good part of the day browsing the shelves, but I set an alarm on my phone so I wouldn't lose track of time. I didn't want to leave Aunt Olivia and the dogs waiting for me for too long, and I was eager to get to the vet clinic.

When I exited the bookshop, with two novels in hand, I nearly ran into Lance and Dean, who were strolling down the sidewalk, take-out coffee cups in hand. As we exchanged greetings, Lance's gaze fixed on something over my shoulder. I turned to see Giles Gilroy standing farther down the street, talking with Jackie, the owner of the Moonstruck Diner.

'Is something wrong?' I asked when I turned my attention back to Lance and noticed that his grip had tightened on his coffee cup.

'Like I said the other day, I don't trust that guy,' he said.

Dean had an expression of mild concern on his face as he watched Giles and Jackie part ways.

'Jackie's a smart woman,' Dean said. 'And she knows enough about Giles to realize she shouldn't trust him.'

'Let's hope that's the case,' Lance grumbled.

'Have a nice day, Georgie,' Dean said to me as they continued on their way down the street.

I wished them the same and then struck off in the opposite direction. I'd passed on Giles Gilroy's message and business card to Aunt Olivia as he'd requested, and she'd told me that she wasn't ready to sell any of her antiques, and might never be. Considering my own suspicions about Giles as well as Lance's and Dean's concerns, I was glad my aunt wasn't eager to take him up on his offer.

Pushing aside thoughts of the antiques dealer, I met up with Aunt Olivia at the coffee shop, where she was finishing up a latte as she chatted with her friends. She accompanied me and the dogs to the Pet Palace, where Flossie and Fancy greeted Cindy with great enthusiasm.

Cindy helped me find a cat carrier to purchase and I picked up a litter box and a bag of kitty litter as well. Then I added in some kitten food, cat toys and a bed. Of course, I couldn't leave the store without buying a treat for Flossie and Fancy. They made sure I didn't pass by the display of specialty dog cookies without stopping and picking out a bone-shaped treat for each of them.

After loading all the purchases into the trunk of my car, I drove us to the Twilight Inn so my aunt could drop off her ticket booklet and all the money she'd collected for the raffle. I waited on the front porch with the dogs while Olivia entered the inn.

I sat down in a white wicker chair and took in the beautiful view of the ocean. The Victorian inn sat on a hill at the southern edge of the cove, giving me a perfect vantage point to enjoy the sight of the sparkling water and the red-and-white lighthouse perched on a point that jutted into the ocean. In a few days, the cove would be the site of an epic battle reenactment between two pirate ships and their crews of scallywags, but today it was a peaceful scene, with only a few pleasure boats out on the water.

Flossie and Fancy lay down on either side of my chair, flopping on to their sides and enjoying the shade provided by the covered porch. I leaned back and relaxed, my thoughts drifting to a story idea I'd had brewing in my mind for more than a week now. As soon as I'd returned my latest screenplay to the producer, I was going to jot down an outline for the new thriller. I hadn't had much of a chance to turn plot ideas around in my head when nearby voices interrupted my thoughts.

'You've got to have a pirate costume, Flynn,' a female voice said. 'It's Dead Eye Days.'

I turned in my seat and saw that the inn's front windows were open. Two shadowy forms moved around inside. I turned my gaze back to the ocean so the people in the house wouldn't catch me staring in at them.

'Annaleigh, you know I'm not into costumes,' Flynn said in response. 'Besides, I refuse to take part in Dead Eye Days in any way.'

'Can't you just relax?' Annaleigh sounded exasperated. 'At least the festival gets kids excited about history.'

'It's not history!' Flynn fumed. 'It's fiction!'

'Argh!' The groan of frustration came from Annaleigh. 'Lighten up!'

It sounded as though she'd stormed out of the room. After her footsteps receded, I heard another set, heavier this time. Seconds later, the front door of the inn flew open. Flynn yanked the door shut behind him and stomped down the steps, never even glancing my way. He climbed into a car parked at the curb and slammed the door. The engine revved and he tore off down the street.

Whether or not Dead Eye Dawson had ever reached these shores, he was certainly sparking a lot of passionate emotions more than two hundred years after his death.

Auntie O and Catherine came out through the front door a few minutes later. The dogs raised their heads but remained lying on the porch. I stood up and exchanged greetings with Catherine.

'Is Rayelle home?' I asked her, wondering if I could have a quick chat with her about volunteering her artistic skills.

Catherine's cheery expression faded. 'I'm afraid not. I don't know where she's gone off to. She's supposed to be helping here at the inn. It's not like her to be so moody and unreliable, but she's really not been herself since Jasper died.'

Aunt Olivia gave the other woman's arm a sympathetic squeeze. 'It's hard to come to terms with. Perhaps she just needs some time to process everything.'

'A funeral might help,' Catherine said. 'That, and having the killer behind bars.'

My aunt nodded. 'Justice and closure,' she said, as if plucking the words right out of my thoughts. 'That's the best we can hope for right now.'

Silently, I added one more hope to that list: that the police were having far more luck than me with achieving those goals.

EIGHTEEN

My heart melted when I lifted the kitten out of the carrier in the farmhouse kitchen. Flossie, Fancy, Gizmo and Auntie O all watched with rapt attention as I cradled the tiny creature against my chest.

'She's adorable,' I said, completely in love already.

'A real sweetheart,' my aunt agreed, gently stroking the kitten's head.

Carefully, I set the little cat down on the kitchen floor, ready to scoop her back up in an instant, if necessary, though I felt certain that the dogs would be gentle with her. After all, they hadn't harmed her when they found her in the cave. If it hadn't been for the spaniels, the poor little thing probably would have perished out there in the wilderness. That was a thought I didn't want to dwell on.

As I'd expected, Flossie and Fancy treated the kitten with great care. They touched their noses to her fur before lying down and watching as she explored the kitchen. She sniffed here and there, wandering around, and then she sat down in the middle of the floor, looked up at me and let out a plaintive meow.

My heart melted again. At this rate, there'd be nothing left of it by the end of the day.

I picked her up and gave her a cuddle.

'I can see she's already stolen your heart,' Aunt Olivia said. 'I'm afraid mine might be in danger too.'

'She's a darling.' I pressed my cheek against her soft fur. 'But she needs a name, even if she's only with us temporarily.' My heart ached as I spoke those last words.

'Unless we find her human, I suspect there won't be anything temporary about it,' my aunt said with a smile. 'But, yes, she certainly needs a name.'

I snuggled my face into the kitten's gray fur and her rumbling purr sent vibrations into my cheek. 'You're like the softest, cutest little dust bunny that ever existed.'

Fancy gave a little yip of agreement. The sound startled the kitten, making her eyes go comically wide.

'And look,' Aunt Olivia said, clearly smitten, 'her hazel eyes are almost the exact same shade as yours.'

I held the kitten away from my chest and saw that Auntie O was right. Now that I had more time to study the cat's markings, I noticed that the white patch on her chest was roughly in the shape of a star.

'You've got a star on your chest and your gray fur reminds me of dust bunnies – in the cutest way possible – so maybe Stardust? Or just Star?'

'I think Stardust is perfect,' Aunt Olivia said, still smiling. 'You can always call her Star for short.'

I held the kitten up in the air and gazed into her eyes. 'What do you think? Should your name be Stardust?'

She gave a tiny little mew.

Fancy added a 'woo' and Flossie woofed and bounced around in a circle.

My aunt and I laughed.

'I'm going to take that as a yes.' I addressed the kitten again. 'I just have one more question: how the heck am I supposed to get any work done?'

I soon found out the answer to my own question. Stardust wouldn't let me focus on answering emails or anything else until I spent some time playing with her. She particularly liked the bunch of soft feathers that dangled from a wand toy, especially when I made the feathers dance around the room.

Finally, after running, jumping, skidding and rolling around like an acrobat, Stardust fell fast asleep on my lap at the kitchen table. Gizmo was chattering away, but I was able to tune out that noise and respond to the new emails in my inbox.

When I'd finished that task, I carefully shifted the kitten to one of the dog beds that occupied part of the sitting area off the kitchen. Stardust squirmed and yawned, exposing her adorable pink tongue, then she went right back to sleep. That gave me enough time to prepare some snacks for later that evening.

When I'd arrived in Twilight Cove, Tessa had invited me to join her group of friends for their bi-monthly game nights. I'd attended only one so far, but I'd volunteered to host the next meetup, so the group would be showing up at the farmhouse later on.

With the snacks prepared – or, in the case of the nachos, ready to go in the oven later – I left Stardust at the house for a short time while I helped out with the evening chores, but then I hurried back for another cuddle session. I followed that up with a shower and then turned on the oven, leaving it to heat up while I set everything except the nachos out on the counter. It would be a self-serve station since we needed the kitchen table free for our games.

Tessa arrived first and immediately lost her heart to Gizmo and Stardust. I suspected that the parrot and kitten would be getting a lot of attention that evening. The dogs too, of course.

'Oh, I nearly forgot,' Tessa said as she stood in the middle of the kitchen, cuddling the kitten as the spaniels watched and Gizmo chattered away. With one hand, Tessa reached into the handbag she'd left on a nearby chair. She pulled out a book and handed it to me. 'Check this out. It's an advance copy of Ajax Wolfgang's upcoming book.'

'How did you get this?' I asked as I checked out the cover, which indeed stated that it was an advance copy and not for sale.

'From Flynn. It turns out that Ajax is his cousin. Ajax brought him a copy, knowing that Flynn's a history buff. Anyway, Flynn's already read it from cover to cover. I ran into him at the grocery store this morning and he mentioned that he was having a barbecue with Ajax that evening. I asked him a few casual questions about his cousin, and then Flynn ran out to his car and got me this.'

'I guess you haven't had a chance to read it.'

'I figured I didn't need to read the whole thing,' she said. 'There's an index at the back, so I just read the chapters that mention Dead Eye Dawson.' She danced around the kitchen, waltzing with Stardust in her arms. 'Shall I summarize for you?'

'Please.'

'According to Ajax, Dead Eye Dawson never made it farther north than Baja.'

'OK,' I said as I thought things over. 'That explains why he doesn't believe that the treasure map is real.'

Tessa held up a finger. 'But there's more.' She addressed the kitten in her arms. 'What do you think, Star? Should we tell Georgie the rest?'

I groaned. 'You know I'm not good with suspense, unless I'm writing it into a screenplay.'

She laughed and stopped dancing. 'OK, I'll spill. According to

Flynn, Ajax's books haven't been selling well. He's looking for his
big break, and if this book can help set him up as a historical pirate
expert, Ajax thinks he might get hired as a consultant for a new TV
show that's in development with one of the big-time streamers.'

'Ah,' I said, understanding.

Tessa's smile brightened. 'I knew you'd catch on right away.'

'If Dead Eye's treasure map is authentic, that would prove Ajax
wrong, and this book could make him look foolish. He certainly
wouldn't have people turning to him for his expertise.'

'Exactly.'

I continued to voice my thoughts out loud. 'Maybe Ajax wanted
to steal the map so there wouldn't be any evidence to refute the
claims he makes in his book. But Jasper caught him in the act and
ended up dead.'

'That's how I see it playing out,' Tessa agreed.

'When I saw him at the beach the other night, it looked like he
was trying to cozy up to Elsie, but she wasn't interested. Maybe he
was hoping to find out if Jasper left behind any copies of the map.'

'Ooh,' Tessa said with appreciation. 'You're probably right.'

'Ugh.' I dropped the book on the kitchen table.

'What's wrong?' Tessa asked.

'You know what this means, don't you? We have to add a name
to our suspect list. I've been wanting to whittle it down, not make
it longer.'

'OK, so that's a pain,' she agreed, 'but if it gets us closer to
putting Jasper's killer behind bars, it's totally worth it.'

I couldn't argue with that.

The back door opened and Callum entered the kitchen.

He greeted Tessa and gave me a quick kiss. Tessa set Stardust
on the floor and the kitten scampered about before creeping
cautiously up to Callum.

'Aren't you a beauty,' he said to her.

She meowed at him and I could tell by the look in his green eyes
that the little kitty had captured his heart as well.

He picked her up off the floor and her purr began right away,
rumbling like a loud engine. She snuggled up against his chest like
she never wanted to leave. I couldn't blame her.

Cindy Yoon and Tessa's other friends arrived within the next few
minutes. Two of them I'd known back in my teens when I attended
Twilight Cove High for one year. Julia Chen came on her own, but

Ava-Kate Kershaw – now with the last name MacIntosh – came with her husband, Steve. He recognized Callum right away and they started chatting baseball. Steve's cousin Jordy was also a member of the group. I'd met Steve and Jordy only once before, at the previous games night, but they seemed like nice, easy-going guys, and it sounded like they were interested in joining our fun league team in the spring.

After Ava-Kate insisted that further baseball talk should be saved for another time, everyone helped themselves to snacks, and then we got settled at the table, starting out with a game of Monopoly. Aunt Olivia had a cupboard full of board games that we'd played when I'd visited as a child and when I lived at the farmhouse with her. The games were a couple of decades old – at the very least – but nobody seemed to mind.

I sat next to Callum, and every time I looked over at him, with the kitten sleeping soundly in his lap, I felt a tugging at my heart. I really needed to slow down the rate at which my feelings for Callum were growing.

As I had that thought, a wave of anxiety hit me. What if things didn't work out between us? Would it be awkward having Callum living on the farm and working at the sanctuary? Would he decide to move away, leaving Auntie O and me to find a new farm manager?

'Georgie,' Tessa said, shaking me out of my thoughts. 'It's your turn.'

'Right. Sorry.' I forced myself to refocus on the game.

After we'd played two other games and the snacks had mostly disappeared, everyone got up to leave. We said our goodbyes and everyone except Tessa, Cindy and Callum headed out. The three of them insisted on helping me clean up the kitchen.

Callum shifted the still-sleeping kitten on to Fancy's dog bed. The spaniels immediately snuggled in next to her, all of them sharing the one bed. Stardust woke up enough to stretch and give a great big yawn. Then she snuggled in against the dogs and went back to sleep.

'I'm not sure I can handle all the cuteness,' I said as I put the last of the dirty dishes in the dishwasher.

'She's adorable, that's for sure,' Tessa said. 'Are you certain you're not going to keep her?'

'I'd love to keep her.' I tore my gaze away from the tiny furball of adorableness. 'But what if there's someone out there looking for her?'

Callum wiped down the kitchen counter. 'Considering where you found her, I think there's a good chance that someone was trying to get rid of her.'

'As sick as that makes me feel, I know it's the most likely scenario,' I admitted.

'People often put up missing pet posters in my shop,' Cindy said. 'Nobody has come by recently looking for a lost kitten, but how about I put up a poster?'

'What if some random person tries to claim her?' Tessa asked, voicing my own concern.

'Unfortunately, that could happen,' Cindy said, 'especially since she's so darn cute. But I won't post a picture, just a general description. If anyone wants to claim her, they'll have to describe the things that make her unique.' Cindy moved closer to the sleeping kitten, who had her chest exposed. 'Like the white star on her chest and that one gray spot on the little white sock on her front paw.'

The suggestion made me feel a lot better about the idea. 'That sounds good. Thanks, Cindy.'

'It's no problem,' she assured me. 'And we don't have to leave the sign up for long. That way, you'll know soon whether she's yours for keeps.'

I tried not to think about how hard it would be to part with the sweet kitten if it turned out that someone had lost her accidentally. That was just another thing to add to the list of things I didn't want to dwell on, some of the others having to do with my relationship with Callum.

Why did I always have to overthink things? Why couldn't I just live in the moment, worry-free?

That was something I wanted to work on, but my brain always seemed to default to fretting.

With the kitchen now clean, Tessa and Cindy got ready to leave. I walked them out to their cars while Callum got the dogs up and took them outside for a final chance to do anything they needed to do before bed.

The sun had set and the breeze slipped over my bare arms and legs with a cool touch.

Tessa reached into the passenger side of her car and pulled out a black hoodie. 'I'm glad I brought this. It totally felt like summer all day, but now I can tell that September isn't far off.'

'It'll be here before we know it,' Cindy said as she gave us a wave and climbed into her car.

Tessa groaned as she pulled on her hoodie. 'I'm trying not to think about that too much. September means back to work. I love my job, but I love summer vacation even more.'

'That's probably true for most teachers,' I said. 'You've still got a couple of weeks of freedom to enjoy.'

'And I plan to make the most of them.' Tessa turned to climb into her car.

When I saw the back of her hoodie, I froze. 'Tessa.'

She must have heard the tension in my voice. She faced me again, looking worried. 'What's wrong?'

'Your hoodie. What's that logo?' I moved in closer and lifted the hood so I could get a better look at the logo on the back of her zipped-up sweatshirt. It featured a somewhat menacing-looking fish with its back and tail curved to hug a partial circle, the rest of which disappeared behind the fish's body.

'It's the Twilight Cove High School logo,' she said. 'New since you and I were students. Go, Steelheads!'

Sure enough, I could now see the school's name written inside the partial circle.

'I saw someone wearing a hoodie just like this the night Jasper was killed,' I said. 'They were in his neighborhood.'

'And you think they might have had something to do with Jasper's death?' Tessa sounded really worried now.

I shrugged. 'Maybe it was an innocent person out for an evening walk, but they were walking briskly, away from the general area of Jasper's house.'

'And we have one person on our suspect list who I know definitely has one of these hoodies,' Tessa added.

We looked at each other and said the name in unison:

'Flynn Smith-Wu.'

NINETEEN

I got Tessa to promise not to question Flynn about whether he was in Jasper's neighborhood on the night of the murder. Not yet, anyway. We needed to take some time to think about how best to approach him. I didn't want to end up with a target on my back if he was the killer, and I definitely didn't want that happening to Tessa.

We agreed to meet the next day to talk things over, after we'd had a chance to sleep on the revelation about the hoodie. Of course, there was always a chance that Flynn wasn't the person I saw in Jasper's neighborhood that night. According to Tessa, almost every faculty member and student at the high school owned either a hoodie or T-shirt with the school's logo on it. Still, Flynn was the only person with a direct connection to the high school who was on our suspect list. We really needed to figure out if he had an alibi.

I didn't sleep well that night, which didn't surprise me. I kept thinking about Flynn and our other suspects, as well as my relationship with Callum. My thoughts also circled around Stardust. I hadn't even had her here at the farmhouse with me for a full twenty-four hours, and already I desperately wanted her to stay permanently. She was currently curled up on the big dog bed in the corner of my room with Flossie and Fancy, her own brand-new bed empty. Usually, the spaniels joined me on my queen bed, but tonight it seemed they wanted to watch over the little kitten. The sight of all three of them snuggled up together put a smile on my face as I climbed into bed, but I soon found myself wishing I could drift off to sleep as easily as the animals did.

Eventually, I fell asleep, but it felt far too early when my alarm went off the next morning. I lay in bed for a while, listening to Herald the rooster crowing outside, but then I decided there was no point in lazing about and doing more overthinking. Keeping busy would be a far better idea. Besides, Star was already awake and flying around the room, trying to climb the furniture and generally being a fuzzy little acrobat under the watchful eyes of Flossie and Fancy. The kitten clearly thought it was time to start the day.

I didn't want to take Stardust out to the barn because I was worried about her getting lost or harmed in some way while I was busy looking after the donkeys. She, however, didn't want to be left behind. When I shut the door on her, taking the spaniels outside with me, she cried pitifully. I stood on the porch, listening and trying to harden myself against the sound so I could get on with my chores, but then Flossie and Fancy started whining too. Flossie touched her nose to the door and then looked up at me, her message clear.

'I'm not sure this is a good idea,' I said.

Flossie stared at the back entrance to the farmhouse. The latch clicked and the door swung open.

I barely managed to keep my jaw from dropping.

'Flossie? Did you do that?'

She and Fancy darted into the house and scooted around behind Star, herding her toward the door. She scampered past me and then stopped dead on the porch, her hazel eyes wide as she took in the sight of the big world.

I shook off my shock and picked her up, cuddling her against my chest. 'Don't worry. You're safe as long as you stick with us.' I addressed the spaniels next. 'Right, girls?'

Fancy's response was a long 'a-woo', and Flossie's was a bark with a wag of her tail.

I took in a deep breath. How many more abilities did the spaniels have that I didn't yet know about? I was both in awe of them and concerned. The more they used any magical powers, the higher the chance that other people would become aware of what they could do. Maybe I needed to tell Auntie O and Callum. Then they could help me protect the dogs.

With a shake of my head, I decided to leave that decision for another day.

I carried Stardust out to the barn, planning to leave her in the tack room with the dogs to watch over her. We ran into Callum before we made it there and he held out his arms for the kitten right away.

'It looks like I might have competition for your affections now,' I said as I watched the adorable sight of Callum cuddling with Stardust.

Callum raised his gaze to meet mine. 'You don't need to worry. You're not about to slip my mind, Georgie Johansen.'

His words set alight a happy glow in my chest and also quieted down some of the worries still circling in my head.

'Can I take you out to lunch today?' he asked.

I accepted without hesitation. Even though I saw Callum every day at the farm, I still craved time alone with him without the distraction of work.

Star didn't end up in the tack room right away, because she insisted on riding around on Callum's shoulder. He let her do that while he was carrying out some light work – and I snapped several adorable photos of them together – but then she had to go into the care of the spaniels, who seemed more than happy to look after their furry little charge.

Later that morning, I managed to read through my script and tweak a few final things before sending it off to the producer. I was impressed that I managed to get that much work done with an energetic and curious kitten scampering around the house and with Gizmo chattering away.

Before departing for my midday date with Callum, I left Stardust and the dogs with Aunt Olivia at the carriage house. She promised she would drop by and visit with Gizmo for a while too, so he wouldn't get lonely.

With all the animals in good hands, I climbed into Callum's truck and he drove us into town. We decided to eat at the Moonstruck Diner. Callum was craving the diner's fish and chips, and I was in the mood for the Mediterranean shrimp wrap.

We were seated in one of the booths, with our food in front of us, when Elsie entered the diner and approached the counter to pick up a take-out order. I would have waved, but she never turned our way.

She perched on one of the stools at the counter while Jackie disappeared into the back to check on her order. As she waited, Elsie's phone buzzed and she answered the call.

I was chatting with Callum, so I didn't pay any further attention to Elsie until there was a natural lull in our conversation and I heard her say, 'I won't get the money right away.'

I zeroed in on her voice as I took a long drink of my soda.

'But I think you should quit your job and focus on your studies,' she continued. 'In a few months, we'll have all the money we need.'

Jackie emerged from the back with a paper bag of food, so Elsie cut short her phone conversation and paid for her order. A minute later, she left the diner, without ever noticing me.

It sounded like Elsie already had plans for the money she would inherit from Jasper. How badly did she need that money? Would she have killed Jasper for it?

I didn't even know if Elsie was aware prior to Jasper's death that he had named her as one of his main beneficiaries. She hadn't indicated either way when Aunt Olivia and I had chatted with her yesterday.

I decided to bring up Elsie's phone conversation when I talked to Tessa later in the day. For the time being, I wanted to stay present and enjoy my time with Callum.

When we left the diner a while later, Callum took my hand and I liked how natural it felt for him to do so.

We walked down the street, heading for Callum's truck. We were nearly there when two women in their twenties came out of the chocolate shop, one blonde and the other with black hair. The blonde looked our way and gave a shriek.

'Callum McQuade? It's Callum McQuade!' She and her friend rushed over to us. 'I'm Brittany and this is Jasmine.'

'We're such big fans!' Jasmine's dark eyes practically sparkled with excitement.

'Nice to meet you,' Callum said, still holding my hand. 'This is my girlfriend, Georgie.'

'Oh my gosh!' Brittany gushed. 'You two are so cute together!'

'*So* cute!' Jasmine agreed. 'Could we get some photos?'

'Of course,' Callum said, completely unfazed.

I snapped photos of the women with Callum, using both of their phones. When I handed the devices back, I thought that would be the end of it.

'Would it be OK if I got a picture of the two of you?' Brittany asked.

'You're adorable,' Jasmine chimed in.

Callum looked my way. 'Georgie?'

'Sure,' I said, surprised that they wanted me in the photo.

I was feeling a bit awkward until Callum put his arm around me and I leaned into him. The smile that appeared on my face in that moment came naturally.

Brittany and Jasmine each took a photo and then beamed at us.

'Thank you so much!' Brittany said.

'You two are the best!' Jasmine added.

They scurried off together, chatting and bubbling with energy.

Callum and I climbed into his truck and moments later we were cruising along Ocean Drive, heading north toward the farm. I drummed my fingers against my leg, my thoughts whirling.

Callum glanced my way. 'You good?'

'Mm-hm.' I was too lost in thought to provide a better answer. I noticed a crease between his eyebrows and realized he was worried about something. That sent my thoughts whirling even faster.

Callum cast another glance my way. Then he flicked on his turn signal and left the highway for a lookout point at the top of an oceanside cliff.

'Is it all right if we get out for a minute?' Callum asked.

'Sure,' I said slowly, my stomach churning as much as my thoughts.

I met him in front of the truck, where we had a stunning view of the Pacific Ocean. Waves crashed against the rocks below us and a couple of seagulls circled overhead. Although the scene should have brought me a sense of calm, I felt anything but.

I couldn't wait in suspense any longer, so I turned away from the view to face Callum. 'Are you OK?'

He studied me with his green eyes, the crease still between his eyebrows. 'That's what I wanted to ask you.' He took my hands in his. 'I know it's not easy with me getting recognized when we're trying to have time to ourselves. I don't ever want to make you feel uncomfortable or like you're not my priority.'

'You don't.' I could tell I didn't have him convinced. 'OK, so sometimes I feel awkward, but that's not your fault. I'm just not sure what to do when I become invisible.'

The intensity in his eyes sent pleasant tingles along the back of my neck.

He moved in closer, letting go of my hands so he could rest his on my hips. 'You're never invisible to me, Georgie. And I don't want you feeling like you are to anyone else either.'

'Your fans want to see *you*,' I pointed out. 'I'm nobody to them and I'm OK with that. Maybe I just need to pull out my phone and scroll through social media whenever it happens. That might stop me from feeling like I have a neon sign flashing the word "awkward" over my head.'

'What can I do to make it easier on you?' he asked. 'I want to include you, but I also don't want to if it's not what *you* want. I introduced you today and then realized I shouldn't have done that until I'd checked with you first.'

'You can introduce me anytime you want.'

That got a brief smile out of him, but then he sobered again. 'Those photos they took of the two of us could end up online.'

I was about to respond to that when I realized I didn't know what to say.

Callum didn't take his eyes off mine and I felt like he was looking deep inside of me. It was both thrilling and frightening at the same time.

'I feel like you've got a lot of thoughts going through your head right now,' he said.

I cracked a smile. 'So many that I don't think I can count them.'

'Can you share any?'

I took a moment to choose my words. 'You're a sports celebrity and I'm . . . very much *not* a celebrity.'

His eyes seemed to darken. 'Georgie, you know that doesn't matter to me. At least, I hope you do.'

'But now those pictures of us together could be on the Internet, and I get the feeling that might worry you. And it's OK if it does,' I added quickly. 'I get it.'

'The only reason it worries me is that I'm not sure how you feel about the attention that might come from it. I'm definitely not ashamed to be photographed with you, Georgie.'

The sincerity in his voice was reflected in his eyes. Knowing that he truly meant those words settled the churning in my stomach and eased the tension out of my muscles.

A new feeling spread through my bloodstream, one that brought me a sense of peace and ease. I realized it was confidence, not necessarily in myself but in what we had together.

'It doesn't matter what comments people post online,' I said, looping my arms around his neck, 'because I don't have to read them.'

He smiled, looking deep into my eyes again.

'Now it feels like you're the one with a lot of thoughts going on in your head,' I said.

'A lot of thoughts about how great you are.'

'Keep those ones,' I advised with a smile. 'What are the others?'

His expression became more serious again. 'Now that I'm retired, I think people will recognize me less and less as time goes by. But in the meantime, I know there's a lot that comes with dating someone in the public eye. I want to do whatever I can to make sure you're comfortable.'

'I think it's going to take a bit of getting used to,' I admitted, 'but I probably will get used to it.'

'If there's ever anything you want me to do or not do in those situations, will you let me know?'

'If I've got it figured out myself, I'll tell you,' I promised. I fingered the collar of his crewneck T-shirt as I worked up the courage to say my next words. 'There was something you said to Brittany and Jasmine that I really liked.'

Callum had his arms around me now, holding me close to him. 'What's that?'

'You called me your girlfriend.'

A slow grin appeared on his face. 'That's another thing I should have talked to you about first. Maybe a while ago, because I've told other people that too.'

'Who have you told?' I asked, curious.

'My parents. My sister. Javi and a few other former teammates. Like I said before, according to Javi, I never stop talking about you.'

I laughed, brimming with happiness. 'I'd like to meet Javi sometime.'

'I'm pretty sure you'll get that chance.' He paused before continuing. 'I know we're in the early stages of our relationship, but my parents want to come for a visit, and I'd love for you to meet them.' He quickly added, 'You don't have to say anything now, and I'll understand if it's too soon, but will you consider it?'

'Of course,' I said, although I was glad that he was giving me time to think it over. It *was* early in our relationship, but I mostly appreciated the time because, for an introvert like me, meeting new people – especially under such important circumstances – sometimes required me to work up my courage. 'When are they coming to Twilight Cove?'

'Not for a few weeks,' he replied.

'I'll definitely let you know soon,' I promised.

'And right now . . . we're OK?' he checked.

'Better than OK,' I assured him.

We shared a kiss on the clifftop and climbed back into the truck, both of us with smiles on our faces.

TWENTY

E ven though I'd decided to take the rest of the day off from writing, I ended up at the kitchen table with my laptop in front of me, drafting a pitch for a new screenplay idea. I'd planned to outline a new thriller script next, but after arriving home from my lunch date with Callum, a different story idea had popped into my head. I figured it was probably my newfound confidence in my relationship with Callum that had stirred up the romantic in me. So now I was jotting down the basic plot for a summertime romantic comedy.

As I worked on the outline, more aspects of my own life crept their way into the pitch. The story would take place in a seaside town in the grip of a pirate treasure craze. Although the two main characters wouldn't end up finding actual pirate gold, they would find their own treasure in the form of love, at the end of a humorous and hopefully heartwarming journey.

I was reading over what I'd written when Aunt Olivia arrived at the back door of the farmhouse. Flossie and Fancy had been snoozing on the kitchen floor, but they jumped up to greet her with their usual enthusiasm. Gizmo, of course, ordered my aunt to walk the plank. Awakened by all the noise, Stardust skidded across the floor, did a crazy flip in the air and then tried to leap up to climb the pretty yellow curtains framing the kitchen window. Fortunately, she wasn't yet able to leap high enough and didn't get her claws in the fabric.

I scooped the kitten up into my arms before she could attempt any other mischief.

'I thought you were taking the day off,' Auntie O said, eyeing the document I had open on my laptop.

'I've taken part of it off,' I said. 'I just couldn't help myself. I had a new idea and I wanted to get it written down before it disappeared out of my head.' I grabbed a glass from the cupboard. 'Can I get you a drink?'

'No, thank you, dear,' my aunt said. 'I just popped by to share some good news.'

Hope rose inside of me. 'The police have caught Jasper's killer?'

'Unfortunately, no.' A shadow of sadness passed across Auntie

O's blue eyes before her expression brightened. 'But I might have found Gizmo a new home.'

'Son of a biscuit eater!' the parrot exclaimed, making us laugh.

'You remember Dean from the auto shop?' my aunt asked.

'Of course. I just saw him yesterday.'

'He has a niece in Eugene who used to have an African grey parrot,' Olivia explained. 'The poor bird died of cancer three years ago when he was just in his twenties. Ginny – that's Dean's niece – would love to come visit Gizmo and see if the two of them would be a good fit for each other.'

'That's fantastic news,' I said with a smile.

If Auntie O thought Ginny would be a good caretaker for Gizmo, I trusted her judgment on that.

'I'm sure you'll make a good impression, Gizmo,' I said to the parrot. 'How could you not?'

'You're so clever and handsome,' Auntie O told him.

Gizmo let out a loud wolf whistle that nearly shattered my eardrums. Then he strutted around his cage and preened.

'He knows it,' I said with a laugh. I thought back to the previous day. 'Dean and Lance seem to be good friends.'

'They grew up together,' my aunt said. 'And neither one has family right here in town, so it's good they've got each other to hang out with. There used to be a rivalry between them, but they seem to have grown out of that.'

'Neither one is married?'

'Lance was married for a short while many years ago,' Olivia replied. 'As for Dean, there was a girlfriend in the past who broke his heart. He's dated a few women briefly since then, but I don't know that he ever got over Patty Buchanan.'

I hoped my heart wouldn't ever break so thoroughly that I never truly recovered. It was thoughts like that one that made me nervous about romantic relationships, but I was now making a concerted effort to not let such worries get the best of me. It was a work in progress, but one I was determined not to give up on.

My aunt and I chatted with Gizmo for a while longer, and then I told her that I was heading out that evening. Tessa and I had arranged by text message to get together at the beachside park. Tessa had more painting to do for Dead Eye Days and I'd offered to lend a hand. Hopefully, we would have the chance to talk about our suspects while working on the face-in-the-hole boards.

'I was thinking of making some jam,' Auntie O said. 'Do you mind if I come and use this kitchen while you're out? That way, I can keep Gizmo and Star company.'

'Of course I don't mind,' I assured her. 'It's your kitchen, after all.'

'More yours than mine now.'

'Either way, it's a great idea,' I said. 'I know Gizmo and Star will love having you here.'

Auntie O and I ate a light dinner together before I headed out with Flossie and Fancy. When I parked in the lot by the main beach, I saw that there was already plenty of activity over on the grass. Lance Earley was up on a ladder, stringing Edison lights around the gazebo.

As I drew closer to the structure, I recognized Dean Haskell standing nearby, a cordless drill in one hand.

'Aren't you a bit old to be climbing ladders?' he called up to Lance.

'If I'm old, you're ancient,' Lance shot back. 'You've got two months on me.'

Dean stroked his gray beard. 'But I've aged so much better.'

Lance shook his head and kept working. 'You're full of it, Haskell.'

Dean let out a deep laugh and headed beyond the gazebo to a temporary fence and gate that had been set up on the grass, surrounding a white tent. A sign above the gate revealed that the fenced-off area would be the location of the beer garden during Dead Eye Days. Large pieces of painted plywood, cut in various shapes, lay on the grass outside the fence.

'How's Olivia's truck running?' Dean asked me when he saw me and the dogs.

'As smooth as butter, according to her,' I replied with a smile.

'Glad to hear it.' He gave me a two-fingered salute as he helped another man lift one of the pieces of plywood.

Tessa appeared at my side. 'The pieces fit together like a puzzle. When it's all set up, the sides of the beer garden will look like the sides of a pirate ship.'

As Dean and the other man affixed one piece to the fence, I could see that she was right.

'It looks like a lot of work,' I commented.

'It's not so bad. The ship pieces were made years ago,' Tessa explained. 'They just need to be put back together each summer.'

I followed her to a quieter spot in the park, where the unpainted face-in-the-hole boards sat on the grass next to several open cans of paint and a couple of brushes.

I'd dressed in my oldest shorts and T-shirt so I wouldn't need to worry too much about getting paint on my clothes. Tessa almost matched me in her denim shorts and blue shirt, but her clothes already had spatters of paint on them. Before my arrival, she'd started on a board featuring a sketch of pirates dancing around an open treasure chest that was filled to the brim with gold and jewels. She showed me a sample drawing so I could see which colors to put in each part of the image. I picked up a paintbrush and got to work painting one pirate's tricorn hat. Flossie and Fancy were content to lie on the grass for a snooze, cracking open an eye now and then to make sure I was still close by.

While we worked, I told Tessa how I'd overheard part of Elsie's brief phone conversation at the Moonstruck Diner earlier in the day. 'I'm guessing she was talking to her son,' I said to finish.

Tessa had stopped painting while she listened. 'She totally could have killed Jasper for the money. Then she took the map to make the police think that's what it was all about.'

'My thoughts exactly,' I agreed.

'I wonder if the police have considered that angle,' Tessa mused. 'I don't suppose Brody would tell me.'

'There's also Flynn,' I reminded her. 'If he was the hoodie-wearing person I saw in Jasper's neighborhood, that puts him near the scene of the crime. There was also the female pirate I saw running from the area.'

Tessa looked over at the costumed actors who were starting to gather for another rehearsal. 'That could have been one of the actors. They were rehearsing that night.'

I swept my gaze over the costumed women present but didn't see a purple sash. 'I don't see anyone who's a match.'

'Let's focus on Flynn for now, then.'

'We need to somehow find out where he was that evening,' I said. 'But without tipping him off that we suspect him of killing Jasper.'

Tessa added some blue paint to the frock coat of one of the pirates on the face-in-the-hole board. Seconds later, her eyes widened and she let out a tiny squeal of excitement. When I followed her gaze, I spotted Flynn strolling across the park, holding hands with a young woman with dark hair and fair skin.

'This is perfect!' Tessa exclaimed, keeping her voice barely above a whisper. 'We can put Operation Alibi into effect right now.'

'I'm surprised Flynn is here,' I said, noting that he was scowling at the costumed actors who had gathered near the gazebo. 'I thought he wanted nothing to do with Dead Eye Days.'

'Annaleigh probably dragged him here. She's helping her mom organize the actors for the festival.'

Now that Flynn and his girlfriend had drawn closer, I saw the family resemblance between Annaleigh and her younger sister, Rayelle. I could also see a bit of Catherine in her features.

Tessa quickly told me her plan as we set our paintbrushes on the trays. I picked up the spaniels' leashes and Flossie and Fancy jumped to their feet. We hurried around the gazebo before slowing our pace so it would look like we'd casually strolled into Flynn and Annaleigh's path by chance as we walked the dogs.

'Oh, hey, Annaleigh, Flynn,' Tessa greeted with what seemed like genuine surprise.

No wonder she taught drama at the high school. She would have had me convinced if I hadn't been part of her ruse.

'Are you taking part in the Dead Eye Days performances?' she asked, sounding as though she didn't already know the answer.

'Not likely,' Flynn muttered.

Annaleigh jabbed him with her elbow, sending him a brief scowl. 'I'm helping direct the scenes, but I'm not acting. Rayelle is, though.' She glanced around. 'If she ever shows up.'

'Annaleigh, have you met my friend Georgie Johansen?' Tessa asked. 'She just moved to town.'

'Nice to meet you,' Annaleigh said with a smile.

'You too,' I said to her before addressing Flynn. 'I think I saw you in the Sunset Heights neighborhood a few nights ago. You were wearing one of those Twilight Cove High School hoodies.'

Flynn's brow furrowed in confusion. 'What night?'

'Thursday,' I said, not adding that it was the night of the murder. I didn't want him to suspect the motive behind my questions.

Flynn shook his head. 'You must be confusing me with someone else. I was at the inn with Annaleigh that evening.'

His girlfriend nodded. 'I was supposed to help out with the Dead Eye Days rehearsals that evening, but I had an asthma attack earlier in the day. Not bad enough to land me in the hospital,' she added quickly when Tessa and I expressed our concern. 'But I wasn't feeling great. Flynn was nice enough to stay with me. We binge-watched *Only Murders in the Building*.' She shuddered. 'We never thought for a second that there could be a real murder happening in our town that night.'

'It was definitely shocking,' Tessa said with a nod. Then she addressed Flynn again. 'But you do have a school hoodie, right? I'm pretty sure I've seen you wearing one.'

'Sure,' he said, 'but I haven't worn it for a while. I loaned it to my cousin when he arrived in town last week. Coming from southern California, he finds the nights here chilly.'

'Your cousin . . .' I said as dots connected in my head.

'Ajax Wolfgang,' Flynn confirmed what I was thinking. 'The writer.'

TWENTY-ONE

'Ajax Wolfgang has got to be the killer!' Tessa whispered once we were alone again.

'He definitely could be the person I saw in Jasper's neighborhood that night,' I agreed as I picked up my paintbrush. 'He's the right height and build. But if lots of people own those school hoodies, that won't be enough to get the police to arrest him.'

The dogs settled down on the grass again, their chins resting on their paws as they watched us work.

Tessa got back to filling in a pirate's frock coat with blue paint. 'OK, true, but it might be enough to get the cops to look closely at him, and that could lead them to finding more evidence.'

She had a good point.

'Do you think we should tell Brody?' I asked.

'Probably.' Tessa set down her paintbrush. 'I'll text him and let him know that we have something we want to tell him.'

Once she'd done that, she returned to painting.

'At least we can cross one name off our suspect list now,' I said with a sense of satisfaction. 'Flynn has an alibi.' I reconsidered that statement. 'As long as we believe Annaleigh.'

'I'm pretty sure we can,' Tessa said. 'I've known her forever and I really don't think she'd cover up for Flynn. I suspect their relationship is on shaky ground. Annaleigh always seems annoyed with him.'

I recalled the brief argument I'd overheard between them at the inn and the way Annaleigh had scowled at Flynn moments ago. 'I've noticed that too and I scarcely know them.'

My gaze strayed to Flynn and Annaleigh, who were now chatting with Lance near the gazebo. It looked as though the electrician had finished stringing up the vintage lights. They were switched on now, and even though it was barely dusk, the effect was already magical. After dark, the lit-up gazebo would look even more amazing.

As the young couple walked away from Lance, they appeared to be arguing again. Watching them, Lance came over our way.

'Those two,' he said with a shake of his head. 'That young man is going to get dumped soon if he doesn't lighten up.'

'They do seem to be arguing a lot lately,' Tessa agreed.

'Lately?' Lance echoed, incredulous. 'It's been weeks. I did the electrical work when Catherine and Roger were renovating the inn. If I had ten bucks for each argument I overheard between Annaleigh and Flynn, I could fund a vacation to Hawaii.' He took in the sight of what we were doing. 'Nice work, ladies. Kids will love these.'

With those final words, he strode off toward the beer garden and began helping Dean and the other man affix the plywood ship panels to the fence.

Since the sun was heading for the horizon now, Tessa and I picked up our painting pace.

'So,' she said after we'd worked in silence for several minutes, 'how are things with you and Callum?'

I was about to answer her question, but then I rethought my response before speaking. 'I was going to say the same as the last time you and I talked, but that's not quite true.'

She shot me a concerned glance. 'Did something bad happen?'

'The opposite.' I filled her in on Callum's latest fan encounter and the conversation we'd had afterward, although I didn't share every single detail.

'I'm so glad the two of you talked about that,' Tessa said when I'd finished. 'I like how happy he makes you but not how much you question if you're good enough for him.'

'There are probably people out there who will still question that, but I'm going to do my best to stop doing it myself.'

'Just don't read any online comments about the two of you and you'll be fine,' Tessa said.

'I'll avoid the comments like the plague,' I promised.

Dusk had fallen now and it was getting harder to see what we were doing, so we decided to call it quits for the day. We'd nearly finished the board we were working on and just one more remained to be painted.

Using the supports at the back, we carried the face-in-the-hole boards inside the beer garden tent for safekeeping. Tessa planned to return the next day to continue painting. Once the boards were all finished, other volunteers would move them to various locations around town in time for the start of the pirate festival.

As we transferred the last of the paint cans inside the fence, Tessa received a message from Brody. They texted back and forth for a minute, ultimately arranging for us to meet him near the ice cream parlor in ten minutes.

'That's the perfect excuse to indulge in some dessert,' Tessa said. 'After all that painting, we deserve it.'

Fancy and Flossie voiced their enthusiastic agreement.

'See?' Tessa said with a smile.

I smiled too. 'I'm not about to argue.'

We reached the ice cream parlor before Brody arrived, so we ordered pup cups for the dogs and cones for ourselves. With our treats in hand, we sat on the bench outside the shop, watching the sky grow darker above the ocean.

Brody pulled up in his cruiser a few minutes later and parked right in front of us.

The dogs greeted him with wagging tails when he climbed out of the vehicle and came up on to the sidewalk. He crouched down to give Flossie and Fancy attention on their level, much to their delight.

'So what's this vital clue you've uncovered?' Brody asked as he straightened up a moment later.

I glanced Tessa's way. 'Vital clue?'

She shrugged. 'It could be.'

'I hope you two haven't been putting yourselves in danger,' Brody said, leveling his dark gaze at us.

'Of course not,' Tessa said. 'Just hear us out, OK? This could be really important.'

'I'm listening.'

'We think the killer might be Ajax Wolfgang,' Tessa informed him.

A line appeared across Brody's forehead. 'Who's that?'

Tessa told him about the writer and then she and I took turns outlining what we'd learned about him, including his possible motive for killing Jasper and the fact that he could have been the hoodie-wearing individual I'd seen in Jasper's neighborhood on the night of the murder.

'But you're not certain it was him you saw?' Brody asked me.

'He's the right height and build, and he has Flynn's school hoodie, but I never saw the person's face,' I admitted.

'Don't you think it's worth taking a closer look at him?' Tessa pressed. 'He's got a motive and he was probably near the scene of the crime.'

'Possibly near the scene of the crime,' Brody amended. 'But, yes, I'll pass this information on to the detectives from the state police.' He crossed his arms over his chest. 'Please tell me you haven't been digging around for information.'

I wasn't sure what to say to that, but I didn't have to worry about it because Tessa apparently didn't have the same problem.

'We hear and see things. When we think it's important, we pass it along to you. Isn't that what you want us to do?' She managed to sound completely innocent, as if we hadn't just questioned Flynn in an effort to find out if he was the killer.

'What I don't want you doing is putting yourselves in danger. This is a murderer we're talking about.' He shifted his gaze to me. 'I don't want a repeat of what happened back in June.'

Flossie gave a woof, lending support to that statement, while Fancy licked my hand and whined. I gave her a pat, hoping to reassure her.

'Trust me,' I said to Brody, 'neither do I.'

He relaxed his stance and Tessa and I got up from the bench.

'We missed you at baseball practice the other night,' I said, with the hope of putting an end to any further attempt to warn us off sleuthing.

'I'm hoping I can make it to the next one.' Brody gave each of the dogs another pat. 'It all depends on my work schedule.'

'I'll text you once we know the day and time,' Tessa said.

After a few more parting words, Brody climbed back into his cruiser and drove off.

'Do you want to stop our investigation?' I asked Tessa as we crossed Ocean Drive during a break in traffic.

'Why would we do that?' she asked, surprised by the question.

'I wouldn't want to cause any friction between you and Brody.'

She cast me a suspicious glance as we reached the other side of the road. 'Why are you worried about that?'

I shrugged. 'In case you want something other than friendship with him.'

'Brody doesn't think of me that way.'

I kept my eyes on her as I asked, 'Do you think of him that way?'

She sent me another suspicious glance. 'Why would you even ask that?'

'You're dodging my questions.'

Tessa attempted to glare at me, but the effect was ruined by the fact that her resolve to keep quiet on the subject was clearly wavering.

I nudged her arm with my elbow. 'Spill.'

Fancy added an 'a-woo' of encouragement.

Tessa let out a sigh of defeat. 'The truth is, I never did think of him that way until a few weeks ago. Remember the dinner we had at the Moonstruck Diner when you arrived in Twilight Cove in June?'

'I remember,' I said. 'When I pointed out that you sounded like you were a fan of Brody, you blushed.'

'I didn't blush.'

'Sorry, Tess, but you totally did.'

Fancy, not to be left out of the conversation, looked over her shoulder at us and let out a 'woo-woo' as she trotted along next to Flossie.

Tessa pressed her hands to her cheeks. 'My face has betrayed me.' She dropped her hands. 'When I said that Brody and I were just friends, I realized maybe I have a little crush on him. But just a little one,' she added quickly. 'And I don't want him finding out.'

'What if he feels the same way?'

'He doesn't,' she said with certainty. When I opened my mouth to argue, she cut me off before I could start. 'Nope. And this is top-secret information.'

'Nobody will hear about it from me,' I promised. 'Your cheeks, on the other hand, aren't as good at keeping secrets.'

Tessa groaned.

Fancy copied the noise, making us laugh.

We walked along the edge of the park, heading toward our cars. Most of the actors and other volunteers had dispersed, but a few hung around chatting near the gazebo, where the vintage lights still shone.

When I glanced toward the corner of Main Street and Ocean Drive, I slowed my pace and put a hand on Tessa's arm. 'Look over there.'

Tessa followed my line of sight and slowed her pace to match mine. 'Elsie and Ajax?'

Although most of the businesses on Main Street were now closed for the night, the streetlamps provided enough illumination to identify the two individuals standing on the corner.

As we watched, Elsie appeared to laugh at something Ajax said. Then, to my surprise, she tucked her arm through his and they walked up Main Street together, with Elsie sticking as close to Ajax as possible while still maintaining her ability to walk.

'I never would have imagined them together,' Tessa said. 'Isn't there quite an age gap?'

'Maybe twenty years?' I replied. 'I'm guessing Ajax is in his mid-thirties. And Elsie . . . maybe mid-fifties like Jasper?'

'Something like that,' Tessa agreed.

I stared across the road at their retreating backs. 'Strange.'

'That Elsie's so into him when Jasper hasn't even been buried yet?'

'There's that,' I said. 'But the last time I saw Elsie and Ajax together, she looked like she didn't want anything to do with him.'

'Maybe he managed to charm her?' Tessa asked, not sounding very convinced by her own theory.

Before I had a chance to answer, Flossie and Fancy growled and pulled on their leashes.

'What's wrong, girls?' I asked with alarm. They rarely growled like that.

The spaniels lunged forward, nearly yanking me off my feet. I scrambled to keep up with them and Tessa hurried along at my side.

'What are you doing?' I asked the dogs.

Flossie and Fancy kept pulling me until we passed a parked white van. Then they stopped so suddenly that I nearly tripped over them. When I regained my balance, I realized they were staring at something up ahead. On the far side of a dark sedan, Giles Gilroy leaned

in close to a cowering Rayelle Adams and said something I couldn't
hear, a nasty expression on his face. Then Giles turned on his heel
and marched away, never spotting me, Tessa or the dogs.

Once Giles was several paces away from her, Rayelle turned and
fled in the opposite direction.

'What was that jerk doing to her?' Tessa asked with a frown.

I was too stunned to acknowledge her question.

In the moments before Rayelle disappeared into the darkness, I
got a good look at her pirate costume with its purple headscarf and
matching sash.

TWENTY-TWO

Tessa and I lingered at the beach for half an hour, talking over
the fact that Rayelle was the female pirate I'd seen running
through Jasper's neighborhood on the night of the murder.
We also talked about what might have been going on between her
and Giles Gilroy.

Despite our long chat, we had no idea why Rayelle would want
to kill Jasper or why Giles would behave in a threatening way
toward her. Maybe the guy was just a jerk, but there could have
been more to it than that.

I tossed and turned after going to bed that night, thoughts swirling
around in my head. It didn't help that Stardust decided she'd had
enough sleep shortly after midnight. She romped around the
bedroom, jumping around, swatting at everything she could find
and generally causing mischief. The dogs chased after her, joining
in the fun.

Finally, after an hour of shenanigans, she curled up on the dog
bed and fell fast asleep. Fortunately, her escapades had also
exhausted me to the point where I managed to drift off. Not so
fortunately, I woke up before my alarm went off, thanks to Gizmo
shrieking down in the kitchen. He'd been good about not screeching
until that moment, but it seemed he was lonely, so we all got up
and trudged downstairs as soon as I was dressed. Well, I trudged.
Flossie, Fancy and Star raced down the stairway, fully recharged
after their night's sleep. I wished I could say the same about myself.

I wasn't hungry enough to eat breakfast at that hour, so I fed the animals and headed out to the barn to get an early start on the farm chores. Callum had already moved the animals out to their pastures for the day and was busy feeding the goats. After stopping to say good morning to him, I fed the donkeys and then moved on to mucking out the stalls in the barn. These days, Callum usually did that job but, despite my lack of sleep, I craved the extra physical work.

'Everything OK?' Callum asked, leaning against the doorframe of the stall I was currently cleaning.

I wiped the back of my hand across my forehead. 'Sure. Why do you ask?'

'You're shoveling that manure like it's somehow offended you.'

I leaned on the shovel, taking a moment to catch my breath. 'I thought some hard work might settle my mind.'

Callum straightened as concern flickered across his face. 'So there *is* something wrong?'

I shook my head, not wanting him to worry. 'I'm just thinking about Jasper's murder again. It's like trying to put a puzzle together when all the pieces are constantly in motion and you're not even sure if they all belong to the same puzzle.' I continued before he had a chance to say anything. 'You're probably going to tell me to leave the puzzle for the police, but I can't help it. Whenever I'm faced with a mystery, my brain wants to figure it out.'

'I'm not going to tell you to leave the puzzle to the police,' Callum said. 'Just all the dangerous stuff.'

'I definitely plan to leave *that* to them.' I suppressed a shudder as vivid memories of my encounter with a killer back in June surfaced. 'And it's probably ridiculous for me to think for a second that I might have a chance of identifying the killer, but my brain's going to keep trying nonetheless.'

'Not ridiculous.' He hooked his thumbs into the pockets of his jeans. 'You're observant. That's probably one of the things that makes you such a great writer.'

'Sometimes I'm observant,' I amended. 'The rest of the time I'm in my own little world and have no idea what's going on around me.'

Callum grinned. 'You get a dreamy look in your eyes when you do that.'

My cheeks flushed, because that dreamy look was probably most obvious when I was thinking about him. Maybe I should have told him that, but instead I just offered him a hint of a smile. Sometimes I said more to him than I planned and other times the words I wanted to say got stuck on my tongue.

'Why don't you let me finish the stalls so you can go do some writing,' he suggested.

'I guess that's what I should be doing, but I'm going to finish helping you with the stalls first. I slipped off one work glove so I could tug my phone out of my back pocket and check the time. It was later than I realized. 'Have you seen Aunt Olivia this morning?'

'I was about to ask you that,' Callum said. 'She's usually out here by now.'

As if we'd magically summoned her, my aunt rushed into the barn.

'Sorry I'm late,' she apologized.

'You're not really late,' Callum told her. 'It's not like we have set hours.'

'But the animals like their food on time.' Olivia set a straw hat on her head. 'I got caught up in phone calls from Dolores and Leona.'

'Is something wrong with one of your friends?' I asked as a whisper of worry fluttered through my chest. Both of the women she'd mentioned were members of her Gins and Needles group.

'No, everyone's fine,' Auntie O said, alleviating my fledgling concerns. 'They just had some news to share.'

'About Jasper's death?' I guessed.

My aunt frowned. 'Possibly. It might all have to do with that darned treasure map again.'

'What happened?' Callum asked, beating me to the question.

'Somebody ransacked Jasper's and Elsie's houses last night.'

I took a second to digest that news. 'Someone who was looking for the map?'

Callum took off his cowboy hat and ran a hand through his blond hair. 'I thought the general theory was that the killer took the map after murdering Jasper.'

'The map was missing from Jasper's house, as far as the police could tell, but nobody knows where it is for sure,' Auntie O said.

'So maybe the killer didn't get the map that night and came back to search again?' Callum theorized.

'And when they didn't find it at Jasper's house, they decided to try Elsie's place?' I added.

'I really have no idea what's going on.' The sadness in Olivia's eyes tugged at my heart. 'But I sure hope the police figure it out soon.'

I came out of the stall and removed my gloves so I could give my aunt a hug. 'I can do your chores today, if you like,' I offered.

'Thank you, hon, but I enjoy the work, and keeping busy is good for me.' Her phone rang as she gave me a quick squeeze. She checked the screen of the device but then declined the call and tucked the phone away. 'Everyone wants to talk about the latest news, but it can wait. Besides, my friends and I have got our Gins and Needles meeting tonight.'

'Gossip central,' I said with a nod and a smile.

My aunt smiled too. 'Especially once the cocktails start flowing.'

She set off to feed the chickens, so Callum and I finished cleaning out the stalls, and then I forced myself to sit down in the farmhouse living room and get some writing done. I was relatively successful, until Gizmo started singing his favorite tune over and over again. That woke up Stardust, who had been snoozing on the rug with the dogs. She scampered around, jumping, rolling and generally treating the living room like a parkour course, while Flossie and Fancy watched with their tails wagging.

I struggled to work through the commotion for a while, but then Gizmo started shrieking, 'Give me the map! Give me the map!'

When his words sank in, I shoved my laptop on to the coffee table and ran into the kitchen, the dogs and Stardust clattering after me.

'What did you say, Gizmo?' I asked.

He shifted along his perch. 'Give me the map! Give me the map, you fool!'

I sank into one of the kitchen chairs.

'Oh, Gizmo,' I said with an ache in my chest. 'Is that what the killer said to Jasper?'

Not for the first time, I pushed aside the thought of the parrot witnessing Jasper's murder. I hoped he didn't understand what he'd seen, but the violence probably unsettled him even if he didn't know what was going on.

'If only you could tell me the killer's name,' I said to him.

'Shiver me timbers!' he said. Then he sang that same old tune again.

With my thoughts back on Jasper's murder, I decided to give up on writing for the rest of the day. I texted Tessa the news about the break-ins at Jasper's and Elsie's houses.

We decided to drop by Elsie's place to see how she was doing. When I mentioned to Aunt Olivia that Tessa and I planned to offer to help Elsie clean up after the intruder, she wanted to come with us.

We were more than happy to include her. Aside from enjoying my aunt's company, I knew that Elsie was more likely to accept our offer of help and more likely to reveal information with my aunt there. Even though Elsie wasn't close to Olivia, my aunt was far less of a stranger to her than Tessa and me.

I didn't want to leave Stardust alone for too long, but when I shared that concern with Callum, he put my worries to rest. He said he'd let her ride around on his shoulder for a while. When she got tired of that, he would bring her back to the house and check in on her every so often. If Star ended up staying with us permanently, I knew there would be times when she'd be alone in the house, but she was so young and mischievous at the moment and I didn't want her getting into any serious trouble. She had Gizmo for company, but the parrot wasn't exactly kitten-sitter material.

Tessa met us at the farm and we set off for Elsie's place in my car, Flossie and Fancy accompanying us. Minutes later, we pulled up in front of Elsie's house. When we knocked on the door, Elsie answered within seconds. She had dark rings under her eyes and her mouth was set in a frown. When she saw Olivia, her frown relaxed, but she still looked tired.

'I appreciate the offer of help,' she said once we told her why we were there, 'but I just finished tidying up. The intruder didn't do any serious damage. They just emptied drawers and book-shelves.'

'I hope you weren't home when they broke in,' I said, determined not to leave without more details.

'Thankfully not.' Elsie rested a hand over her heart. 'I drove up to Portland to see my son and stayed overnight. Well, part of the night, anyway. When the police called to tell me about the break-in, I started for home right away.'

'You must be exhausted,' Olivia said.

Elsie tucked her hair behind her ear. 'I probably will be once I stop to breathe. The police were here for ages, dusting for finger-prints and looking for other evidence. Once they were done, I wanted to get the house cleaned up right away. I'm heading over to Jasper's place next. The police said I could clean up there too.'

'Isn't it still a crime scene?' I asked.

'Not anymore,' Elsie said. 'The police returned the key that Jasper gave me.'

'We're sorry we're too late to help you here,' Auntie O said, 'but please let us help you with Jasper's house.'

Elsie seemed relieved by the offer and agreed to meet us at Jasper's place with the key. When she led us into his house through the front door, I paused on the threshold, an unpleasant chill seeping through my bones. I couldn't help but remember the last and only other time I'd been in the house.

Auntie O rubbed my back and I could see in her eyes that she was having similar thoughts to mine. I was there to help not just Elsie but also Jasper and my aunt, I reminded myself. I did my best to push the unpleasant memory aside as I followed Elsie and Tessa deeper into the house. We did a quick walk-through and found that the intruder had ransacked every single room. Drawers had been emptied, furniture had been upturned, and every book had been tossed from the shelves to the floor.

In the kitchen, we found a boarded-up window with a pile of broken glass beneath it. I tightened my grip on the leashes when Flossie and Fancy tried to lunge toward the sharp debris.

'Stay back, girls,' I told them. 'I don't want you getting your paws hurt.'

The spaniels put their noses to the floor and tugged me off to the side. They stopped near the open kitchen cupboards and Fancy let out an 'a-woo' as she looked up at me. I realized that they were trying to direct my attention to clumps of reddish-brown mud that had dried on the linoleum.

When I took a closer look at the kitchen floor, I spotted more mud with the same red tinge. I peered over the island at the scattered glass beneath the boarded-up window. Bits of the mud were mixed in with the shards. That was probably why the spaniels had tried to pull me in that direction. While the others got busy putting items back in the cupboards, I did another walk-through of the house and found bits of the same dirt in almost every room.

When I returned to the kitchen and pointed out the mud, Elsie put her hands on her hips and shook her head. 'I cleaned these floors yesterday after the police took down the crime scene tape.'

'So this mud was tracked in by the intruder or the police,' Tessa said.

'I'm betting it was the intruder.' I pointed out the mud mixed in with the broken glass. 'The police probably wouldn't have walked over the shards, but the intruder would have stepped there after climbing in the window. Was there any mud left in your house?' I asked Elsie.

'Some,' she replied, 'but not this much.'

Maybe that meant that the intruder hit Elsie's house after searching Jasper's place. That would make sense if the person was searching for the treasure map or a copy of it.

Auntie O leaned in for a closer look at one of the clumps of mud on the kitchen floor. 'There's only one place around here with mud that color.'

Tessa nodded. 'Hollyburn Hill.'

'Is that a popular place?' I asked, never having heard the name before.

'It's kind of out of the way,' Tessa said. 'You have to hike to it.'

'And not everyone knows how to get there,' Auntie O added.

Although I refrained, I wanted to hug my aunt and friend.

We might have stumbled upon an important clue.

TWENTY-THREE

Elsie set to work cleaning up the kitchen floor and Aunt Olivia started putting the living room back together. Tessa and I decided to work together in the study, even though I wasn't keen to go in that room again. During the first walk-through and while looking for more mud, I'd hovered in the doorway, never actually setting foot in the room. This time, I didn't let myself hesitate and walked right in after Tessa.

'Is it awful being back here?' she asked as we stood in the middle of the room.

I noted that the Persian rug was missing. The police had probably removed it, since Jasper had died on it. I was glad that Jasper's blood had gone with the rug.

'It's not easy,' I replied, 'but we're here for a purpose and that helps.'

All the desk drawers had been emptied on to the floor, Jasper's books had been tossed into piles, and his collection of artifacts and antiques had also been thrown from the shelves. A few were broken or damaged, but others had survived intact.

'Someone mentioned that Jasper had a safe, but I haven't seen one yet.' I crossed the room to where a painting of a pirate ship hung on the wall.

'Maybe it's hidden,' Tessa suggested.

'That's what I'm thinking.' I nudged the painting away from the wall, but there was nothing secreted behind it.

We surveyed the rest of the room. My sweeping gaze halted when I noticed that one of the wide wood panels on the wall had larger gaps around it than others. When I pressed on the panel, it swung away from the wall like a door.

'A secret hidey-hole!' Tessa exclaimed with excitement.

'Unfortunately, this one's just hiding an electrical panel.' I shut it, disappointed.

'But where there's one . . .' Tessa pointed to another section of wood paneling with gaps around it.

I hurried over and opened it with a press of my hand. This time we found the safe, unlocked and empty. It made sense that the police would have removed the contents if there'd been anything inside when they arrived on the scene of Jasper's murder.

We searched for other hiding spots, but found none, so we got to work cleaning up the mess the intruder had left. Although I hoped to uncover more clues as we tidied up Jasper's study, we also used the time to discuss the potential significance of the mud tracked into the house.

'If there's a way to find out if any of our suspects have been to Hollyburn Hill recently, that could point us to the killer,' I said as I began replacing books on the shelves.

Tessa picked up pens, pencils and other office supplies that lay scattered on the floor around the desk. 'So now we have to check all our suspects' shoes?' She didn't sound as though she relished the idea.

'First, we can try to find out if any of them are hikers,' I said. 'And Ajax isn't from Twilight Cove, so what are the chances he would know about Hollyburn Hill and how to get there?'

'He wouldn't,' Tessa said, dropping a bunch of writing utensils into a penholder. 'But Flynn is his cousin, and Flynn does a lot of hiking.'

I followed her line of thought. 'So Flynn easily could have taken Ajax to Hollyburn Hill.'

Tessa nodded. 'Maybe we're back to checking everyone's boots?'

'Maybe,' I said, wishing we had a better plan. I lowered my voice to ensure that it wouldn't carry beyond the study. 'Do you know if Elsie hikes?'

'No idea. She doesn't look outdoorsy, but that doesn't mean she's not.' Tessa stopped rifling through a pile of papers. 'Her house was ransacked too. Are you thinking she might have staged the break-in at her place so she'd look like a victim rather than a suspect?'

'I guess that's a possibility,' I said, 'but why bother staging a break-in here? She has a key. She could have searched the place high and low yesterday when she was here cleaning the floors.'

'Good point.' Tessa shoved the papers into a desk drawer. 'So Elsie probably wasn't responsible for last night's break-ins. Does that mean we can scratch her off the suspect list for the murder?'

'I'm not sure. I keep going back to the question of why the killer would be searching Jasper's and Elsie's houses if they took the map when they killed Jasper?'

'As Callum suggested, maybe the killer didn't get the map on the night of the murder,' Tessa said. 'And everyone thinks it's missing because Jasper was really good at hiding it? Or the killer is now looking for something else?' She shook her head. 'That last part doesn't seem likely.'

'Not impossible, but I feel like this all has to do with the treasure map, especially in light of what Gizmo said this morning.' I filled Tessa in on what I'd heard the parrot say. Then I held a pile of books in my hands as I took a moment to think. 'You and Callum could be right. Perhaps the killer never did get the map because Jasper hid it so well that even the police didn't find it when searching this place.'

'Or because Jasper hid it somewhere else,' Tessa speculated.

'Like at Elsie's house,' I added. 'The problem is, we have no way of knowing if the intruder found what they were looking for this time.'

'This is all so befuddling.' Tessa shoved a book on to one of the shelves. 'I'm tempted to leave it all to the police like Brody wants us to do.'

'We probably should,' I said with a sigh.

Tessa heard what I'd left unsaid. 'But . . .'

'But I want to get closure for Auntie O.'

'And I want to help with that,' Tessa said. 'But it feels like we're spinning our wheels.'

I sighed again. 'I know what you mean.'

We spent the next two hours focused on tidying and cleaning, not talking about suspects, clues or theories. That didn't stop thoughts of such things from going around and around in my head like a carousel. That was another reason I didn't think I could drop my investigation. Unsolved mysteries always tended to weigh on my mind. This one, hitting close to home as it did, would pose a distraction to me until I had answers to all the questions rattling around in my head.

When we finally left Jasper's house, all of us hungry and ready for a late lunch, I noticed a slender white woman with chin-length platinum-blonde hair power-walking along the sidewalk, watching us as she drew closer. She appeared to be in her late fifties and wore a dark purple tracksuit. When we reached the driveway where I'd left my car parked behind Elsie's and Jasper's, the woman approached us.

'Elsie, hon, I heard about the break-ins,' she said in a sympathetic voice. 'Like you needed anything more to deal with.

'Thank you, Mary Rose.' Elsie introduced Aunt Olivia, Tessa and me before adding, 'Mary Rose lives next door to Jasper. She's the one who reported the gunshot on the night of Jasper's death.'

'I also called the police about the break-in,' Mary Rose said with a note of pride in her voice. 'There was an unusual amount of activity in the neighborhood last night.'

'What do you mean?' I asked, my curiosity piqued.

'There were some teenagers out doing stunts on their bikes, but that was before I went to bed. Then, as I was calling my cat in for the night, I saw a car parked out in the back alley. I wouldn't have thought too much about it, except someone ran across Jasper's yard, out into the alley, and then drove off in the car.'

'Did you get a good look at the person?' I asked, trying to sound casual when really excitement was bubbling up inside me at the prospect of new clues.

'No,' Mary Rose said, disappointing me. 'It was just a shadowy figure in the darkness. But I thought it was peculiar, especially because of Jasper's murder. So I scurried across the grass and peeked over the fence as the car's engine started and its lights turned on. I still didn't get a look at the driver, but it was a silver sedan.'

'You didn't get the license number?' Elsie asked, and I was glad I wasn't the only one questioning Jasper's neighbor.

Mary Rose shook her head, making her platinum-blonde hair swing. 'But I told the police there was a sticker on the back windshield.'

'What kind of sticker?' I asked.

Mary Rose looked pensive. 'There was a scalloped shell, or maybe one of those trumpet-like flowers. Then there was a box or square beneath that with some writing below the design.' She shook her head again. 'The car drove off so quickly and the only light to see by came from the vehicle itself.'

Tessa shared a glance with me. 'But that all happened around the time of the break-in?'

'I assume so,' Mary Rose said. 'Because of the murder, I decided to call the police right away. After they checked out Jasper's house, they came to my place and told me that someone had broken in.' Her eyes gleamed as she addressed Elsie. 'Why would someone break into your house and Jasper's house on the same night? I assume the same person is responsible.'

'I have no idea,' Elsie said.

I couldn't tell if she was being truthful or not.

Although Mary Rose wanted to keep us chatting about the break-in and the murder, Auntie O made our excuses and we climbed into our cars as Jasper's neighbor resumed her power walking. I'd parked behind Elsie's vehicle in the driveway, so I backed out first and we drove off so she could leave too.

Tessa came back to the sanctuary with us and she and I wandered into the farmhouse to visit Gizmo and Stardust after Olivia headed for the carriage house. We found the parrot in his cage, as expected, but there was no sign of the kitten. I texted Callum and he assured me that Stardust was safe and sound with him in the barn. Tessa and I grabbed an apple each and munched on them while we strolled over to the barn, talking over our latest information on the way.

'So there's a good chance that the person who broke into Jasper's and Elsie's houses drives a silver sedan with a sticker on the rear window,' I said to start.

'And there's also a good chance that the intruder is the person who killed Jasper,' Tessa added before biting into her apple.

'Did Mary Rose's description of the sticker ring any bells for you?' I asked.

'No,' Tessa said, sounding disappointed. 'But I'll be looking at the back window of every silver sedan I see.'

'Same. Unfortunately, I'm betting there's a lot of them in Twilight Cove.'

'Especially with all the tourists in town right now.' Tessa sighed, but then her face brightened. 'I'm sure I can find out if Flynn has taken Ajax to Hollyburn Hill.'

'Just be careful,' I warned her. 'We don't want either of them knowing why you're asking about it.'

'I'll be careful,' she promised as we tossed our apple cores into a compost bin.

'I guess I need to get in touch with Brody,' I said. 'I haven't told him that Rayelle was the woman running through Jasper's neighborhood on the night of the murder.'

Tessa pulled out her phone and we paused by the entrance to the barn as she tapped out a text message.

'I'll mention that to him now,' she said. 'If he wants more details from you, he can get in touch.'

As she sent the message, we got distracted from our conversation by the sight of Callum walking through the barn toward us, with Stardust perched on his shoulder.

Tessa clutched my arm with one hand and fanned herself with the other. 'Georgie, how can you handle a sight like that?'

'My heart is fluttering,' I admitted.

Callum on his own was enough to give me butterflies. Seeing him with the adorable kitten riding around on his shoulder was almost too much for my heart to handle.

I pulled out my phone and took a photo as Callum approached us. He grinned when he saw what I was doing, and I got a picture I was tempted to print and frame.

Stardust meowed at me, so I lifted her off Callum's shoulder and cradled her against my chest, where she closed her eyes and purred. We caught Callum up on the latest news, but then Tessa had to hurry off to a hair appointment. She promised to text me to let me know if she managed to get any information out of Flynn.

As much as I wanted to make progress on piecing together the puzzle of Jasper's murder, I decided to buckle down and put in a few more hours of writing before the day ended. Any more sleuthing on my part would have to wait.

TWENTY-FOUR

I didn't know how much time had passed when I surfaced from the fictional world of my latest screenplay. I'd knocked out page after page, so lost in the grip of the story that I'd forgotten about the world around me. Apparently, I'd also forgotten to eat, other than the apple I'd had while Tessa was still at the farm. My stomach wasn't happy with me for ignoring its rumbles, which had probably been carrying on for far longer than I'd noticed.

Before sitting down to write, I'd let Flossie and Fancy outside at their insistence. The last I'd seen of them, they were bounding off in the direction of the barn, no doubt going in search of Stardust and Callum. I decided I should go out and check on them. They'd probably be wanting their dinner soon.

When I reached the kitchen on my way to the back door, a delicious aroma reached my nose, setting off a series of louder rumbles in my stomach. I glimpsed movement through the window and smiled in anticipation. I stayed inside long enough to feed Gizmo and then I stepped out on to the back porch.

Callum stood at the barbecue, his back to me as he grilled a variety of vegetables and marinated tofu. I walked up behind him and slipped my arms around him, resting my cheek against his broad back. I felt more than heard his low rumble of laughter as he placed one hand over mine where it rested on his stomach.

'If you're going to sneak up on a guy, that's the way to do it,' he said.

'I wasn't sneaking. You're just intent on your grilling.' I released my hold on him, though I kept one arm loosely around his waist, so I could join him at his side and get a closer look at our cooking dinner. I breathed in the divine aromas. 'And it looks like your focus is going to pay dividends to my stomach.'

'I hope you don't mind me doing this,' he said. 'I figured you were probably so caught up in writing that you forgot about dinner.'

'You know me well.'

He caught my gaze with his. 'And hopefully even better as time goes on.'

I smiled, liking his words, but a sudden attack of shyness caused me to avert my gaze from his.

'Where's Stardust?' I asked. 'And the dogs?' The animals were conspicuously absent.

'Over at the carriage house,' Callum replied. 'Olivia wanted some kitten time and the dogs decided to join her.' He set down the metal spatula. 'Dinner will be ready in a minute. In the meantime, I brought you something.'

'In addition to the food? Now you're spoiling me.'

He laughed. 'It's something you might not even want.' He picked up a paper shopping bag from one of the wicker chairs. Despite his grin, he hesitated slightly before handing me the bag. 'You don't have to keep them.'

I peeked into the bag and smiled as I pulled out two garments. 'Your T-shirts?'

'So you don't have to worry about getting your jersey dirty.'

I held up the first one. It was a raglan baseball tee in white with black sleeves. On the back was the name McQuade and the number thirty-three. It appeared to be the right size for me.

'My sister had those made up a few years back when I had a bunch of friends and family coming to a game in Colorado,' Callum explained as he grabbed the barbecue tongs and flipped the tofu on the grill. 'I asked her if she had any left over and she sent that one.'

'That was fast shipping,' I said.

His sister still lived in Colorado.

'She sent it by courier. I think she got a bit excited.'

'About sending a T-shirt?' I asked with mild surprise.

He set down the tongs. 'About the fact that I have a woman in my life she really likes.'

'She's never met me,' I pointed out, although I liked hearing his words nonetheless.

He briefly touched two fingers to my cheek. 'But I've told her a lot about you.'

'Only good things, I hope.' I was mostly joking.

'Of course only good things,' Callum said. 'What else is there?'

I laughed at that. 'I don't want to spend the whole evening making a list, so we'll just move on.'

He took hold of my shoulders and looked me in the eyes. 'I wish you could see yourself the way I do, Georgie.'

Heat rushed to my cheeks, as much from the intensity of his gaze as his words.

He gave my shoulders a gentle squeeze and released them, breaking the momentary trance his green eyes had lulled me into.

My tongue suddenly refusing to work, I pulled the second T-shirt out of the bag. This one was a short-sleeved, gray crewneck. It also had Callum's last name and number on the back, but this one was larger than the other.

'And that's one of mine,' he said as I held it up against myself.

'That you've actually worn?' I asked with hope.

'Many times.' He rubbed the back of his neck, looking a little unsure of himself. 'I didn't know which you'd prefer – one of mine or one that might fit you.'

'Do I have to choose?'

He grinned at that. 'You're welcome to both. I just wasn't sure . . .'

I kissed him before he could finish his sentence, hoping to erase any remaining traces of his doubt. 'I love them, so I'm going to be greedy and keep them both.' I kissed him again. 'Thank you. Now I can have some McQuade magic whenever I want.'

'You can anyway,' he assured me. 'Now that I'm back in Twilight Cove, I'm never more than a text message away.'

My heart swelled with emotion. I was trying to find a way to put my feelings into words when Callum turned to the barbecue.

He grabbed the tongs and checked the food. 'These are ready now.'

I squelched the jumbled words that were trying to make their way out of my heart and up through my throat. So many times he'd reassured me about his feelings with his words and actions. I wanted to do the same for him, but words were hard for me. Sure, I worked with words for a living, but writing was different than speaking from my heart. A script could be edited any number of times before sharing it. Pouring my heart out on the spot didn't come with such a luxury, and that knowledge often tied my tongue up in knots.

As Callum handed me a plate of grilled deliciousness and we sat down on the porch swing to eat, I silently vowed that I would find a way to let him know how I felt about him.

Soon.

* * *

By the time I said goodnight to Callum that evening, Flossie and Fancy had returned to the farmhouse, and Aunt Olivia had carried Stardust over before returning to the carriage house. The animals grew restless as Callum and I shared a prolonged kiss in the kitchen, so we finally parted, my body – and especially my heart – humming with happiness.

Upstairs in my bedroom, I changed into a pair of pajama shorts and the gray T-shirt Callum had given me. The oversized shirt was soft against my skin and filled me with thoughts of him and the words I wished I could say out loud.

Hit by a sudden shot of inspiration, I dug through my closet until I found a shoebox that held a collection of beads and other supplies for making bracelets. I'd gone through a brief phase when I'd made several bracelets for myself, but I hadn't touched the beads in a long time. I was glad I'd kept the supplies, because I had an idea and I didn't want to wait to execute it, in case I lost my nerve.

I sat cross-legged on my bed with the box before me. Flossie and Fancy curled up next to me while Stardust scampered around the room, swatting at her toys, which were now scattered across the floor. I figured it was a good thing she was keeping busy. That was better than having her decide she wanted to 'help' me with the beads.

I grabbed my phone and did a quick search on the Internet to find the reference I needed. Then I set to work, stringing beads on to a leather cord. The task soothed me, untangling and quieting my thoughts about Callum and the murder. Once I had the bracelet completed, I put away the supplies and climbed into bed, my mind growing hazy with sleep. I was glad to drift off quickly. I would need my rest, because the next day would be for sleuthing and gathering my courage to give Callum the gift I'd just made for him.

TWENTY-FIVE

The first place I visited the next morning was the Treasure Trove. Even though Jasper's murder and the recent break-ins occupied much of my thoughts, I hadn't forgotten about my quest to find out more about Flossie and Fancy, if at all possible. Fae was busy with a customer when the spaniels and I entered the shop, so I spent a few minutes browsing. A rotating rack near the door held a variety of greeting cards with designs painted or drawn by local artists. I chose a card for Tessa since I knew her birthday was coming up in September, just a couple of weeks after my stepmother's. As I approached the sales counter, the other customer shared a few final words with the shopkeeper and then left the store.

Fae came around the counter to greet the dogs, crouching down so she could accept kisses on her cheek and give them smooches on their snouts.

I watched with a smile as I set the birthday card on the counter. 'I hiked the path you marked for me,' I said as she and the spaniels wrapped up their extended greeting. 'Thank you again for the map.'

Fae straightened up and returned to the other side of the sales counter. 'My pleasure. Did Flossie and Fancy go with you?'

'They did, and they were great hiking companions, of course. They even found an abandoned kitten in the woods.'

Fae pressed a hand over her heart. 'Oh, my stars! The poor creature!'

'She's fine,' I rushed to assure her, 'and living with us at the farm for the moment. Maybe permanently, if she doesn't turn out to be someone's missing cat.'

Fae smiled. 'If she ends up staying with you and these beautiful girls, I know she'll have a great home.'

Fancy voiced her agreement and Flossie wagged her tail.

'Did you find any wild blueberries?' Fae asked.

'I didn't notice any,' I said, 'but I wasn't looking.'

'It's a great place for berry picking. Hollyburn Hill is too.'

My ears perked up at that. I could have sworn the dogs' ears did as well.

'I've heard Hollyburn Hill mentioned a couple of times,' I said. 'Is it a popular place?'

Fae considered the question. 'I suppose it is with hikers and foragers, but I still have the place to myself most times when I'm there.' She scanned the birthday card I'd chosen. 'Did you feel the energy of Witch's Peak?' Fae asked.

Fancy let out another 'a-woo', as if answering the question.

'Of course *you* did,' Fae said, leaning over the counter to direct her smile at the dogs.

'Energy?' I echoed. I remembered how recharged I'd felt after soaking my feet in the stream up in the hills, but I didn't mention that.

'Oh, yes,' Fae said. 'That's a very powerful place. Ley lines converge there, you know. I like to go there whenever I need some healing vibrations.'

Two women came into the shop at that moment, and that came as a relief to me because I didn't know what to say to Fae. I *had* felt something while sitting by the stream and maybe that energy was the key to Flossie's and Fancy's unusual abilities. Perhaps they were born in that spot or drank from the stream beneath a full moon. All I really knew was that Witch's Peak, where the ley lines converged, likely had something to do with the dogs' powers.

I paid for the birthday card and thanked Fae as one of the other customers approached the counter.

'I see you got the lights fixed,' I heard the woman say to Fae as I left the shop with the dogs.

Out on the sidewalk, I paused and drew in a deep breath of fresh air that carried a hint of saltiness. If I didn't know about Flossie's and Fancy's abilities, I probably would have dismissed what Fae had told me. I'd never really believed in magic before I'd met the dogs, but they were irrefutable proof that there was far more to the universe than I'd previously realized.

While I strongly suspected that I'd never find out exactly how Flossie and Fancy had come into their powers, knowing that the place up in the hills likely had something to do with the origin of their abilities made me feel better. Natural magic of the universe was a far better explanation than experiments conducted in a lab somewhere.

'I think I'm going to have to learn to be content with not having all the answers,' I said to the spaniels.

Flossie gave a woof and Fancy let out a long 'woo-woo'. I was pretty sure they were putting their support behind my statement. Being content without answers to all of my questions didn't come naturally to me. I always wanted to know the explanation behind things, and that's probably why I enjoyed writing about mysteries and crimes, because I was in control of the story and could always ensure that everything was explained and wrapped up at the end. This time, though, I didn't have complete control over the narrative, and yet I sensed that I would learn to be OK with that in time.

I couldn't, however, be at peace with not knowing the answer to the question of who had killed Jasper. As long as the murderer's identity remained a mystery, that person would be on the loose and could, potentially, harm someone else. That seemed like a real danger considering that someone – who might well have been the killer – appeared to still be searching for the treasure map.

After moving out of the way of the light foot traffic on the side-walk, I sent a text message to Tessa, asking if she'd had a chance to speak with Flynn yet. She probably hadn't, since it was barely mid-morning now, and she'd likely text me once she'd chatted with him, but an anxious need for answers hummed through my blood-stream and made it hard for me to wait without checking in.

Tessa didn't reply right away, so I tucked my phone in my pocket and started off down the street with Flossie and Fancy.

'How about we stop in at the Pet Palace now?' I said to the spaniels.

It was a good thing I was already moving. Otherwise, the dogs probably would have pulled me off my feet when they lunged toward their favorite shop.

Laughing, I hurried after them, keeping a firm grip on their leashes.

Once inside the store, I spent several minutes chatting with Cindy. So far, no one had claimed to be missing a kitten of any description, let alone one that looked like Star. Cindy had taped a poster to the window of the shop and another near the sales counter. I felt a bit guilty about how relieved I was to know that no one had yet tried to claim Stardust. Cindy suggested leaving the posters up for another few days, and I hoped that the sweet kitten would get to stay with me and the dogs on a permanent basis. She had wriggled and meowed her way right into my heart.

Of course, we couldn't leave the Pet Palace without buying some treats for Flossie and Fancy. I also picked up a few more supplies for Star and a toy for Gizmo. The toy was essentially a roll made of layers of seagrass that Gizmo could enjoy demolishing. There was room inside the roll to stuff it with nuts and other parrot-friendly treats.

Although I felt a hint of sadness at the prospect of saying goodbye to Gizmo if he ended up going to live with Dean Haskell's niece in Eugene, I knew it would be for the best as long as the parrot and Ginny were a good match. I'd developed plenty of affection for Gizmo during our short acquaintance, but a parrot didn't fit into my life as well as cats and dogs and the farm animals did. A forever home with a caring and dedicated parrot lover would be the best outcome for him.

As I left the Pet Palace with Flossie and Fancy, I found myself humming the tune that Gizmo so often sang. I stopped on the sidewalk to check my phone and opened a new text message from Tessa. She hadn't yet spoken to Flynn, but he was known to frequent the local coffee shop, Déjà Brew, and she was on her way there to see if she could find him. I let her know that I was in the area too and we arranged to meet up a little later. First, I wanted to head over to the Twilight Inn to ask Rayelle if she'd be interested in volunteering her artistic skills to make posters for the animal sanctuary's upcoming fall fundraising event.

I was about to start walking east toward the inn when a dark shape moved overhead, causing the morning sunlight to flicker. I shaded my eyes against the brightness of the summer sky and watched Euclid circle in the air above us.

If we'd been completely alone, I would have called out a greeting to the owl, but there were pedestrians not too far away and I didn't want to draw any attention to us or to Euclid, mostly because I didn't want anyone to realize that I was following an owl. I knew that was what Euclid wanted me to do when he swooped down lower and then back up to a higher altitude before winging his way over the line of shops.

Flossie and Fancy also knew what Euclid wanted and dashed ahead, nearly pulling me off my feet.

'Wait for me, girls!' I said as I hurried after them.

The spaniels slowed their pace just enough so I could keep up with them. It took me by surprise when Euclid led us into an alley behind a row of shops. He glided down to land on the edge of the roof and blinked his yellow eyes as the dogs and I drew to a stop below him. Right in front of me, posted on the exterior wall of the building, was a small sign declaring the business to be Gilroy's Antiques.

'What is it you're trying to tell me?' I asked the owl as I looked up at him.

Without providing me with any further clues, Euclid took off from his perch and flew away.

Fancy let out a short howl, drawing my attention back to her and her sister. They tugged me across the small, three-stall parking lot behind the building until we reached the only occupied spot. A silver sedan sat there, facing the back of the antiques shop. Flossie barked and raised one paw, her nose pointing toward the rear of the car.

I stepped closer to the vehicle for a better look at the sticker displayed in the rear window. It bore the logo of the antiques shop, which featured a gramophone with the words 'Gilroy's Antiques' below it.

'Thank you, girls,' I whispered to the dogs. 'And thank you, Euclid,' I added, glancing up at the sky.

Although the sticker featured a picture of a gramophone, in low light or when glimpsed very briefly, the gramophone's horn easily could have been mistaken for a scalloped shell or a trumpet-like flower.

TWENTY-SIX

My thoughts whirled like a tornado inside my head as I waited impatiently on the street corner. I'd texted the new clue to Tessa, along with photos of the sticker and the silver sedan's license plate. I'd also sent the photos to Brody via text messages, along with a brief explanation. Tessa had responded within a minute or two, but with only a brief message saying she'd meet me on the corner shortly. I'd already been standing there with the dogs for close to five minutes, and all three of us were growing antsy.

Fortunately, I saw the door to Déjà Brew open, and Tessa emerged from the coffee shop. She spotted us right away and hurried to meet us on the corner.

'I'll walk with you to the inn,' she said, knowing that was my next destination.

I fell into step with her as the dogs trotted along in front of us.

Tessa tugged an elastic off her wrist and fastened her hair into a ponytail as we walked. 'Sorry my message was so short. I was in the middle of talking to Flynn.'

'It's fine,' I assured her before bringing up the topic weighing on my mind. 'Giles must be the person who broke into Jasper's and Elsie's houses, right?'

'Well, we know his car was in the alley behind Jasper's house on the night of the break-ins,' Tessa said. 'And Mary Rose saw the driver run through Jasper's backyard before getting in the car. As far as I know, Giles is single and doesn't have any family in Twilight Cove, so it doesn't seem likely that someone else would be driving his car.'

'Maybe not impossible, but I agree with you,' I said. 'I texted the photos of the sticker and license plate to Brody. Hopefully, the police will follow up on the information soon.'

'So does this mean that Ajax couldn't have been the burglar?' Tessa asked.

'Giles does seem to be a more likely suspect,' I said. 'But how did things go with Flynn?'

'I had coffee with him,' she replied. 'I made it seem like I randomly bumped into him at Déjà Brew. I started talking about hiking and asked if he'd been to Hollyburn Hill recently. He volunteered that he'd taken Ajax there, among other places. Ajax is as keen a hiker as Flynn is, apparently.'

'Did he give any indication as to when he and Ajax were at Hollyburn Hill?'

'Three days ago,' Tessa said. 'I wanted to ask if that was the most recent hike they'd been on, but I couldn't figure out how to phrase the question without potentially making Flynn suspicious, so in the end I didn't ask.'

'That was a good decision,' I assured her. 'We need to be careful about what we say.' I considered her information. 'Three days ago . . . If they haven't hiked elsewhere since, Ajax definitely could have been tracking red dirt around on the soles of his boots two nights ago.'

'I thought he had to be the burglar, until you texted me about the sticker.'

'If I didn't know about the sticker on Giles's car, I'd have Ajax pegged as the number-one suspect too,' I said. 'And we can't rule him out entirely, but I think Giles belongs at the top of our list now.'

'Definitely,' Tessa agreed. 'If not for his alibi, I'd still suspect Flynn. He was complaining about the map and historical inaccuracies again.'

Flossie and Fancy sat down at the next corner and waited for a car to drive by. When the road was clear, we all stepped off the curb.

'I'm glad we were able to take him off our list,' I said. 'That's some progress, at least. And hopefully, the police will know soon if Giles really was the person who committed the burglaries.'

Tessa said she was holding on to the same hope.

We'd reached the Twilight Inn by then, so Tessa stayed out on the front porch with the dogs while I stepped inside the Victorian mansion. Nobody sat behind the registration desk in the foyer, but Catherine appeared before I had a chance to ring the bell on the desk.

She smiled as she came down the hall toward me. 'Georgie, how nice to see you again. What can I help you with?'

I quickly explained the purpose of my visit.

'I'm sure Rayelle would be glad to help with the posters for the fundraiser,' Catherine said. 'She's in her studio. You're welcome to go out there and see her.'

Catherine told me that Rayelle's studio was located in a small outbuilding at the back of the property. She invited me to pass through the inn to get to the backyard, but I told her I'd walk around the house since I had the dogs with me.

Tessa joined me as I made my way around the Victorian inn with the dogs. A cute outbuilding painted cream and light gray to match the house sat beyond a rose garden and the dog run – which was currently empty. The building had large windows as well as skylights, and the door stood open.

Flossie and Fancy sat down as soon as we reached the door, and I knocked on the frame before poking my head inside. Rayelle sat at a desk by one of the windows, sketching with a pencil. When I first glimpsed her, she appeared sad, but she smiled when she saw me, and her expression grew even brighter when Flossie and Fancy peeked inside as well.

'Come on in,' Rayelle invited.

The dogs wasted no time accepting the invitation and ran straight to her for attention. I followed more slowly and Tessa brought up the rear.

'You can let the dogs off their leashes,' Rayelle said to me as she stroked the spaniels' fur. 'I don't mind them being loose in here.'

I unclipped the leashes and the dogs scooted closer to their new friend until they were sitting on her feet and leaning against her legs. Rayelle seemed pleased by their affection and continued to fuss over them.

I sneaked a glance at the drawing she'd been working on. A

crying woman who closely resembled Rayelle stood in the rain with her face turned up to the sky as tears ran down her face. It was a somber sketch but also a beautiful one.

'Wow,' Tessa said as she glanced around the studio. 'This is a nice set-up.'

The desk was at one end of the rectangular room and a couch sat against the opposite wall. In between were a couple of easels and a rolling, adjustable stool. Shelves of art supplies lined one wall and several canvases leaned up against the shelving unit. The studio also had a workbench with a large sink set into it.

'Thanks,' Rayelle said. 'I love it. My mom says I basically live here in my studio and she's probably right. Some nights I even sleep here on the couch.' She got up from her desk. 'But I'm sure you're not here for a tour.'

I quickly explained why we'd come to speak with her. I was glad to see a spark of enthusiasm in her eyes when I finished.

'I'd love to help out!' she said. 'I love animals, so the sanctuary is a cause close to my heart.'

She asked a few questions about what exactly Auntie O and I were looking for in the posters and I answered as best I could. While Rayelle and I chatted about the project, Tessa wandered slowly around the studio, checking out the various paintings and drawings. Flossie and Fancy sniffed around, exploring the space with their keen noses.

'How about I come up with a couple of preliminary sketches over the next couple of weeks?' Rayelle suggested. 'I can email them to you and you can choose which one you like best and let me know if any changes are needed.'

'That sounds great.'

We exchanged phone numbers and email addresses so we could easily keep in touch.

As I tucked my phone away, Flossie came over and bumped her nose against my leg. When I looked down, I saw that she held a slightly crumpled piece of paper in her mouth. She dropped it and it drifted down to land by my foot.

'Flossie, that's not yours,' I admonished as I picked up the piece of paper. 'I'm so sorry,' I added to Rayelle.

I was about to say more when the writing on the page caught my eye. It appeared to be an invoice, but what really got my attention was the name of the seller: Venturini Vintage Paper.

I ran my eye down the page and saw that the invoice was for several sheets of paper that dated back to the 1820s.

Rayelle took the invoice from me, her face flushing bright pink. 'That should be recycled.' She shoved it beneath the sketchbook lying open on her desk.

I glanced at Tessa, who stood beside me. I could tell by the expression on her face that she'd managed to get a glimpse at the invoice as well.

An awkward silence fell over the room.

Tessa drew in a breath and I could tell she was about to speak, but then Fancy trotted over our way and looked up at me with bright brown eyes, a hiking boot held in her mouth.

'Fancy!' I took the boot away from her. 'I'm so sorry,' I said to Rayelle. As I apologized, I turned the boot – in what I hoped was a subtle movement – so I could check its sole. It was completely clean, not a speck of dirt on it.

'I don't know what's got into them today,' I continued as I handed the boot to Rayelle. 'They've become a pair of snoopers.'

Rayelle's blush had faded slightly, but her face was still quite pink. 'It's all right,' she said as she accepted the boot from me. 'No harm done.'

Despite those words, I detected a flicker of fear in her eyes.

'Do you do a lot of hiking?' Tessa asked after giving me a nudge with her elbow.

'Sure,' Rayelle said as she set the boot down next to its partner on a mat by the door. 'I get a lot of inspiration from nature.'

'Do you ever go to Hollyburn Hill?' I asked. 'I've heard it's a nice place.'

'Now and then. I was just up there last week.'

Tessa and I shared a weighty glance while Rayelle busied herself with tidying her already neat desk. She was definitely nervous and uncomfortable.

Worry wriggled around inside of me. Rayelle seemed like a nice young woman and I didn't want to suspect her of any wrongdoing, but I'd seen her in Jasper's neighborhood on the night of the murder. The other red flags were impossible to ignore as well.

Tessa and I could have left right then and shared our concerns with Brody, but I sensed that it might not take much to get Rayelle to crack in that moment, so I forged ahead.

'That vintage paper you ordered,' I said, 'did you use it to make the treasure map?'

Rayelle's eyes widened. 'No! Of course not!'

Despite her protestations, I was certain I was close to getting the truth from her.

I continued to press her. 'If the map was a fake and you made it, I can understand why you'd break into Jasper's house to get it back.'

'Is that what you did?' Tessa asked.

Rayelle stared at us with wide, frightened eyes for a beat or two.

Then she burst into tears and cried, 'I never want to see that map again!'

TWENTY-SEVEN

'So you have seen the map,' I said, picking up on the phrasing of Rayelle's last statement.

She flopped down on to the couch and dropped her head into her hands, still crying. 'It's my fault that Jasper's dead.'

Tessa glanced my way before saying, 'You didn't kill him, did you?'

Rayelle's head jerked up, her face streaked with tears. 'Of course not! I never would have harmed him on purpose.' Another sob shook her body. 'But it's the map that got him killed and he had the map because of me.'

Flossie and Fancy rested their chins on Rayelle's knees, wagging their tails and letting out quiet, worried whines. She wiped her tears away with the back of her hand before petting the dogs. Right away, I saw some of the tension drain out of her.

I perched on the arm of the couch and Tessa sank down on to the rolling stool.

'Rayelle,' I said carefully, 'I saw you running from Jasper's neighborhood right around the time he was murdered.'

Her forehead creased with confusion, but then it smoothed out again as understanding dawned in her eyes. 'I was visiting my boyfriend. He lives near Jasper. I lost track of time and realized I was late for the rehearsal at the park. That's why I was running. I never went to Jasper's house that night.'

That sounded like a plausible explanation, but I still had so many questions.

'Did you forge the treasure map?' I asked.

Between her artistic skills and the vintage paper she'd ordered, I figured that was a logical conclusion. However, she quickly set me straight.

'No way. I swear I didn't. I get why you'd think that after seeing that invoice, but the map is real.' She reconsidered what she'd said. 'Well, I don't know if it was made by Dead Eye Dawson, or if it even dated back to the 1700s, but I didn't make it and it was probably in our attic for a long time.'

Flossie and Fancy continued to comfort Rayelle as she went on with her story.

'While the inn was undergoing renovations, we found out there were problems with the roof and rafters. We moved a bunch of stuff out of the attic so the workers would have room to get around easily. There were some boxes that my grandfather had stashed there and nobody had touched since. I'm not even sure if he knew all of what was inside. I went through the boxes and found the map. Of course, I know the Dead Eye Dawson legend, so I thought maybe I could make some money off the map and help my family.

'The renovations ended up costing way more than we expected,' she continued. 'And I know it's put a strain on my parents financially. So I sold the map to Giles Gilroy and then he sold it to Jasper, probably for a profit. I should have thought of selling it to Jasper directly, but Mr Gilroy was the first person that came to mind when I thought about getting some money for it.' Her tears had stopped now, but she still seemed weighed down by guilt and sadness. 'And then Jasper was killed because of the map.' Tears welled in her eyes again, but they subsided before spilling out on to her cheeks. 'That's what everyone thinks, isn't it?'

She was right about that, but I didn't bother voicing any confirmation for fear of making her feel even worse.

'The only person responsible for Jasper's death is the murderer,' Tessa said gently.

'But if I'd kept the map in my family and hadn't tried to make money off it, nobody ever would have killed Jasper.' Rayelle leaned forward to press her face against the dogs' heads.

They kissed her cheeks and that brought a wobbly smile to her face.

I tried to sort out the thoughts in my head. They were all tangled up with each other, but I did my best to tease them apart one by one. 'If you didn't fake the map, why did you order that vintage paper from the early 1800s?'

'Because, apparently, I'm full of terrible ideas.' When Rayelle saw the lack of understanding on my face and Tessa's too, she explained what she meant. 'After I sold the map, I thought I could make more money by forging some old documents and selling them to Mr Gilroy. An awful idea, I know, and dishonest. That's why I never actually went through with it. By the time my order of nineteenth-century paper arrived, I knew I couldn't do it.'

'Then why was Mr Gilroy threatening you?' I asked.

'We saw the two of you down by the beach the other night,' Tessa explained when Rayelle appeared surprised and puzzled.

'Oh, that.' Rayelle stroked the dogs' fur, appearing calmer now. 'He didn't want me telling anyone that he sold the map to Jasper. He doesn't want anyone knowing he ever had it in his possession.'

'Why not?' Tessa asked.

I added a question of my own. 'And how, exactly, did he threaten you?'

'He wasn't very specific with the threat,' Rayelle said. 'He just told me I'd regret it if I didn't keep it a secret. I figured he was worried he'd be a suspect in Jasper's murder if anyone found out, because maybe people would think he'd wanted the map for himself.'

I continued with that line of thinking. 'Maybe he wanted money for the map so he sold it to Jasper, but he also wanted the map for himself, so he tried to steal it back and ended up killing Jasper in the process?'

Rayelle shrugged. 'I guess that's what he was worried people would believe.'

'It could be exactly what happened,' I said, mostly to Tessa. She nodded and I knew she was thinking about the fact that Giles's car was seen by Jasper's house on the night of the break-in.

'But he didn't find the map on the night of the murder, so he went back to search again,' Tessa added.

It made sense.

'But did he find it when he broke into Jasper's and Elsie's houses the other night?' I wondered out loud. 'If the mud is any indication, he hit Jasper's house first, so the fact that he moved on to Elsie's house suggests he didn't find what he was looking for at the first location. Elsie claims Jasper didn't leave a copy of the map with her. If that's the truth, Giles wouldn't have found anything at her house either.'

'But why would he need to steal the map back?' Tessa asked. 'The smart thing would have been to dig up the treasure or at least make a copy of the map before selling it to Jasper.'

'Maybe Giles wanted to sell it to someone else so he could make even more of a profit,' I speculated.

A thought struck me and I looked at Rayelle. The guilt on her face as she met my eyes told me she knew what I was thinking.

'I made a copy of the map and took photos of it before I sold it to Giles,' she admitted without any further prodding. 'I was selling him the map, not any guarantee that I hadn't dug up the treasure first. I figured if I could sell it *and* find the treasure, I could really help out my family. I don't know if I'd legally get to keep and sell the treasure, but people would probably want to interview me and stuff, and they might have paid me for that.'

I wasn't sure about the laws surrounding buried treasure either. Something still bothered me about Rayelle's story.

'But didn't Giles ask you if you'd looked for the treasure yourself?' I thought Giles was shrewd enough to have considered that possibility before handing over any money for the map.

'Sure, he asked,' Rayelle replied. 'And I didn't dare lie to him. I figured he would know if I did, and the guy gives me the creeps. I told him the truth – that I tried to find the treasure but came up empty.'

'There is no treasure?' Tessa asked with obvious disappointment.

Rayelle shrugged. 'Not where I looked, and I'm pretty sure I followed the map correctly.'

'But even knowing that, Giles might have tried to find it himself,' Tessa said.

'You're probably right about that,' I agreed.

'So, either there is no treasure or Giles has probably found it by now,' Tessa mused. 'But if he did find the map at Elsie's house, then that means she lied. Unless Jasper stashed it at her house without her knowing. That might be a bit of a stretch.'

'Maybe Elsie knew the map was at her house and already tried to find the treasure.' I remembered her telling someone – presumably her son – over the phone that they no longer had to worry about money problems. I'd assumed that was because she was inheriting half of Jasper's estate, but what if she had also found buried treasure?

'Do you think I'll go to jail?' Rayelle asked with trepidation, looking close to tears again.

Flossie whined and snuggled closer to her and Fancy let out a soft 'woo' before resting her chin on Rayelle's knee again.

'I doubt it,' I said, hoping to reassure her. 'All you've done is sell a document that was in your family's possession and dig without result.'

'But I might as well have killed Jasper with my own hands.' She blinked back fresh tears.

'You couldn't have known what would happen,' I said, wishing I could assuage some of her guilt. 'If Giles is the killer, it was his greediness that got Jasper killed. If Giles isn't the murderer, Jasper would likely still be alive if he hadn't announced the fact that he had the map in his possession.'

Rayelle had managed to hold back her tears, but she still looked miserable. 'I wish I could turn back time, but I know I can't. If there's anything I can do to make things right, even just a little bit, I want to do it. I'm glad my secret is out in the open now. It was eating me up inside.'

Tessa joined Rayelle on the couch and put an arm around her. 'We're glad you told us. I think the best thing to do would be to tell the police everything. It could help them put the killer behind bars, especially if that person is Giles Gilroy.'

Rayelle's guilt and anxiety didn't fade away completely, but there was a spark of determination in her eyes when she nodded. 'I'll talk to the police. I'll tell them everything I know.'

TWENTY-EIGHT

Tessa phoned Brody and we waited with Rayelle until he arrived with a detective from the Oregon State Police. Before the officers got to the inn, I asked Rayelle if we could see her copy of the map. She shared it with us and even made me a copy of my own using the all-in-one printer on her desk. I had the map tucked away in my pocket by the time the police showed up. Tessa and I stayed with Rayelle while she repeated everything that she'd told us to the officers. Flossie and Fancy remained close by her, and I could tell that they were providing her with real comfort.

The detective wanted Rayelle to go to the local police station to provide a formal statement, so at that point, Tessa, the spaniels and I took our leave. I was glad that Rayelle never mentioned to Brody or the detective that she'd given me a copy of the map. I suspected the detective would have taken it away from me if he'd known. I wasn't sure if studying the map would do me any good, but having it to look at would at least satisfy some of my curiosity.

Tessa also wanted to see the map, so we examined it while we slowly walked back to where we'd left our cars. The map showed the coastline as well as some landmarks rather than all the details of the area. A dotted line marked a path from the ocean to a spot I assumed was a short distance inland at the northern edge of Twilight Cove.

'Does it make sense to you?' I asked as I handed the paper to Tessa so she could take a closer look.

She turned the map this way and that, studying it from different angles. 'The shoreline does look like our cove.' She touched a finger to the point of land that jutted out into the ocean at the southern end of the cove. 'And this is where the lighthouse is now, though it's not shown on the map. That makes sense, if this is the real deal or even a decent fake, because the lighthouse wasn't built until the 1800s, after Dead Eye Dawson was supposedly in the area.' She traced her finger along the dotted path, pausing at a wiggly line that joined up with the ocean. 'This must be Starfall Creek.'

The X on the map sat near the line Tessa had just identified as the creek. There was also what I thought was a jagged rock drawn near the X.

I pointed to it. 'Does that look familiar to you?'

Tessa frowned at the map. 'No, but I don't know the area all that well. Brody might recognize it. He and some of his friends grew up roaming the woods at that end of town.'

'If Rayelle dug for the treasure, maybe she recognized the landmark.' I sent her a quick text message, asking her about the jagged rock, or whatever it was meant to be. I didn't expect an immediate reply since she was on her way to the police station, but I hoped she'd get back to me later in the day.

Maybe I was catching treasure fever, but I didn't think so. It would be exciting to uncover Dead Eye Dawson's stash of loot, but I was more interested in knowing whether Rayelle was the only person who had tried digging up the treasure. Maybe if she accompanied me to the spot marked on the map, she would be able to tell if the ground was more disturbed than it had been when she'd left the area empty-handed.

If no one else had tried digging for the treasure, my question would be why hadn't Giles given it a go? Even if he didn't now have the map in his possession and never made a copy for himself, surely he would have studied it before selling it to Jasper. Of course, if he didn't currently have the original map, then its whereabouts remained unknown. Perhaps Jasper had simply hidden it so well that nobody had found it yet, but the theory of Giles being both the killer and the burglar would feel a whole lot tidier to me if it turned out that he did now have the map.

I wouldn't have thought it possible, but all my jumbled thoughts about the map and the murder flew from my mind when I arrived home. The bracelet I'd made the night before sat on the kitchen table, where I'd left it that morning. I stood in the middle of the room, caught between wanting to hide the bracelet in a drawer and longing to immediately take it to its intended recipient.

Nervous butterflies fluttered in my stomach, but I pocketed the bracelet anyway and marched out the back door, Flossie and Fancy on my heels. When we reached the barn, I peeked into the tack room, wondering if I would find Stardust there. Sure enough, she was curled up on a blanket, sound asleep. When the dogs burst into the room, the tiny kitten lifted her head, gave a great yawn and let out a tiny meow. Flossie and Fancy hurried over to her and touched their noses to her gray fur.

Satisfied that all three of them would be fine in the tack room for the time being, I shut the door and continued on through the barn. When I strode out the back door, I almost ran right into Callum, who had a bag of animal feed over his shoulder. His truck was parked a few feet away, and I figured he'd probably just returned from the farm supply store.

'Hey,' he greeted as he set the heavy bag down by his feet. 'Did you have a good time in town?'

'It was productive,' I said.

I knew from the crinkle in his forehead that he was wondering what I meant by that, but I didn't give him a chance to ask. I also didn't give myself a chance to chicken out.

'I have something for you.' I dug the bracelet out of my pocket, but kept it hidden in my hand. 'After you gave me the shirts, I wanted to give you something in return.'

'You didn't have to do that,' Callum said, his voice warm.

I took a deep breath and then pressed the bracelet into his hand. 'You absolutely don't have to wear it.' As he took a look at the bracelet sitting in his palm, I kept talking in a rush. 'I know you don't usually wear jewelry of any kind, but making bracelets was a hobby of mine at one time, and last night I had the urge to make one for you. It's not much, but there's meaning behind it, even though that might not make much sense and . . .'

Callum stopped my barely coherent stream of chatter with a kiss on my lips.

'Georgie,' he said, tucking a lock of hair behind my ear with a gentleness that made my heart ache, 'I love it. Thank you.'

He slid on the bracelet, and I was relieved to see that it managed – barely – to fit over his hand.

He admired it for a moment, fingering the beads, before grinning at me. 'Every time I look at it, I'll think of you. Not that I really need a reminder, but it's nice to have one anyway.'

'I'm glad you like it,' I said with a smile. I gave him a quick kiss. 'Now I'll let you get back to work.'

'Hold on a moment.' He took my hand. 'Have you seen Dexter's new talent?'

Dexter was one of the sanctuary's adorable pygmy goats.

'No,' I said, curious.

'You need to check this out.'

He left the bag of feed where it sat on the ground and led me out of the barn, my hand still in his. When we reached the goat pasture, Callum released my hand and climbed over the fence. This particular fence was higher than the others. It needed to be, since the goats were mischievous creatures and good climbers. I stepped up on to a small platform outside the fence that allowed me to see over the top rail.

Callum stopped to pat one of the goats on his way across the pasture to where a large rubber ball sat on the ground. He picked it up and called out, 'Hey, Dexter!'

Then he threw the ball.

It hit the ground and rolled a few feet before coming to a stop. Dexter immediately ran for the ball. He tried to leap on to it, but lost his footing and fell to the ground.

'Oh no!' I exclaimed with worry, but the pygmy goat was already back on his feet.

Undeterred, he hopped on to the ball again, keeping all four legs moving in a running motion. This time, he managed to stay on the ball for several seconds, spinning it beneath him like a log roller.

I laughed and clapped as he lost his balance and jumped to the ground.

'Way to go, Dexter!' I called out.

Callum strode over my way. 'He's very proud of himself.'

'He should be. That's quite the talent.'

Callum stopped by the water trough and removed his cowboy hat just long enough to run a hand through his hair. He was about to say something when a blur of movement caught my attention, a split second before Dexter leapt into the air and head-butted Callum right in the stomach. Callum staggered back a step. His legs hit the edge of the water trough and he fell into it with a splash.

Gasping, I clambered over the fence as Callum raised his head out of the water, spluttering. I grabbed his hand and hauled him to his feet. Water poured off of him in rivulets and his cowboy hat lay on the ground near my feet.

'Are you OK?' I asked, my eyes wide.

Callum coughed and wiped water from his eyes. 'I'm fine.' He checked his wrist. The bracelet appeared to be none the worse for wear. 'Nothing's broken and the bracelet's fine, so it's all good.'

We looked at each other as water continued to drip from his hair and clothes. Then we both burst out laughing.

'You're a naughty boy,' I called to Dexter when I had enough breath to speak.

The pygmy goat was now grazing innocently across the pasture as if nothing had happened.

'He's got personality, that's for sure.' Callum laughed again.

I picked up his cowboy hat and went up on tiptoes so I could place it on his head. On my way back down to the flats of my feet, Callum caught my wrist in his hand, his thumb skimming over my pulse point.

'Thanks for saving me from drowning,' he said with one corner of his mouth quirked upward.

'I'm pretty sure you could have saved yourself, but you're welcome.'

His face was mere inches from mine and I was sorely tempted

to kiss him. From the look in his eyes, I had a feeling he felt the same. But then I realized that Dexter was moseying over our way. 'I suggest we bail,' I said, my gaze now fixed on the goat. Callum glanced over his shoulder and then boosted me over the fence. He climbed over to join me before Dexter had a chance to carry out a repeat performance.

'Sorry about your clothes,' he apologized.

I now had a couple of damp spots on my shirt and shorts, thanks to him helping me over the fence. 'They'll dry,' I said, unconcerned. 'As for your clothes . . .' I eyed his waterlogged shirt and jeans. 'You should probably change.'

He wrung out the front of his T-shirt, giving me a brief and tantalizing glimpse of his six-pack. 'I'm thinking that's a good idea.'

I took a step back, trying to ignore the way his soaked shirt clung to his muscular frame. 'I'll leave you to it, then.'

It took all my willpower, but I managed to walk away.

When I glanced back and saw the way Callum was looking at me, contentment warmed me from the inside out, and I was glad beyond measure that I'd been brave enough to give him the bracelet.

TWENTY-NINE

After I fetched the animals from the tack room, my thoughts unsurprisingly meandered their way back to the mystery surrounding the treasure map and Jasper's murder. All the questions circling in my head threatened to drive me crazy. I was hoping that Rayelle, and perhaps Brody, would be able to address at least a couple of those questions.

Waiting for answers wasn't my strong suit, but I didn't have much choice. I kept busy with writing and farm chores, but by the middle of the next day I was itching for news. I was glad when I received a text message from Tessa, inviting me to meet up with her and Brody at the town's main beach. Brody had been working overtime since Jasper's murder and likely would be again in the coming days, but he had a day off to enjoy at the moment.

Even if I hadn't received the invitation, I would have spent some time walking around town. It was the first day of the pirate festival, and I wanted to get a taste of the event's atmosphere. I was mostly looking forward to the battle reenactment scheduled to take place two days from now, but I knew there would be plenty of other things to see and do as well. If I could concentrate on the festivities. I was hoping that Brody had something he was willing to share with Tessa and me, and my mind would likely be preoccupied until I spoke with him.

My eagerness caused me to arrive at the beach fifteen minutes before I was supposed to meet Tessa and Brody. That gave me time to take the dogs for a short walk. I could see from the beach that Main Street was busy, with very few parking spots available and plenty of pedestrians making their way in and out of the shops. I spotted several people wearing pirate costumes and, from time to time, I heard shouts of 'Ahoy, matey!' and 'Shiver me timbers!'

Gizmo would have felt right at home here.

I planned to leave my costume at home until the final day of the festival when I would come into town to watch the pirate battle reenactment take place in the cove. Flossie and Fancy, however, hadn't allowed me to leave the farmhouse without first tying on their Jolly Roger bandannas. They got plenty of attention as we walked along the beach, with children running up to pet the dogs and a few adults asking to snap photos. Flossie and Fancy lapped up the attention, their eyes bright and their tails wagging.

When the dogs' newfound friends went on their way, we continued walking along the beach. I was about to turn around and head back to meet Tessa and Brody when I noticed Elsie Suárez jogging along the wet sand at the water's edge, coming our way.

I waved and called her name. She slowed to a walk and pulled wireless earbuds out of her ears.

'Do you mind if we walk with you for a minute?' I asked.

'Sure,' she said as she tucked her earbuds into the pocket of her running shorts. 'I was just winding down anyway.' She fell into step with us.

'Is there any news about the murder investigation?'

'None that the police have shared with me,' she replied. 'Although I stopped in at the grocery store earlier and heard that Giles Gilroy has been arrested.'

That was news to me, but I was relieved to hear it.

'I don't know if that has anything to do with the murder, though,' Elsie added.

'Would you be surprised if Giles is the killer? Were there any issues between him and Jasper, or do you think the map would have been the sole motive?' I held back a wince, hoping she wouldn't think I was pelting her with too many questions.

Fortunately, she seemed unperturbed by my interrogation. 'He might have just wanted the map, but who knows with Giles Gilroy?'

'What do you mean?' I asked, my curiosity piqued.

Elsie hesitated before replying. 'Jasper didn't like the guy and neither do I.'

'My friend saw him with you the day after Jasper died. Was he bothering you?'

Elsie frowned at the memory. 'I certainly wasn't enjoying his company. He was trying to butter me up, probably in the hope that he could scam me out of any antiques I might inherit from Jasper.'

That seemed to fit with what I'd heard about the man from other sources.

'Why didn't Jasper like him?' I asked.

'Truth be told, I didn't want to talk about this earlier, because I didn't want Giles finding out that I'd spread rumors about him. There's no telling what he'd do if that happened.' She rubbed her arms as if trying to ward off a sudden chill, despite the warm sunshine. 'But now that he's in police custody . . .' She paused, but then, to my relief, continued. 'Jasper thought Giles was untrustworthy, up to some sort of dodgy business.'

My curiosity threatened to bubble out of me. 'What kind of dodgy business, exactly?'

'Jasper never said. He just told me not to trust Giles and that he hoped one day people would see the man for who he really was. Jasper was a bit obsessed with trying to expose Giles. It was a bone of contention between us. I thought he should let sleeping dogs lie, you know?' A buzzing sound grabbed Elsie's attention. She dug her phone out of her pocket and checked the screen. 'Sorry, I need to take this call.'

'No problem,' I said, my mind spinning as I digested the information she'd given me. 'Have a nice day.'

The dogs and I continued along the beach, leaving Elsie by the water's edge to take her phone call in private. I checked my own phone as we walked and saw that I had a response from Rayelle. In her message, she said that she'd figured that the map symbol that looked like a jagged rock was a cliff near Starfall Creek. Although the cliff didn't have the exact shape shown on the map, she figured it could have changed over the past couple of centuries. She said she might have doubted that the mark represented the cliff – because of the discrepancy in the shapes – but the placement of the creek on the map suggested that the cliff was the right place.

I thanked her for the information and tucked my phone away again. The spaniels and I had just reached the parking lot when I spotted Tessa and Brody near one of the many food trucks parked along Ocean Drive. I waved to them and picked up my pace.

Maybe Brody could tell me more about Giles Gilroy's arrest.

THIRTY

'Has Giles Gilroy been arrested for killing Jasper?' I asked after I'd exchanged greetings with my friends. I wasn't sure if I should believe the rumor Elsie had heard at the grocery store.

Brody grinned and shook his head. 'I knew it wouldn't take long for the interrogation to start.'

'Hey,' Tessa protested. 'I've been on my best behavior. I've been here with you for nearly three minutes and I haven't asked you a single question about the case.'

Brody fought to suppress his grin. 'And I'm suitably impressed.'

'You're leaving us in suspense,' I accused.

Brody gave in. 'He hasn't been arrested for anything.'

'What?' Tessa exclaimed in disbelief. 'But that was his car in the alley.'

'We brought him in for questioning,' Brody said, 'and when we confronted him with that information, he admitted that he was at Jasper's house on the night of the burglary.'

'So why didn't you throw the book at him?' Tessa demanded.

Brody didn't seem annoyed by her question. In fact, he appeared to be fighting another grin. 'There's still a chance he'll be charged with breaking and entering, but he claims he went there to peek in the windows and see if he could get a look at some of Jasper's antiques. He said he's hoping he can get Jasper's heirs to sell some of the collection to him. But – according to Gilroy – he saw the smashed window and took off.'

'You believe that story?' I asked, not hiding my incredulity.

'Sounds pretty flimsy to me,' Tessa said, her opinion the same as mine.

'We're not sure if he's telling the truth,' Brody admitted, 'but we're holding off on making any further moves for the time being.'

'Why?' Tessa asked with disbelief.

'I can't say.' Brody leveled his gaze at us. 'And I'd appreciate it if you didn't repeat that to anyone.'

We both promised we wouldn't, but the decision on the part of the police still surprised and puzzled me.

'So, for now at least, Giles is free to commit other crimes,' Tessa said with a frown.

'He's being watched,' Brody said, 'so you can rest easy. And please don't mention that to anyone either.'

Again, we promised we wouldn't.

'I was just talking to Elsie Suárez,' I said. 'She mentioned that Jasper suspected Giles of something.'

'Something criminal?' Tessa asked.

'She wasn't sure,' I replied, 'but she said Jasper advised her to keep her distance from Giles because he was up to no good, and Jasper was hoping to prove it. Elsie didn't say anything about it before, I think because she's scared of Giles, but she heard he'd been arrested so she thought it was safe for her to talk about him now.'

Tessa nudged Brody's arm with her elbow. 'See, Giles really could be the killer. Maybe he found out that Jasper was going to expose him and he stole the map just to make it look like that's what the murder was about.'

'But then why ransack the two houses later?' Brody continued before either of us could come up with a response. 'Never mind. You don't need to be answering that question or any others related to the case. Leave it to the professionals, OK? I don't want either of you getting hurt.'

Tessa and I exchanged a glance.

Instead of agreeing to his request, I jumped in with another question.

'Did you ever figure out what the note in Jasper's journal referred to?' I asked.

'No.' Brody shot me a suspicious glance. 'Have you?'

'No. I haven't given it much thought lately.'

'Good,' he said. 'Think about other things. Things that aren't the domain of the police, who have been trained to investigate crimes and deal with dangerous people.'

Tessa rolled her eyes, but she was smiling.

'Don't hate me,' I said to Brody, 'but I can't stop thinking about the map.'

He glanced up at the sky and sighed. 'You and the rest of the town. Three times now, we've had to respond to calls of trespassers digging on private property.'

'People who've seen the map?' Tessa asked with surprise.

'Nope, but there've been a few rumors flying around town about where the treasure might be buried. It seems most of those rumors originated at the pub, probably after a few drinks were consumed.'

Tessa cast a longing glance toward the food trucks. 'Speaking of drinks, I could really use one.'

'Isn't it a bit early?' Brody asked.

'I meant of the non-alcoholic variety.'

The teasing twinkle in his eyes suggested that he'd known that all along. 'And I could use some food.'

'I thought you already had lunch,' Tessa said.

'Sure, but that was an hour ago.'

Tessa smiled at that. 'You always did have a hollow leg.'

Flossie woofed and Fancy 'woo-ed'.

'Brody's not the only one,' I said with a smile.

We spent the next several minutes ordering food and drinks from a couple of the trucks. Brody bought fries and all three of us ordered cherry slushies. I had a bottle of water for the dogs, but I told them they'd have to wait until dinner time to have any food. Fancy heaved out a dramatic sigh and lay down by my feet as I waited for my drink. I laughed but didn't give in.

A family that had been eating at one of the park's picnic tables cleared up their trash and vacated the spot, so we swooped in and claimed the table for ourselves. All the others were occupied by families, and many of the children wore pirate costumes and had their faces painted. A small band was set up in the gazebo and played sea shanties while children and adults danced in time to the music. On the far side of the gazebo, near the beer garden, vendors had set up booths where they were selling everything from tricorn hats to locally sourced honey. A small fortune teller's tent was also set up among the vendors. A sandwich board sitting outside the tent stated that Fae would be doing tarot and palm readings there at certain times during the festival.

'You're not selling any of your art?' Tessa asked Brody as we settled at the wooden table.

Brody was a talented painter and woodcarver and sometimes sold his Native American art at the local farmers' market.

'I didn't know if I'd have time,' Brody said as he emptied a packet of ketchup over his fries. 'But my sister's got a booth and she's selling some of my stuff.'

'I'll go say hi to her later,' Tessa said.

A cheer rang out from the small crowd by the gazebo. The band had paused between songs and a pirate made his way unsteadily through the crowd, looking as though he'd had a touch too much rum. Several other pirates, both men and women, followed after him, calling out to the crowd and interacting with them.

'Dead Eye!' some of the children cheered as the lead pirate staggered past them.

The kids – and a few adults – trailed along with the pirates as they wound their way through the park.

'Who's playing the part of Dead Eye Dawson?' I asked, unable to recognize the actor behind the costume and makeup.

'It's Lance Earley this year,' Tessa said.

'But not every year?'

'He and Dean Haskell have been trading back and forth each year for the last while,' Brody said. 'It's a coveted role, but the rule is you have to have been a member of the local theater group for at least three years before you can try out for the part.'

I watched the pirates disappear into the distance. 'I hope it's not a heated rivalry.' The last thing Twilight Cove needed was more deadly drama.

Brody quickly put that worry to rest. 'Nah. Lance and Dean are friends. They've both been president of the local hiking club at some point too. I think Dean is the current president.'

Tessa nodded as she took a sip of her drink. 'I heard that Lance scaled back his hiking because of his bad back, but he's still active with the theater group.'

'He's helping connect Aunt Olivia and me with actors for our fall fundraiser,' I said.

With the pirates gone and the band taking a break, the park quieted down.

I took a long drink of my slushie and immediately regretted it.

I winced when the brain freeze hit me and Fancy whined with worry when she saw me cringing.

'It's OK,' I assured her and her sister once the pain had passed. She and Flossie lay back down on the grass.

'Small sips only,' Tessa warned.

'I should have known better,' I admitted. After taking another sip – tiny this time – I addressed Brody. 'Tessa tells me you're familiar with the woods to the north of town. Did you recognize the spot marked on the map?'

'I only got a brief glimpse of it. The state police have been keeping the map close to their chests. I think they're worried that the treasure fever some townsfolk have might spread through the local department.'

I looked Tessa's way and she shrugged, understanding my silent question.

'Well . . .' I tugged my copy of the map out of the pocket of my shorts.

Brody guessed what it was before I even had it unfolded. 'Of course you have a copy.'

'Hey, if it weren't for us, you wouldn't have all that information from Rayelle Adams,' Tessa reminded him.

I handed Brody my copy of the map and he smoothed it out on the table in front of him.

I tapped at the landmark drawn near the X. 'Rayelle thought that was a cliff near Starfall Creek, even though the cliff doesn't quite have that shape.'

Brody shook his head right away. 'That's not the cliff. Rayelle wasn't looking in the right area.' He pointed to the line depicting the waterway. 'That's Starfall Creek, all right, but Rayelle was missing one vital piece of information: the creek's path was diverted several decades ago.' He tapped a finger on the landmark. 'I know exactly where that is.'

THIRTY-ONE

Tessa leaned forward with excitement. 'Does this mean we're going treasure hunting?'

'Nope.' Brody folded up the map but didn't hand it back

to me. 'You can't just go around digging wherever you want. There are laws about that, even when it's not private land, which is what we're dealing with here. Eagle Rock – the one shown on the map – is on Dean Haskell's property.'

'So we take the map to Dean and get his permission,' Tessa said, still eager. 'I'm not worried about keeping any treasure – I know it wouldn't belong to us – but Dean might let us help him dig.'

'Dean won't be digging either.' Brody held up the folded map. 'And I'll be keeping this.'

'What?' Tessa said with dismay. 'Why can't we keep it?'

'Because I don't want anyone ending up in danger because of it.' He extricated his long legs from the picnic table and stood up. 'I'm surprised you haven't already heard, considering the way news spreads in this town.'

'Someone already found the treasure?' I guessed.

Brody shook his head. 'Someone broke into Rayelle's studio last night.'

A frisson of alarm shot through me. 'Is she OK?'

'She's fine,' Brody said. 'Fortunately, she was sleeping in the main house at the time. But she didn't remember until she discovered the break-in that she'd left a copy of the map tucked inside her sketchbook.'

'Did the burglar find it?' Tessa asked.

'It's gone, so we assume so.'

'But maybe that's not a bad thing,' I said. 'Whoever stole it is likely the killer and now they're probably going to dig for the treasure.'

Brody tucked the map in one of the pockets of his jeans. 'Which is why the state police have got someone watching the spot where Rayelle was searching.'

'But if the burglar knows about the stream diversion . . .' I trailed off.

'Then they'll be digging on Dean Haskell's land, and nobody's got an eye on that spot.' Brody produced his phone from another pocket. 'But we will soon. I'm going to get in touch with the detective in charge right away.'

'They should have let you look at the map in the first place,' Tessa said. 'Now it might be too late to catch the treasure hunter in the act of searching.'

Brody scrolled through his contacts. 'Let's hope not.'

After a few more words, Brody left us, talking on his phone as he walked away.

'We should have asked how long Giles was at the police station,' I said, thinking things over. 'But since he wasn't arrested, I doubt they kept him overnight.'

Tessa finished my thought. 'So he could be the one who broke into Rayelle's studio.'

'How do you feel about taking a look at some antiques?' I asked.

The dogs jumped up and Flossie gave an excited yip.

Tessa smiled. 'I'm totally in.'

When we reached Gilroy's Antiques, I paused in the shop's vestibule so I could tie the dogs' leashes to the ring on the wall. Tessa pushed through the next door, going in ahead of me. I secured Flossie's leash to the ring, but then Fancy lurched after Tessa and her lead slipped out of my grasp.

Fancy!' I hissed as a wave of panic hit me.

The door drifted shut, but it was mostly glass, and Fancy's brown-and-white body seemed to disappear before my very eyes. I knew from experience that she was still there, and when I looked closely, I could see her brown eyes as she glanced back at me. She wasn't invisible, but she had camouflaged herself so she blended in with her surroundings. Fortunately, Tessa hadn't noticed Fancy slip through the door behind her and also hadn't witnessed the dog's transformation.

'What is she up to?' I whispered to Fancy's sister.

Flossie sat down and looked up at me, her tail swishing against the floor.

'Don't get into any mischief,' I warned. 'I'm going to find your sister.'

I entered the shop with caution, trying not to be obvious about the fact that I was looking around, trying to find my camouflaged dog.

Tessa stood off to the left, admiring an old spinning wheel. Giles was nowhere to be seen, but the door behind the sales counter stood open. The slightest quiver of movement drew my gaze to the right of the counter. The scene before me flickered slightly, as if colors were shifting.

A second later, Fancy's nose touched my bare leg. I almost gave a yelp of surprise, but managed to bite it back. A small rectangle of cream-colored paper drifted to the ground, and I knew that Fancy had dropped it. As I bent down to pick it up, I whispered, 'You need to get back with your sister.'

Tessa glanced over my way as I straightened up.

'I think I heard Flossie whine,' I said, hoping that gave me a good enough excuse to open the door to the vestibule. It was the truth. Flossie was whining, sounding as if she felt left out.

I opened the door and felt Fancy brush past me as she joined her sister. Once she was in the vestibule, her camouflage faded away and she became fully visible as she sat next to Flossie. I hurried to tie her leash to the ring, not wanting her to get up to any further mischief. Only then did I take a look at the sturdy bit of paper Fancy had brought me. It was a business card and, fortunately, it was only slightly damp from being held in my dog's mouth.

My breath caught in my throat as I read the fancy script printed on the card above a phone number and email address.

Samuel M. Kilduff, SMK & Associates. Wealth Management Solutions.

SMK.

Those were the initials on the pen Euclid and the dogs found on Old Birch Road.

'Nice find, Fancy,' I whispered.

She raised her head proudly and swished her tail from side to side. I gave each dog a pat on the head and then slipped back into the store, tucking the business card into the pocket of my shorts for safekeeping. Giles Gilroy was still nowhere to be seen, although I did hear a low murmur of male voices coming from somewhere in the back.

As casually as possible, I made my way over to Tessa, who was now checking out a display of vintage costume jewelry. I was about to whisper to her, to tell her that I had a clue, when the male voices drew closer. Deciding to keep quiet for the moment, I joined my friend in pretending to be interested in the antiques on display.

A second later, Giles emerged from the back room, wearing a dress shirt and tie with gray trousers. A tall, gray-haired white man in a dark blue suit accompanied him. I didn't recognize him, but I didn't like the look of his cold blue eyes.

The unknown man glanced at Tessa and me, but his stony expression didn't change. He strode out the door, through the vestibule and on to the street, not even glancing at Flossie and Fancy.

'Welcome back, ladies,' Giles said. 'Anything I can help you with today?'

'We're just browsing, thanks,' I said quickly.

I was itching to get out of the shop so I could show Tessa the business card. I'd have to tell her that I found it, since she didn't know about the dogs' abilities, but I definitely wanted her to know about it.

Thankfully, the door to the shop opened and Dean Haskell walked in, so Giles turned his attention away from us.

'Dean,' Giles said in greeting. 'Your antique diver's helmet is ready for you.'

He disappeared into the back and Dean smiled at Tessa and me. 'Ladies.'

We exchanged pleasantries with him and then we ducked out of the shop, taking the dogs with us.

Tessa released a breath as soon as we reached the sidewalk. 'I really wanted to tell Dean that he might have pirate treasure buried on his land, but not with Giles potentially within earshot. If he's the killer and he stole the map from Rayelle, he might not know the real location of the loot.'

'Plus,' I added, 'Brody wouldn't be pleased if we spilled the beans.'

'If the police are going to have someone watching his land, maybe they'll tell him why,' Tessa said, looking pensive.

I could tell she had a plan forming in her head. 'What are you thinking?'

She smiled. 'Maybe once the police have talked to Dean and have had a chance to check out the spot near Eagle Rock, Dean might have some information to share.'

'Do you think he would talk to us about it?'

'Sure,' Tessa said. 'Especially if we take some baked goods. The guy loves his cookies.'

I liked the sound of that plan. 'OK, but we know he's not home right now.'

'And we need to give the police time to get organized. So maybe we should go over there this evening?'

We agreed to do just that, and then I pulled the business card out of my pocket.

'This was on the shop floor.' That at least was the truth. I *had* picked it up off the floor after Fancy dropped it, and she'd likely found it on the floor too.

Not for the first time – or the last – I wished I could be completely honest with Tessa.

We'd reached the end of the street and Tessa drew to a stop as she studied the card. I saw the moment when the dots connected in her head.

She looked up from the card. 'SMK. Weren't those the initials on the pen you found?'

I nodded my confirmation. 'Maybe this Samuel guy is Giles's investment advisor?'

'What would an investment advisor be doing on Old Birch Road?'

'Maybe someone from the firm is a hiker?' I suggested. 'Or one of their clients is?'

'Maybe.' Tessa didn't sound convinced. 'I don't think that's a local firm, though. I've never heard of it.'

I pulled out my phone and did a quick search on the Internet. When I got to the site for the wealth management firm, I looked up its location. 'It's a Portland firm,' I said. Next, I navigated to the page that introduced the advisors who worked there. 'Check out Samuel Kilduff's photo.'

I angled my phone so she could see the screen.

She recognized the man immediately. 'That's the guy who left the antiques shop while we were there.'

A gaggle of tourists, some of them wearing pirate costumes, ambled past us, so we turned the corner on to a quieter street and found some shade next to a building. The dogs sat down, their tongues lolling out.

'Elsie said that Jasper thought Giles was up to no good,' I said. 'And Jasper made a note in his journal about Old Birch Road.'

'Giles clearly knows this Samuel guy,' Tessa added. 'And there's a connection between Samuel and Old Birch Road.'

'So maybe Jasper really was investigating Giles – or Giles and Samuel – and Giles found out.'

'Giles is totally the killer.' Tessa shuddered. 'I'm not going back in his shop. Too creepy.'

'We should tell Brody about Samuel Kilduff and his connection to Giles and the pen I found,' I said.

Tessa whipped out her phone. 'I'm on it.'

THIRTY-TWO

I felt bad about giving Brody so much information to pass on to the state police on his day off, but I also knew that we needed to share everything we'd discovered with the official investigators. After Tessa's phone call – during which she'd assured Brody that we came across the business card by chance and not because we were snooping – we decided to head to the Treasure Trove. Tessa wanted to buy some scented candles as a gift for her cousin Valentina, who had a birthday coming up at the end of the month, and I wanted to talk to Fae about crystals.

Earlier in the day, while trying to outline a new screenplay, I'd run into a snag. I couldn't quite get all the plot elements tied together and it felt like I was beating my head against a brick wall whenever I tried to think of a solution. It occurred to me that there might be a crystal that could help me with my creative block.

A few months ago, I would have dismissed the idea as nonsense, but my freshly charged amethyst was helping to keep me free of headaches – or so it seemed – and I figured that if an amethyst could help me with that problem, other crystals might assist me with other troubles.

As Tessa and I walked down the street with the dogs, the afternoon sun beat down on us. I needed to get the spaniels a drink of water soon and I wanted to get them out of the heat. Myself, too. After we stopped in at the gift shop, I'd take the dogs home for a rest in the air-conditioned farmhouse.

As we neared the Treasure Trove, I noticed a black SUV with tinted windows parked near the Moonstruck Diner on the other side of Main Street. Two men in dark suits climbed out. They wore sunglasses and they both removed their jackets and draped them over their arms as soon as they were on the sidewalk. They didn't look like tourists and they were definitely overdressed for the weather. I figured they were on a break from work or maybe in town on a business trip. Seconds later, they disappeared into the Moonstruck Diner and I soon forgot about them.

When we reached Fae's shop, located a short distance off Main Street, stepping inside came as a relief. Fae had the air conditioning on and the store felt like an oasis after being out in the hot sun. The dogs perked up once inside and I was grateful that Fae allowed them in the shop. Otherwise, I would have had to save my crystal shopping for another time so I could take Flossie and Fancy home.

Three other customers, all of them women, were browsing the shop, but Fae came over to greet us and fuss over the dogs. When she saw their tongues hanging out, she hurried into the back and returned with a bowl of water, which she set down next to the sales counter. Flossie and Fancy greedily lapped up the water and I thanked Fae for her thoughtfulness.

After the spaniels had their fill of cool water, they wandered with me toward the back of the store, where Tessa was perusing the selection of scented candles. On our way there, we passed the doorway with the beaded curtain. Flossie and Fancy sat down by the door and raised their noses to sniff the air. When I stopped and focused on my sense of smell, I noticed a scent lingering in the air around us. My pulse picked up its pace.

Tessa appeared at the end of the aisle. 'Georgie, I could use your help choosing scented candles for Valentina. There are so many nice ones that I don't know what to pick.'

'Sure.' I didn't move. 'What's that smell?'

Tessa came closer and sniffed the air. 'Oh, that's just incense. Fae always burns it when she does tarot readings.' She nodded at the beaded curtain. 'That's the room where she does the readings.'

As Tessa returned to the shelf at the back of the store, I followed, eager to tell her something.

'Tessa,' I whispered when I reached the display of candles, 'that's the same smell I noticed in Jasper's study when Auntie O and I found his body.'

Tessa's eyes widened. 'What do you think that means? I don't remember seeing an incense burner in the study.'

'Neither do I.' I thought for a moment. 'The scent was so faint. Do you think it could have been clinging to the clothes of the killer?'

Tessa considered that. 'It's possible, especially if they were close to the burning incense for a while shortly before going to Jasper's house. If the killer was there minutes before you and Olivia arrived, that could be why you could still smell the incense.'

'So either the killer burned incense or they were near someone else's incense before going to Jasper's house.'

'Time to do some subtle questioning?' Tessa suggested.

'I'd say so.' I backtracked a few steps so I could peek around the corner toward the sales counter. Fae was busy ringing up purchases for two of the other customers. 'Later, when Fae's not busy,' I said to Tessa.

'In the meantime, tell me which one you like better.' She held out two candles for me to sniff and I chose my favorite.

We went through that process with a few other pairs until she'd chosen two candles for her cousin. By that time, we were the only customers remaining in the store.

We headed over to the sales counter together and Tessa set her candles next to the cash register while I moved aside to check out the display of crystals. Each type was held by a small bowl, and the crystals came in all colors of the rainbow. Next to each bowl was a small card, giving the name of the crystal and some information about it.

'Oh, I love these scents. Good choice,' Fae said to Tessa as she rang up the candles. Then she addressed me. 'Are you looking for something in particular, Georgie?'

'Oh . . .' I wasn't sure what to say. I didn't want Tessa to think I was strange for having an interest in the crystals.

It turned out that I needn't have worried.

Tessa tapped her credit card to pay for the candles and then came over to join me by the display. 'I love crystals. I didn't know you were into them too, Georgie.'

'Back at you,' I said with relief. 'I really only got introduced to them by Dorothy back in June. She gave me an amethyst, and I swear it helps me with my headaches.'

Fae joined us by the crystals and passed Tessa the paper bag holding her candles. 'Dorothy probably cast a spell on the amethyst to make it extra powerful. She was talented with things like that.' She gestured at the display. 'I have crystals here to fill just about any need. Are you looking for something in particular?'

'Is there something to help with creativity?' I asked. 'I have a bit of a block today.'

'Say no more.' Fae moved closer to the crystals. 'You want something to remove the block and get that creativity flowing again.'

Tessa picked a transparent crystal out of one of the bowls. 'Clear quartz is good for so many things.'

Fae nodded in agreement. 'One of which is amplifying ideas.'

Tessa placed the quartz in my hand.

Fae pointed to a bowl full of yellowish stones. 'Citrine helps with concentration and encourages a refreshed state of mind.' Next, she indicated some gorgeous blue crystals. 'Lapis lazuli is great if you need to think outside of the box.' She pointed to another bowl. 'And azurite helps to clear any negative energy that might be interfering with your creativity. There are others, of course, but I sense you might be getting overwhelmed.'

She was right about that.

'What about courage?' I asked. 'I could use help with that too.'

Tessa shot me an inquiring glance, but I didn't want to explain myself in front of Fae. Despite my new confidence in my relationship with Callum, I still struggled to voice my feelings and truly open my heart without fear.

Fae pointed to a bowl of blue-green stones. 'Aquamarine helps with bravery and self-expression.'

I picked out one of those.

'And carnelian is also good for courage and taking action,' Fae added.

That definitely fit the bill.

'What exactly am I supposed to do with them?' I asked. 'Other than recharge them under a full moon?'

'You can place them on your desk or wherever you're working when you want your creativity to flow,' Fae explained. 'Or, for courage, you can carry them with you, in your pocket or in the form of one of these bracelets.' She pointed out a neighboring display of crystal jewelry. 'You can also hold them while you meditate and focus on your intentions.'

That sounded simple enough. 'OK, I'll take this quartz and aquamarine and one each of the others you pointed out.'

'Would you like to select your own or would you like me to choose for you?' Fae asked. 'Sometimes the crystals will call to you.'

I wasn't sure if that was happening, but when I peered more closely at the dishes of crystals, I picked out one of each kind that caught my eye. They were cool in my hand and smooth to the touch. 'These ones, thanks.'

The crystals didn't cost much. As I handed the money over to Fae, I decided it was time to get back to sleuthing.

'I noticed the smell of incense at the back of the store,' I said. 'Does it come in different scents?'

'Oh, yes,' Fae said as she fetched a small paper bag from beneath the sales counter. 'I can order some in for you if you'd like. The type I use isn't one of the most common scents, but it's a mixture that I particularly like.'

I politely declined the offer. 'I was just curious, really.'

'Let me know if you ever change your mind.'

I assured her that I would. 'Did you hear about Giles Gilroy getting questioned by the police?'

'Valentina was here this morning for a tarot reading,' Fae said, referring to Tessa's cousin who worked at the police station. 'She told me all about it.' Fae shook her head. 'I don't trust that man. He gives off negative energy.'

'Does he ever come in your shop?' Tessa asked.

Fae laughed at that. 'Never, and I'm quite OK with that. I don't go in his shop either.'

I thanked Fae when she handed me the small bag containing my crystals. 'What about the writer, Ajax Wolfgang? You mentioned before that you'd spoken to him. Did he visit your store?'

'He was in here one time, looking at the local interest books,' Fae replied. 'He was pleased to see that I had some of his books for sale.'

'Was that last Thursday, by any chance?' I asked, acting like I'd just remembered something. 'I thought I saw him coming out of your shop that day.'

Fae thought for a second. 'I'm really not sure which day it was.'

Tessa voiced another question, managing to sound like she was simply making casual conversation. 'Did you know that Flynn Smith-Wu is Ajax's cousin?'

'I didn't,' Fae admitted, 'but I don't know much about Flynn. I'm not sure I've ever talked to him.'

'He doesn't shop here?' I asked.

'No, but the vast majority of my customers are women.'

'I think I might have seen Elsie Suárez here one day,' Tessa said. 'It must be so hard on her, dealing with what happened to Jasper.'

Fae clicked her tongue. 'I know. The poor woman. She does shop here and she comes in for a reading from time to time.'

The bell above the door jingled as a blonde woman entered the shop with her equally blonde preteen daughter. Both wore tank tops and shorts and looked as though they'd had a little too much sun.

'Thanks for the crystals,' I said to Fae, deciding it was time to go.

The dogs took a few more laps of water from the dish Fae had provided and then we headed out on to the sidewalk. Once the door had closed behind us, I spoke to Tessa in a low voice as we strolled up the street.

'Tell me I'm not crazy for thinking that Jasper's killer was probably in Fae's shop before committing the murder.'

'Not crazy,' she said, keeping her voice quiet as well. 'It's possible that someone else burns that particular type of incense in Twilight Cove, but it's not likely.'

'But Giles wasn't in her shop that day or any other,' I pointed out.

'That does put a wrinkle in our main theory.'

'It couldn't be Fae, could it?' I asked, the question laced with doubt.

'She seems like such a gentle soul,' Tessa said, voicing my own feelings about the woman.

Fancy 'woo-ed' her agreement.

'So maybe Elsie or Ajax are more likely culprits?'

Tessa didn't miss the confusion in my voice. 'It's got me baffled too.'

'Let's hope the police catch someone digging on Dean's land,' I said. 'Because otherwise, I'm out of ideas.'

THIRTY-THREE

I took the dogs home and they flopped out on the kitchen floor, enjoying the farmhouse's central air conditioning that Auntie O had installed a few years back. Tessa met us there after she made a stop at the bakery to buy a selection of cookies to take to Dean. We spent some time chatting with Gizmo and playing with Stardust before heading out to the barn to take care of the evening chores. Tessa insisted that she wanted to help, so I texted Auntie O and told her to take the evening off. I missed having Roxy around, not just because she was a great help with the animals, but because I'd developed a lot of affection for the teen over the summer. I hoped she was having a good time visiting her dad.

As we fed the animals and refilled water troughs, Tessa and I caught Callum up on everything we'd learned that day. When he heard what we had planned for the evening, he took off his cowboy hat and ran his hand through his hair.

'Mind if I tag along?' he asked.

'Of course not,' Tessa said.

'I was hoping you'd want to join us,' I added.

Maybe it was silly, considering that we lived on the same property, but I felt like I hadn't seen enough of Callum over the past couple of days.

After all the animals had been taken care of and Callum had gone back to his cabin for a quick shower, the three of us piled into his truck and headed for Dean's place. Auntie O's farm was located on Larkspur Lane, and we followed that road farther from the center of town as it curved away from the coast and then back toward the ocean again.

Tessa, sitting in the back seat, leaned forward to talk to Callum and me. 'I'm hoping the killer gets caught digging for treasure, of course, and I'm excited to know if there really is pirate treasure, but I'm also looking forward to seeing Dean's house up close. I've only ever seen it from the water, but it looks amazing. It's basically a mini-mansion.'

'Really?' That surprised me. I barely knew the burly, gray-haired mechanic, but if I'd given it any thought previously, I would have pictured him living in a humble home, maybe surrounded by woodland.

'How does a mechanic afford an oceanfront mini-mansion?' Callum asked, voicing the question that had just popped into my head.

'You know, I'm not sure,' Tessa said. 'Maybe his business is extraordinarily successful?'

'You don't suppose . . .' I started to say.

Callum glanced my way before focusing on the road again. 'That Dean found the pirate treasure on his land a while back?'

Tessa leaned between the two front seats again. 'No! Dean?'

I shifted in my seat so I could see her. 'You don't think it's possible?'

She sat back, thinking. 'Sure, I guess it's possible. He could have secretly found a buyer for the gold or whatever it was and used the money to build his dream home. But how do you stumble upon buried treasure?'

'Maybe he was digging a well or preparing to build a shed or workshop,' Callum suggested.

'You might be on to something.' Tessa leaned between the front seats and pointed up ahead. 'I think that's Dean's driveway.'

Callum slowed the truck. Sure enough, a red mailbox at the end of the driveway bore the name 'Haskell'. Callum turned off the road and followed the long dirt driveway, which cut through a swathe of thick woodland.

Before heading out on this trip, I'd checked Google Maps and discovered that Eagle Rock sat in the midst of the wooded area on Dean's property. I tried to get a glimpse of it as we drove along, but the trees grew too thickly for me to see anything other than the forest.

The driveway curved a couple of times before the trees opened up to an expanse of grass. Up ahead, a gray house with lots of floor-to-ceiling windows sat perched at the top of a cliff, overlooking the ocean. It really was a big house for one person. It would have been large even for an average-sized family.

Callum stopped the truck and whistled at the site of the mini-mansion. 'You weren't kidding, Tessa.'

'I hope we get to go inside,' she said.

Callum drove forward again. As we moved out of the wooded area, I noticed movement off to my right.

'Hold on,' I said. 'What's going on over there?'

Callum slowed the truck to a stop again. A short distance away from the driveway, two police cruisers and one unmarked vehicle were parked near the tree-line. The sight took me by surprise. I would have thought the police would want to keep a low profile if they were trying to catch the killer digging for treasure. The sight of the vehicles made me wonder if something else had happened.

Hope filled my chest. 'Maybe they've already caught the killer digging.'

'Maybe we'll see who it is,' Tessa said with excitement.

Callum parked the truck at the edge of the driveway. 'If they haven't already transported the person to the police station.'

Tessa pointed toward the house. 'Look. Here comes Dean.'

The mechanic was striding across the grass from his house.

By unspoken agreement, we all climbed out of the truck and walked toward the unoccupied police vehicles.

'Maybe we should stay back,' Callum cautioned. 'If they don't have the killer cuffed yet, we don't know what might happen.'

That thought was enough to scare me into slowing my pace. I didn't want to get caught up with a killer. I'd done that once and I had no desire to repeat the experience.

We decided to wait a stone's throw away from the parked vehicles, with them between us and the trees, and Dean soon joined us.

'Hi, Dean,' Tessa said in greeting. 'We were stopping by to ask if the police had caught someone digging for treasure yet, but it looks like maybe they have.'

'If they have, they haven't told me about it,' he said, frowning at the police cruisers. 'I knew they were planning a stakeout in the woods, but that's it. I was watching a movie and didn't notice all these vehicles until it was over a few minutes ago. How did you know about the treasure being on my land?'

'We were with Brody Williams when he realized that the map led here rather than a little farther north,' Tessa explained.

I quickly introduced Dean and Callum, and they shook hands. The whole time, Dean's brow remained furrowed. 'I have a hard time believing that the pirate treasure even exists, let alone that it could be buried on my land.'

'Maybe we'll find out what's going on soon,' I said as I noticed Isaac Stratton, the chief of the local police force, emerging from the tree-line.

Chief Stratton was a tall man with deep brown skin, graying hair and some extra pounds around his middle. Although I couldn't see his eyes at that moment, I knew they were dark brown and both kind and discerning.

A uniformed officer followed behind the police chief, but stopped by one of the cruisers. When Stratton saw the four of us standing there, he frowned and altered his path so he could stride toward us.

'What's going on here?' he asked.

'I was about to ask you that same question, Chief,' Dean said. 'Did you catch the person you were watching for?'

'No, we didn't.' He shifted his gaze to Callum, Tessa and me. 'And what are you folks doing here?'

'We came to talk to Dean and then saw the cruisers.' Tessa wisely left out any further details about why we were there.

'I'm going to have to ask you to leave.' Chief Stratton spoke sternly but not unkindly. 'As for you, Mr Haskell, I'd appreciate it if you went back to your house. I'll come and explain things to you shortly.'

'There's not a killer loose on my land, is there?' Dean asked.

'I'll tell you more when I speak to you at your house.' Chief Stratton turned his attention to the rest of us. 'Please head on home.'

'Of course,' Callum said. 'We don't want to get in the way.'

Reluctantly, Tessa and I followed when he headed back to his truck. On our way, we passed one of the cruisers, where the uniformed officer had stopped and now stood with the driver's door open. He was talking into his radio, and as we passed him, I overheard him say, 'We're going to need a crime scene unit here. Instead of pirate treasure, we've got human remains.'

THIRTY-FOUR

I had trouble sleeping that night. My mind was too wrapped up in thoughts about the human remains found on Dean's land. Of course, I didn't have any information beyond that, so it was impossible for me to figure out what was really going on. Instead, my imagination conjured up about a dozen possibilities. In one such imagined scenario, a treasure hunter in possession of either the original map or a copy of it found another person already digging on Dean's land and killed that person so they could lay claim to the treasure. However, I wasn't sure that the police would have referred to what they'd found as human remains if the victim had been recently killed.

Another thought that passed through my head was that perhaps Dean had killed someone – maybe for the money he used to build his house – and buried them in his yard. Or the person seeking out the treasure had stumbled upon an ancient burial ground. Maybe that was the most likely of all the scenarios that ran through my head during the night.

Stardust decided shortly after five o'clock that it was time to play. Since I was tossing and turning instead of getting any real rest, I gave in to the kitten's antics and got up for the day. She tore out of the bedroom and down the stairs, with Flossie and Fancy racing after her. I took the time to get dressed before following the animals and hoped that I wouldn't find the main floor of the house in ruins once I got down there.

Luckily, the only thing amiss, once I got downstairs, was a book that had been knocked off a side table in the living room. I fed the animals, chatted with Gizmo and then checked my phone while the parrot sang his favorite tune.

To my disappointment, I didn't have any new text messages. I didn't know why I hoped I would. It wasn't as if Tessa or Callum had had a chance to find out anything new. It wasn't even five thirty yet.

I wanted to talk to Aunt Olivia about the previous night's news. She was out the evening before and didn't arrive home before I went to bed, so I hadn't seen her since before going to Dean's place. Antsy energy made it impossible for me to sit around in the house, so I decided to get an early start on my farm chores. To my surprise, Callum was already in the barn.

'Looks like I wasn't the only person who couldn't sleep,' I said as I entered the barn with the dogs.

Flossie and Fancy bounded forward to greet Callum. I let them have their turn and then moved in for a quick kiss.

'I got a few solid hours,' Callum said as he ran his hands down my arms, 'but once I woke up, I couldn't stop thinking about the human remains.'

I leaned against his chest with a sigh and he wrapped his arms around me.

'Same,' I said. 'I wonder who it could be.'

A wave of sadness washed over me. If the remains weren't from an ancient burial where someone had been peacefully laid to rest, then there was a good chance that the person was the victim of foul play. I didn't want that to be the case, but if it was, I hoped the police would be able to identify the poor soul and find out what had happened to them. If there were any family members out there wondering about their lost loved one, maybe they could at least get some closure.

Callum kissed my forehead as I forced myself to straighten up.

'Hopefully, it's not a murder victim,' he said, echoing my thoughts.

'I don't know how the police will catch the person who stole the map from Rayelle's studio,' I said. 'It won't be long before the whole town knows that the cops are crawling over Dean's property. No one would dare go there looking for treasure.'

'Who's looking for the treasure?' Aunt Olivia asked from behind me.

I stepped out of Callum's arms and turned around. 'You're up early.'

She came farther into the barn. 'I always find it hard to sleep past five in the summer. Did someone find the treasure?'

'Not the treasure, no,' I said. 'Something else.'

I told Aunt Olivia everything, starting with the copy of the map Rayelle had given me and ending with what I'd overheard at Dean's place the night before.

When I mentioned the human remains, my aunt pressed a hand to her chest. 'Oh no.'

'It might be a Native American burial ground that the treasure hunter accidentally uncovered,' Callum said.

'Or . . .' My aunt trailed off, her face going pale.

Alarmed, I tucked my arm through hers. 'Are you OK, Auntie O?'

'I just had a thought.' She shook her head. 'But no, Dean never could have hurt Patty.'

'Patty?' I echoed.

'Patty Buchanan,' Aunt Olivia explained, the name sounding vaguely familiar to me. 'She was Dean's girlfriend back in the eighties. He was completely in love with her and, I found out later, was thinking of proposing to her. But then she took off without even saying goodbye to him. She left a brief note for him, but that's all. It broke Dean's heart.'

'But now you think maybe she didn't leave?' I guessed. 'That maybe she's been buried on Dean's land the whole time?'

Olivia shook her head. 'It couldn't be her.'

It sounded like she was trying to convince herself more than anyone else.

'How long has Dean owned that land?' Callum asked.

'Since before Patty disappeared,' Auntie O replied. 'At first, there was just a humble little house on the property. Dean eventually tore it down and built the one that's there now. That was maybe ten or fifteen years ago.'

'Did anyone ever hear from Patty again?' I asked.

'Not a soul,' Olivia said. 'But she didn't have any family here, and she left the note and took all her belongings, so it's probably not her.' She gave Callum a weak smile. 'You're probably right about the Native American burial ground. That's got to be the explanation.'

I didn't point out that if someone had killed Patty, they could have taken her belongings and faked the note to make it look as though she'd left of her own accord.

My phone buzzed in the pocket of my jeans. When I saw the text messages that Tessa had sent me, I knew that my aunt's last words were wrong.

We need to meet, the first message read. *Valentina's got news to share.*

The texts that followed sent a chill slithering up my spine.

It's not an ancient burial ground.

It's murder.

THIRTY-FIVE

I agreed to meet Tessa at the Moonstruck Diner as soon as the restaurant opened. That gave me enough time to finish my chores and change from jeans into shorts. Callum and Auntie O were just as eager to find out what Valentina had to say, but Callum needed to fix a panel of fencing and my aunt had arranged to have breakfast with friends at another restaurant.

I left the dogs and Stardust with Callum and drove into town, butterflies leaving my stomach unsettled. The thought of another murder sent anxiety humming through my body and threatened to wipe out my appetite. Even if this murder had happened years ago, it meant that someone had managed to get away with the crime. If that person was still in town, did we have two murderers in our midst?

When I got to the Moonstruck Diner, Tessa and Valentina were already there, occupying the booth at the very back of the restaurant. A couple of other tables and booths were occupied by early risers, but no one sat near my friend and her cousin. That was good, since we wouldn't want anyone overhearing our conversation.

I waved to Jackie Jenkinson, the owner of the diner, on my way past the counter with its chrome-and-turquoise stools. When I reached the booth at the back, I slid on to the bench seat, next to Tessa and across from her cousin. Valentina was a curvy woman with round cheeks and shiny dark hair that was currently piled up on the top of her head. She wore false eyelashes and shimmery eyeshadow. Her nails were painted red, the shade matching her lipstick perfectly.

I'd never met Valentina before, though I'd certainly heard of her, so Tessa quickly introduced us. I could tell she wanted to jump right into our conversation once the introductions were over, but Jackie stopped by the booth to take our orders. Valentina couldn't stay long, so she ordered a cup of coffee and no food. Tessa and I, however, asked for the smoked salmon eggs Benedict. I was hoping my appetite would return by the time our food arrived.

We waited until Jackie had gone away and returned with our drinks before getting down to business.

'Any idea who the victim is?' I asked in a voice barely above a whisper.

'The remains haven't been formally identified yet,' Valentina said, also keeping her voice low, 'but there was a metal plate in the victim's leg and a distinctive charm bracelet found with the remains, so everyone's pretty sure who it is.'

'Patty Buchanan?' I guessed.

Valentina looked disappointed. 'How did you know that?'

'My aunt Olivia wondered if it might be Patty,' I explained. 'But having some confirmation of her identity is helpful.'

That seemed to ease Valentina's disappointment.

'Wait until you hear how the police discovered the remains.' Tessa gave an encouraging nod to her cousin.

The encouragement was probably unnecessary, as Valentina was all too eager to keep talking. 'The police were there to keep watch for someone coming to dig up the treasure, but when they arrived, they saw that the ground had already been disturbed. It didn't take much looking for the officers to find the bones. Apparently, it looked as though someone was digging, found the remains and then hastily tried to cover them again.'

'So maybe whoever was looking for the treasure got there before the police could set up their stakeout, but the treasure hunter got spooked when they found Patty's remains,' I said.

Tessa nodded. 'That's what we're thinking.'

'And it's what the police are thinking,' Valentina added. 'Dean Haskell was Patty's boyfriend back in the day. He identified the charm bracelet as belonging to Patty, and he confirmed that she had a metal plate put in her leg after a car accident. Now the police have got him in for questioning.'

'They think he killed Patty all those years ago and then pretended that she'd left him?' I guessed.

'That's the theory,' Valentina confirmed. 'There hasn't been an autopsy yet, but there was obvious trauma to the skull, so it might have been a blow to the head that killed her.'

I digested that information and then continued voicing my thoughts in a low voice. 'So we have two completely separate murders here? One from the eighties and one from last week?'

Valentina shrugged. 'Seems so.'

She drank down the last of her coffee and grabbed her handbag as she scooted along the bench seat. 'I need to get to work. Tessa, I'll let you know if I hear anything more.'

Valentina started to remove her wallet from her bag, but Tessa waved her off.

'The least I can do is pay for your coffee,' Tessa said.

'Gracias, prima.' Valentina tapped the side of her nose. 'Remember, we never had this conversation.' She winked at us before heading out of the diner.

'That girl's going to lose her job one day,' Tessa said with a shake of her head.

A pang of guilt hit me as I scooted around the table to take Valentina's vacated seat across from Tessa. 'I guess we shouldn't be encouraging her to spill police secrets.'

'I know,' Tessa said, 'but her intel's so good.'

Jackie brought our food, so we waited until she was gone again before resuming our conversation. Fortunately, the sight of my breakfast brought my appetite rushing back and my stomach gave an eager rumble as I unwrapped my cutlery.

'I was really hoping Jasper's killer would be caught by now,' I said as I dug into my eggs Benedict. 'Do you think there's any chance that the two murders are connected?'

'They're separated by decades,' Tessa pointed out. 'And if it's Jasper's killer who was looking for the treasure, why would they dig where they had previously buried a body?'

I thought over what she said. 'Maybe because they were trying to move the body before any treasure seekers found it?'

'Huh,' Tessa said. 'I hadn't thought of that. So, decades ago, Patty's killer buried her in the woods and uncovered the pirate treasure in the process. Then Jasper announces that he's found a map that will lead him to Dead Eye Dawson's loot. Patty's killer knew the treasure was already gone but also knew that the map would lead Jasper right to Patty's body. The killer then goes after Jasper, but Jasper refuses to hand over the map before he dies.'

I picked up the theory. 'The killer searches Jasper's house for the map without success and so returns to search again, trying at Elsie's house too. Somehow the killer knows or finds out that Rayelle had the original map at one point, so they search her studio in the hope of finding and destroying any copies.'

Tessa nodded, but then the light of excitement in her eyes dimmed. 'But why didn't they finish moving Patty's remains? It would be too risky to leave her there, knowing that the original copy of the map is still out there somewhere.'

'Maybe the killer did find the original map hidden at Elsie's house, and once they stole the copy from Rayelle, they figured they no longer needed to move Patty's remains.' I immediately noticed a hole in that theory. 'Except . . . somebody did at least start to dig up the remains, whether accidentally or on purpose.'

'Because the killer's worried there might be another copy floating around? After all, there's the copy that you gave to Brody.'

'That's true,' I agreed. 'Maybe the killer was in the process of digging up Patty's remains when the police arrived at Dean's place, scaring them off before the job was done.'

'I bet that's it,' Tessa said, her excitement returning. 'I think we've cracked the case!'

I hated to dampen her spirits. 'Not quite. Even if we're right, we don't know the killer's identity.'

'Dean's the most likely culprit, now that Patty's involved.' She paused, her excitement dimming again. 'I always thought he was a nice guy.'

'Don't forget that Giles was at Jasper's place on the night someone ransacked his house and Elsie's too.'

Tessa sighed. 'That's true, but I still think the pirate treasure would account for how Dean could afford to build such a nice house on a small-town mechanic's income. Not that I want Dean to be a killer.'

'All I know for sure is that Ajax and Flynn are too young to have killed Patty Buchanan.'

'Elsie's a bit young for that too,' Tessa said. 'She would have been in her early to mid-teens. Plus, she didn't grow up here. I don't remember exactly when she moved to Twilight Cove, but it was probably within the last five years.'

'What about Giles?' I asked. 'Did he live in Twilight Cove back in the eighties?'

'I'm not sure,' Tessa replied as Jackie approached our booth.

'How's everything?' she asked.

'Delicious,' I said, and Tessa agreed, even though we'd both forgotten about our food over the last couple of minutes.

'Hey, Jackie,' Tessa said before she left us, 'how long has Giles Gilroy lived in Twilight Cove?'

Jackie thought for a moment. 'His family moved here when he was pretty young. I know he went to high school here. Did you hear the latest?'

'About Giles?' I asked.

'No, about the police being out at Dean Haskell's place. I just heard from Marlene Hooper that they found human remains that might be Patty Buchanan. Though, of course, you two never would have met Patty.'

'Dean's girlfriend, who supposedly upped and left him, with only a note to say goodbye?' Tessa said.

Jackie nodded. 'You've heard the story. Sounds like maybe she never left, though I just can't bring myself to believe that Dean hurt her.'

'Do you know Dean well?' I asked.

'Sure, I've known him my whole life, practically. He was a few years ahead of me in school, but I dated him for a while before I married Lance. That was a few years after Patty supposedly left. Things never would have worked out between me and Dean because his heart still belonged to Patty. That's why I can't believe he hurt her.' A wistful expression crossed her face. 'Plus, he was always so kind to me.'

'You're married to Lance Earley?' I asked. Her last name was Jenkinson, so I'd never made the connection.

'I was in the past.' She held up her left hand and wiggled her ringless fingers. 'I'm free as a bird now and not about to give that up again.'

Two customers came into the diner, so Jackie flashed a smile at us and hurried off to greet the newcomers.

'So what do we do now?' Tessa asked as she stabbed her fork into one of her eggs. 'If we don't know if we've got one killer or two, how are we supposed to figure this thing out?'

'I guess we just have to wait and hope the police sort it out,' I said.

'In that case, let's talk about the sanctuary's Halloween fundraiser,' Tessa suggested. 'I've got some ideas to share.'

I gladly listened to what she had to say, but despite the pleasant change in topic, Jasper's murder and the grisly discovery on Dean's land were never far from the front of my mind.

THIRTY-SIX

'd left my car parked on a side street, near the local bakery, so after leaving the Moonstruck Diner, I decided to pick up some croissants. Once I had my bag of treats in hand, I crossed the road and headed for my car. As I hit the key fob to unlock the door, a large bird glided in to land on a nearby utility pole. I wasn't surprised to look up and see that it was Euclid.

There were no other people nearby, so I decided it was safe to speak to the owl without people thinking I was strange. 'Morning, Euclid.'

He gazed down at me with his big yellow eyes.

'Are you trying to tell me something again?'

Euclid took off from the utility pole and into a nearby alleyway. It was the one that ran behind the antiques shop and other Main Street businesses.

I locked my car and followed the majestic bird. As I rounded the corner into the alley, Euclid flew up into the sky and disappeared over the rooftops. I jerked back around the corner of the nearest building as soon as I realized that Giles was getting out of his silver sedan, which was once again parked behind his shop. Whether he was a murderer or not, there was something shifty about the man and I didn't want to find myself alone in an alley with him.

I chanced a peek around the corner and saw that Giles had his phone to his ear as he shut his car door.

'I told you not to come to the shop,' he groused into his phone. After a pause, he added, 'I don't need to be micromanaged.'

He opened the trunk of his car and grabbed a briefcase before locking up the vehicle.

'I've got what you want,' he said into his phone. 'Tonight. Usual time, usual place.'

After another pause, he said, 'Fine. See you then.'

He ended the call and pulled a ring of keys out of his pocket as he approached the back door to his shop. When he disappeared inside, I turned away and wandered slowly back to my car, thinking.

The spaniels had found a pen with the initials SMK on it on Old Birch Road, and Samuel Kilduff – who was in Giles's shop the other day – had those same initials. Then there was the note in Jasper's journal about Old Birch Road and the fact that he thought Giles was untrustworthy and possibly a criminal of some sort.

I wondered if Giles's upcoming meeting would take place on Old Birch Road and if it had to do with some sort of unlawful activity. Was Giles about to sell off some pirate treasure?

A wave of fatigue hit me, one that was more mental than physical. I really was better off leaving the murder case to the professionals. It was too confusing for me to figure out. But I did want to know what Giles was up to and whether it had anything to do with Jasper's murder.

When I got back to the farmhouse, I spent a few solid hours writing. With the muddled state of my mind, I expected to have difficulties working out the plot problems I'd run into the day before. I didn't know if it was the new crystals I'd placed next to my laptop or just the fact that I was looking at the project with fresh eyes, but new ideas kept popping into my head and I soon had all the major plot points of the story worked out. I also managed to complete some edits on another screenplay and answered a couple of work-related emails. All in all, it felt like a successful day in terms of my writing career. I couldn't say the same for my sleuthing.

Late in the afternoon, I met up with Callum to take the dogs for a walk through the woods and down to the beach. Although the day was warm, it wasn't quite as hot as previous days, so I knew it would be OK for the dogs to walk in the shade, especially since we would take a dip in the ocean once we reached the beach. Nevertheless, I carried a small backpack with their collapsible water dish and two bottles of water.

As soon as I saw Callum, I noticed that he was wearing his bracelet. The sight set off a warm glow in the center of my chest. While we strolled through the forest, holding hands, I told him everything I'd learned from Valentina as well as what I'd overheard Giles say in the alley. Callum was as confused as I was about the murder case, but he agreed that Giles was up to no good.

'Do you think I should tell Brody about Giles?' I asked. 'It's not like I have any solid evidence that he's breaking the law, but there's a link between Giles and Samuel Kilduff, between Samuel Kilduff and Old Birch Road, and between Old Birch Road and Jasper.'

'I think you should give him all the information and let him decide if it needs looking into,' Callum advised.

I thought that was a good suggestion, so I called Brody while we walked.

He listened to everything I had to share and then said, 'Georgie, don't worry about Giles Gilroy.'

'You don't think it's at all fishy?' I asked with surprise and maybe a hint of disappointment.

'I didn't say that,' Brody replied. 'I'm just advising you to leave that situation alone. The murder case too.'

'The murder case is too confusing for me to even think about anymore,' I said, even though I didn't know how long that would remain the truth. 'I just wanted to give you the information about Giles in case it was important.'

'I appreciate that,' Brody assured me.

We said goodbye and ended the call.

'He doesn't think it means anything?' Callum asked as I tucked my phone away.

'I don't know. He seemed worried about me sticking my nose where it doesn't belong, but not so much about what Giles might be up to.'

Callum squeezed my hand. 'Maybe that means there's no cause for concern.'

'But I can't shake the feeling that there *is* something going on there.'

We left the woods for the beach and found that we had the place to ourselves, as usual. Flossie and Fancy charged ahead of us and galloped straight into the ocean, sending water spraying into the air, where it glittered in the sunshine.

'What are you thinking?' Callum asked when we stopped at the water's edge, still holding hands.

I smiled at him. 'How do you feel about a stakeout tonight?'

Callum grinned. 'Not the most typical of dates, but I'll take what I can get.'

THIRTY-SEVEN

After a refreshing swim in the ocean, Callum, the dogs and I returned to the farmhouse for a quick dinner. Then we took care of all of the evening chores and enjoyed some time relaxing on the back porch of the farmhouse, waiting for dusk. I suspected that whatever the purpose of Giles's meeting might be, it would most likely take place after dark.

We were getting ready to head out and find a place to surreptitiously watch Old Birch Road when Lance Earley's truck pulled into the driveway. Aunt Olivia came out of the carriage house to greet him, and Callum and I followed more slowly. Flossie and Fancy didn't bother to get up from where they lay snoozing in the shade.

'Lance is here to chat about how many actors we might need for the fundraiser,' Auntie O explained.

'I've made a list of characters that we've come up with so far,' I said. 'I can print out a copy, if you like.'

'That would be great,' Lance said. 'Then I can start putting out some feelers to see who might want to volunteer for the roles.'

We all headed into the farmhouse, where I printed out an extra copy of the list.

Gizmo hopped around in his cage, excited by the sudden crowd in the house.

'Shiver me timbers!' he squawked before singing the opening notes to 'Yo Ho (A Pirate's Life for Me)'. Then he switched back to his favorite tune.

Lance gave the parrot an odd look. 'The bird's caught pirate fever too?'

'He was Jasper's,' Aunt Olivia explained. 'Jasper had pirate fever all year long.'

'That he did,' Lance said with a chuckle. Then he became more somber. 'I wish Jasper was still here to enjoy Dead Eye Days.'

Gizmo's hopping became more frantic and his squawks became louder.

'He's not used to having so many people in here all at once.' I handed the freshly printed sheet of paper to Lance. 'He'll settle down in a minute.'

'It's all right, Gizmo,' Auntie O said to the bird. 'We're going now.' She addressed Lance as she led the way out the kitchen door. 'How about a glass of iced tea over at the carriage house?'

'Your homemade brew?' he asked, sounding hopeful.

'Of course.'

'Then that's a definite yes.'

As Lance and Auntie O headed for the carriage house, I said goodbye to Gizmo and Stardust before shutting and locking the back door. Callum and I got into his truck with the dogs and set off.

It didn't take long to reach Old Birch Road. I didn't see any other vehicles on the way or any cars at the foot of the forest road. We ended up backtracking and parking Callum's truck out of sight, a few feet off Larkspur Lane on an overgrown dirt track that was barely wide enough to fit the vehicle. Then we returned to Old Birch Road on foot. There was still no sign of anyone else in the area, but it was early yet, with a hint of light still in the sky.

We made our way along the forest road, Callum and I holding hands and each of us in charge of one leashed dog. Flossie and Fancy had their noses to the ground and their tails wagging as we made our way through the growing darkness.

'Apologies in advance if we end up sitting in the woods half the night for nothing,' I said, speaking quietly even though we seemed to be the only people on the road.

'Time alone with you is never wasted,' Callum said.

He sounded so sincere that I had to stop to give him a kiss.

Fancy let out an 'a-woo'.

'Right,' Callum said with a nod at the dogs. 'Not completely alone. We do have our chaperones. I guess that means we can't get up to too much mischief.'

'Too bad,' I said with a grin as I took Callum's hand and started walking again.

A twig snapped somewhere nearby.

I stopped walking and tightened my grip on Callum's hand. 'What was that?' I whispered, hoping we hadn't accidentally interrupted Giles Gilroy's clandestine meeting.

The dogs stood with their muscles tense and their noses pointed toward the woods to our left. Fancy let out a low growl that sent a tremor of fear down my spine.

'Maybe we should . . .' Callum started to say.

Four men dressed in black burst out of the forest, two from each side of the road.

'FBI! Hands where we can see them!' one of the men shouted.

I raised my hands as my heart nearly skidded to a halt in my chest. Beside me, Callum raised his hands as well, his muscles taut. The FBI agents converged on us. My pulse pounded in my ears as terror raced through my bloodstream. The agents wore bulletproof vests and carried guns that glinted in a menacing way in the light of the rising moon. At least they weren't pointing the weapons at us.

'Flossie, Fancy, sit,' I said, managing to keep the wobble in my voice to a minimum.

They did as they were told, but they were clearly uneasy and Fancy let out a quiet whine.

'What's this all about?' Callum asked as the agents checked us for weapons.

I was impressed by how calm and steady he sounded.

The agents didn't bother to answer his question.

When they were satisfied that we posed no danger to them, they backed off a few paces. I brought my arms back down to my sides with relief, and Callum did the same.

'What are you doing here?' the tallest agent asked in a no-nonsense voice.

'Walking our dogs,' Callum replied, still calm and collected.

I was grateful he'd spoken up. My knees were trembling and my voice probably would have done the same if I'd tried to use it.

'In the dark?' another agent asked, skeptical.

'We like moonlit strolls,' Callum said, managing to sound completely innocent. 'We weren't expecting it to be quite this dark here in the woods.'

The tallest agent spoke again. 'We have to ask you to leave the area.' He touched a hand to his earpiece. After listening for a moment, he swore under his breath. 'No time.' He spoke into his radio next. 'Everyone back in position.' He addressed Callum and me again. 'You two, come with me and make sure your dogs stay quiet.'

I kept a firm grip on Callum's hand as we followed the tall, broad-shouldered agent. He led us off the road and on to a narrow trail that had likely been made by wildlife. After a short but brisk trek through the woods, we arrived at a clearing. Two black SUVs were parked there. They looked just like the one I'd seen parked outside the Moonstruck Diner the day before. Come to think of it, the agent escorting us looked vaguely familiar, and I suspected he was one of the two dark-suited men I'd seen exiting the vehicle on Main Street.

Beyond the SUVs was a rutted dirt track that disappeared into the trees. I could see it only because of the powerful flashlight our guide had turned on.

The agent opened the back door of one of the SUVs and ushered us into the vehicle. 'Sit tight and don't make a sound,' he ordered before shutting the door. He remained standing outside the vehicle and shut off his flashlight.

The dogs climbed up on to the seat with us, Fancy sitting on Callum's lap and Flossie lying across mine. They whined quietly and we stroked their fur in an attempt to calm them.

'It's OK, girls,' I whispered.

I could tell that the agent outside the vehicle was talking into his radio, but I couldn't make out his words. Then he fell silent. Minutes ticked by, ever so slowly.

Callum's hand sought mine in the darkness. 'You doing OK?' he asked, his voice barely audible.

'A little jittery,' I admitted, 'but otherwise fine. You?'

He gave my hand a squeeze. 'Not quite the evening we planned, but I guess this is just a plot twist, right?'

'I prefer my plot twists in books and movies, rather than real life,' I said.

That got a low chuckle out of Callum, and he leaned over to kiss my cheek.

Several more minutes passed in silence. Then shouts erupted in the darkness.

I heard multiple agents call out, 'FBI!' but I couldn't make out what else they said.

We sat tensely in the vehicle, the dogs whining again. A few minutes later, the commotion had finally died down.

The agent stationed outside the SUV opened the back door. 'I'll give you a ride to your vehicle. Where is it?'

Callum gave him directions and the agent nodded. He shut the door and spoke into his radio before climbing into the driver's seat. He turned the SUV around and followed the dirt track slowly through the woods, branches brushing against the sides of the vehicle along the way.

'What was that all about?' I asked. 'Did you arrest someone?'
I was hoping the agents had caught Giles Gilroy in the act of
whatever criminal activity he was involved with, but I didn't want
to let on that we knew anything about that.

'You picked the wrong night for a romantic stroll through the
forest,' the agent grumbled.

'Did you just bust a smuggling ring or something?' Callum asked,
also pretending we didn't know anything.

'In a sense. We're talking black-market antiquities, though, not
drugs.' The agent didn't offer any further details, but that was enough
to satisfy my curiosity.

Eventually, we reached Callum's truck and we climbed out of
the SUV with the dogs.

'Maybe stick to moonlit strolls on the beach from now on,' the
FBI agent advised.

We didn't bother to comment, instead bundling into Callum's
truck and getting the heck out of there.

'That was an adventurous date,' Callum remarked once we were
back on Larkspur Lane, heading home.

'For our next date, how about we just order pizza and watch
baseball?' I suggested.

Callum laughed. 'I'm all for that.' He glanced my way. 'I'm
assuming Giles Gilroy is one of the people they arrested, so I guess
that solves one mystery.'

I nodded. 'We now know why he was having meetings on Old
Birch Road. Probably with Samuel Kilduff. But is Giles also a killer?'

Callum turned the truck into the farm's driveway. 'I'm sure you'll
figure that out.'

I leaned back in my seat. 'Nope. I'm planning to leave everything
to the police from now on. I like solving mysteries, but getting
tangled up in an FBI operation was a little too much excitement for
me. My only plan at the moment is to enjoy the rest of Dead Eye
Days like a normal person.'

Callum parked next to the farmhouse. 'I'd usually say that normal
is overrated, but in this case, I'm right there with you.'

We made no move to get out of the truck. I slipped my hand into
my pocket and fingered the aquamarine and carnelian crystals I'd
put there earlier in the evening. Then I mustered the courage to take
a leap.

'And I'm right here with you.' I shifted in my seat so I could face him. 'Meaning, it's not too soon and I'd really like to meet your family.'

Even with only the moonlight to see by, I didn't miss Callum's smile or the happy glint in his eyes. He leaned in to kiss me, putting a hand to my face and running his thumb over my cheekbone. As our lips touched, my eyes drifted shut, but then Fancy 'woo-wooed' at us from the back seat.

Our laughter interrupted our kiss, but we made up for that a few minutes later when we said goodnight on the back porch. Once the dogs and I were in the farmhouse and heading upstairs to bed with Stardust, I pulled the aquamarine crystal from my pocket and ran my thumb over its smooth surface, a big smile on my face.

THIRTY-EIGHT

'What do you think?' I asked Flossie and Fancy the next morning as I checked my reflection in the full-length mirror in my bedroom.

Fancy yipped and bayed while Flossie gave a woof of approval and danced around in a circle.

I smiled at the dogs' reflections in the mirror. 'I'd say the same about you too.'

They wore their Jolly Roger bandannas and I'd brushed out their fur that morning until it gleamed.

I smoothed out my skirt and decided that I approved of my appearance as well. I'd ordered the costume a couple of weeks earlier, after spending a lot of time searching online for the right one. I didn't want anything too revealing, but I also didn't want to end up with heatstroke from walking around in a too-warm outfit on a summer's day.

In the end, I'd settled on a costume of a knee-length black skirt with a jagged hem, a peasant blouse that I wore off my shoulders and a front-lacing, red corset with metal fasteners in the shape of skulls. A black-and-gold striped sash tied at my waist and I'd put gold hoops in my ears. The ensemble probably would have looked best with tall boots, but because of the weather, I'd opted for a pair of worn combat boots instead.

As I took one last look at my reflection, Stardust scampered across the room, leapt into the air and swatted at the hem of my skirt. Her claws got caught in the fabric and she swung like a trapeze artist.

I grabbed her and held her in a gentle hold as I carefully dislodged her claws from my skirt. She left a couple of small holes behind, but I didn't think anyone would notice.

'As for you, scallywag,' I said as I nuzzled my nose against the kitten's head, 'I'm afraid you're staying home with Gizmo. Maybe he'll teach you how to talk like a pirate. Arrr!'

Stardust looked at me with her hazel eyes and let out a pitiful mew.

My heart melted, but I couldn't change my mind. A pirate festival was no place for a kitten. I wasn't even sure if the dogs would like it. I was in Los Angeles on the fourth of July, but Auntie O had told me that the fireworks hadn't bothered Flossie and Fancy. Still, if they showed any sign of distress when the cannons and guns started firing during the battle reenactment, I'd bundle them into my car and bring them home.

When Flossie, Fancy and I arrived in the center of town, it took me several minutes to find a parking spot. Tourists and locals had flocked to the area to take in the final festivities, with the biggest draw being the reenactment out in the cove. Adults and children – many dressed as pirates – clogged the sidewalks on Main Street and filled the park by the beach. Finally, I found a free spot a few blocks away from Main Street, and we walked over to the park, where I'd arranged to meet Tessa.

The throngs of people didn't seem to faze Flossie and Fancy. I was probably more uneasy than they were. Getting mixed up in a big crowd of people wasn't my favorite thing to do. I wished Callum had come with us, but he had a few more jobs to take care of on the farm, so he would meet up with us later on, hopefully in time for the battle reenactment.

We eventually made our way over to the gazebo, where a band was once again playing sea shanties. I spotted Tessa – decked out in her pirate costume – and I waved to catch her attention. She hurried over to meet us and fussed over the dogs while they wagged their tails and looked up at her with adoring eyes.

'Let's get a little farther away from the music,' Tessa suggested, having to shout to be heard.

I was more than happy to agree with her. The band sounded

great, but close to the gazebo the music was too loud to be comfortable. We wound our way through the crowd until we neared the line of stalls where vendors sold their wares. A short line outside Fae's fortune teller's tent suggested that she was open for business that day. We walked until the music faded to pleasant background noise and the crowd had thinned enough that we had some space to ourselves.

Tessa tucked her arm through mine as we strolled along. 'Valentina called me an hour ago,' she said. 'The word at the police station is that the FBI have been investigating Giles Gilroy for a while. Apparently, dealing in black-market antiquities isn't a new endeavor for him. Good thing I bought that vintage dress already. I don't think his shop's going to reopen for a while, if ever, and I wouldn't shop there again anyway.'

'I'm glad that's one mystery wrapped up,' I said. 'If Giles is also the killer, at least he's in custody. Hopefully, the police can add more charges soon.'

'With luck, all the mysteries will be solved in short order.' Tessa perked up and waved to someone. 'There's Brody.'

I followed her line of sight and waved when I saw Brody, in his police uniform, patrolling the park. He waved back at us and then disappeared into the crowd closer to the gazebo.

'There's supposed to be some sword fighting starting in a minute,' Tessa said, leading the way over to a small stage set up beyond the line of vendor booths.

The stage was empty as we headed that way, but by the time we reached it, two men fully decked out as pirates, with swords at their belts, ran on to the platform and started shouting insults at one another. They drew their swords, still trading insults, and then rushed toward each other, blades raised. More people gathered around the stage once they realized that a show was underway.

The choreographed scene drew plenty of laughter and awe as the pirates dueled and delivered humorous lines. I spotted Ajax Wolfgang in the crowd. He seemed to be enjoying himself but, unsurprisingly, his cousin wasn't with him. I turned my attention back to the scene playing out on the stage, but then glanced at Ajax again. He moved through the crowd and approached a woman who was also watching the stage. When he touched her shoulder and she turned around, I realized the woman was Elsie.

Ajax leaned in and said something to her with a grin on his face.

She shook her head and said something back, looking annoyed. As she walked away from him, Ajax appeared confused, but he soon wandered off in the opposite direction from the one Elsie had taken.

The actors drew their scene to a close, with one pretending to die dramatically, ending by rolling off the back of the stage. The audience laughed and clapped.

'It's getting hot,' Tessa said, fanning herself. 'How about I grab us a couple of slushies?'

That sounded like a great idea to me. Tessa told me that she'd get the drinks while I waited near the stage with the dogs. I noticed that Elsie had stopped by one of the closest vendor booths, one selling handmade jewelry. I led the dogs over to join her.

'Hi, Elsie,' I greeted. 'How are you doing?'

She gave me a sad smile. 'All right. It's hard to be here without Jasper, but I know he wouldn't want me to miss out on Dead Eye Days, especially with the big reenactment coming up shortly.'

'This is my first pirate festival,' I said. 'I hear the battle is quite a sight.'

'It's always a crowd pleaser. Jasper wanted to be part of it, but it's a professional group of performers they bring in for it.'

I wasn't surprised that it was a reenactment for professionals. I'd seen videos online from previous years. There were canons and muskets firing, and pirates swinging from ropes and running around the ships. What looked chaotic and spontaneous was likely well choreographed and thoroughly practiced.

I decided to steer the conversation in another direction. 'Was Ajax bothering you a moment ago?'

'Oh, him.' Elsie waved off the question. 'Nothing I can't handle. I probably confused him, though.'

'Because you seemed friendlier with him the other day?' I asked.

She looked embarrassed. 'Yes, I'm not proud of it, but I did pretend for a while that I was enjoying his company because I was hoping to find out if he had killed Jasper.'

Maybe it shouldn't have surprised me that I wasn't the only one doing some amateur sleuthing, but I hadn't expected Elsie to say that.

'Did you get any good clues?' I asked, not sure that she'd share them with me even if she had managed to get important information from Ajax.

'Not a thing,' she said. 'And I couldn't keep up the pretense any longer. The guy is full of himself, not to mention way too young for me.' She waved at someone in the crowd closer to the gazebo. 'Sorry, I'm meeting some friends.'

'No problem,' I managed to say before she hurried off.

A new scene was starting to play out on the stage, so the dogs and I wandered back in that direction.

I was smiling and laughing at the actors' antics when a familiar tune started playing behind me.

The smile slipped from my face. It was the song I'd come to think of as Gizmo's tune.

I whipped around to see where the music was coming from.

About ten feet away, Lance Earley hit a button on his phone. The ringtone stopped abruptly.

As Lance raised the phone to his ear, his gaze locked with mine.

It was as if his gray eyes hardened to stone as I looked into them.

My heart thudding, I turned away from him and tugged on the dogs' leashes.

'This way, girls,' I said, a note of urgency entering my voice as I led them through the crowd of spectators who'd gathered to watch the latest sword-fighting scene.

When we broke free of the thickest part of the crowd, I glanced back. I could no longer see Lance.

My heart rate grew slightly less frantic, but I couldn't shake the fear buzzing through me. I hurried over to Fae's fortune teller's tent at the far end of the line of vendor booths. There was currently no queue outside, so I peeked in through the open flap.

Fae, wearing a gauzy scarf over her hair and with more bangles on her wrists than usual, sat at a small table in the middle of the tent, which was lit only by flickering battery-operated candles.

'Georgie!' she exclaimed when she saw me. 'Would you like me to read your cards?' She gestured at the deck of tarot cards sitting on the purple velvet cloth spread over the table.

'Actually, I can't stay,' I said quickly. 'I just have a question for you.'

'I'll answer it if I can.'

'Does Lance Earley ever visit your store?'

The question clearly surprised her. 'I don't recall him ever shopping there.'

My shoulders sagged and I wondered if I could be wrong.

'But,' she added, 'he was there recently fixing an electrical problem.'

My pulse picked up again. 'Was that the day Jasper was killed?'

She thought for a moment. 'I think it was, now that you mention it. But in the evening, after I closed the shop.'

'Were you burning incense that day, by any chance?'

'You do ask the most interesting questions,' she said as she regarded me closely. 'Does this have something to do with the murder?'

'It might,' I said, anxious energy buzzing through me.

'Yes, I burn incense most days, and I know I did that day because I was doing several readings in the afternoon, including a couple after hours.'

'Thank you, Fae.' I ducked out of the tent before she could question me further about the reason for my brief interrogation.

I looked left and right, but I didn't see Lance anywhere. I moved off to the side of Fae's fortune teller's tent and sent a quick text message to Tessa before calling Brody. I wasn't surprised when he didn't pick up since he was on duty and I'd called his personal number.

A loud cheer rang out and the crowd in the park surged toward the beach. I checked the time on my phone. The battle reenactment was about to begin. I tried to spot Tessa or Brody in the river of people, but it was hopeless. I backed away from the vendor booths, moving closer to the beer garden, so Flossie, Fancy and I wouldn't get tangled up in the flood of people hurrying across the park.

I turned my attention back to my phone and put a call through to Chief Stratton.

To my relief, he answered after three rings.

'Chief, it's Georgie Johansen,' I said as the first cannon fired in the cove. Musket and pistol fire followed. 'I'm at the park near the beach.'

'Sorry, Georgie,' Stratton said. 'I'm having trouble hearing you. There's a lot of background noise.'

Flossie let out a low growl as she glared at a spot behind me. I was about to turn around when something cold and hard pressed into my back.

Then Lance spoke into my ear, his voice low and menacing.

'Drop the phone.'

THIRTY-NINE

When I didn't budge, Lance moved the gun so I could see it, and pointed it at the spaniels. Both dogs were growling now.

'Georgie?' I could hear Chief Stratton say on the other end of the line.

I dropped the phone on the grass.

Lance kicked it and it skittered away, coming to rest beside the beer garden fence.

'Call off the dogs,' he ordered next.

When I hesitated again, he added, 'Do you really think anyone will notice a few more gunshots?'

The battle reenactment was in full swing now, with shouts and cheers joining the sharp report of gunfire and the loud booms from the cannons. The park seemed to have emptied, with everyone watching the scene out on the water.

'Flossie, Fancy, go find Tessa,' I said, somehow managing to keep my voice steady.

The spaniels looked at me, uncertain, before growling at Lance again.

'Go find Tessa,' I repeated more urgently.

The dogs backed away, glancing between me and Lance.

'Go!' I urged, terrified that Lance might lose his patience and use his gun.

With one last worried look at me, the dogs trotted off, their leashes trailing behind them.

My sigh of relief was cut off when Lance pressed the butt of the gun into my side. He used his free hand to hold my arm in an iron grip.

'Now walk,' he ordered.

I wanted to scream for help, but I knew if I made a sound, he'd shoot me. He was right that one more gunshot would probably go unnoticed, even if a handgun didn't sound quite like the muskets and pistols being fired off by the actors on the ships.

Lance half dragged me around the perimeter of the beer garden. At the back of the fenced-off tent, I spied a police cruiser among the vehicles sitting in a volunteer parking area. The spark of hope that lit up inside of me was snuffed out almost immediately. The cruiser and all the other vehicles were empty.

Lance let go of my arms but kept the gun trained on me as he pulled a set of keys out of his pocket and hit the fob. A pickup truck unlocked with a beep. He yanked open the passenger side door and motioned with his head for me to climb in.

'Get behind the wheel. You're driving.'

I glanced around, but there was no one in sight, no one to help me.

Lance pressed the butt of the gun into my back, so I climbed into the truck, seeing no other option. I scooted across the center console and into the driver's seat. Lance climbed in after me, always keeping his weapon pointed my way. He passed me the keys, and I briefly wondered if I could use them as a weapon, but they'd be no match for the gun.

I started the engine and gripped the steering wheel so hard that my knuckles turned white. It was the only way to keep my hands from trembling.

Lance ordered me to maneuver the truck out of the parking area and on to Ocean Drive.

'Step on it!' he commanded when I tried to move us along at a snail's pace.

Again, I saw no other option but to obey. Of course, Ocean Drive – which was busy when I arrived at the festival earlier – was now empty. As we left the center of town behind, a sickening sensation spread through my body. I had to grip the steering wheel even harder to keep myself from shaking like a leaf.

'None of this would be happening if not for that damn bird,' Lance said as he kept the gun pointed at my side.

'He learned to sing your ringtone when you were at Jasper's house on the night of the murder,' I said, certain I was right about that.

'I knew you had put two and two together. I saw it in your eyes back there at the park when I answered my phone.' Lance shook his head, annoyed. 'I've already changed my ringtone, but I'll have to take care of the bird next, just to be safe. Who knows what else he'll give away?'

That sent a flicker of anger through me. He wouldn't have a chance to harm Gizmo. Not if I had anything to do with it.

'This is all about Patty Buchanan, isn't it?' I guessed.

'Even without the parrot, you know too much,' Lance said, his voice hard. 'You should learn to mind your own business.'

My fingers began to ache from gripping the steering wheel so hard. 'I will, if you let me go.'

'I can't do that.' There was a hint of what might have been regret in his voice when he spoke again. 'I'm not a bad guy, you know.'

I glanced at the gun, incredulous. 'You murdered Patty and Jasper, and now you're about to kill me.'

'Patty was an accident.'

I glanced his way again. 'What happened?'

While I wanted to keep him focused on anything other than the gun he had pointed at me, I was also genuinely curious. Apparently, my curiosity could survive even during a life-threatening situation like the one I found myself in now.

'I waited for her one day when she was at Dean's place and met up with her as she was leaving. I tried to convince her that she was a fool to stay with Dean Haskell. She would have been so much better off with me. But she couldn't see it. She claimed he was the love of her life.' Lance scoffed. 'That man always gets whatever he wants. Beautiful women, money – they just drop into his lap. It's always been that way. I wanted Patty to see that I was the better man. I thought she might just need a little extra convincing, but then she started fighting with me. I gave her a shove and she fell. It was just bad luck that she hit her head and died.'

'So you buried her there on Dean's property,' I said, my voice blunt. 'Did you find the treasure while you were at it?'

'I didn't find anything because there's nothing there.' Frustration radiated off of him. 'That map has got to be a hoax. If I could get my hands on the person who made it . . .' He shook his head. '*They* caused this mess.'

I didn't think anyone was to blame other than him, but I didn't bother saying so. Antagonizing him probably wasn't a good idea.

'Take the next right,' Lance ordered.

I was surprised by the demand. I'd expected him to direct me to drive far out of town, not a mere few minutes away from Main Street.

I did as I was told and realized we were heading for the lighthouse at the southern point of the cove. A long paved road led toward the white-and-red light tower. Even though I hadn't been out this way since moving to Twilight Cove, I knew that the lighthouse was unmanned. With tourists and locals alike transfixed by the pirate battle reenactment, the point of land that jutted out into the ocean appeared to be deserted.

When I glanced to my right, I saw the gorgeous tall ships out in the cove, with costumed people moving about on the decks. Cannons still boomed and guns still fired. As long as the reenactment continued, Lance would be able to shoot me without anyone noticing the noise of the gun going off.

'Pull around the other side of the lighthouse,' Lance instructed as we drew close to the majestic tower.

That would put us out of sight of anyone in or around the cove who might glance our way. I could try crashing the vehicle, hoping to hurt Lance more than myself, but most likely that would only set off the gun, which remained pointed at my side.

I drove around the lighthouse and parked, hoping I could figure out a way to save myself. So far, any viable ideas escaped me.

Lance climbed out of the truck first and gestured for me to follow him out the passenger side door. I left the truck door standing open and moved toward the front of the vehicle when Lance instructed me to do so. That left me with the truck before me, the lighthouse to my left and steep cliffs to my right and behind me. Despite the noise from the reenactment, I could hear the waves crashing against the rocks below.

A sea breeze ruffled my hair and the sun warmed my shoulders. The beautiful summer's day was distinctly at odds with the gravity of my predicament.

'So you killed Jasper because you didn't want him finding Patty's remains?' I asked Lance, hoping to buy myself some time.

'I couldn't risk him digging Patty up, now, could I? I destroyed that stupid map as soon as I got home that night.'

'You weren't worried about the other copies?'

'Copies?' Lance said with disdain. 'There weren't any. Jasper's safe was unlocked when I was there. I checked it and there were no copies.'

Apparently, it hadn't occurred to him that someone else might have a copy.

'But how did you know where the map led?' That was something I couldn't figure out.

'I stopped by Jasper's house to give him a quote on replacing an electrical panel in his study. He had the map out on his desk, the fool. I got a glimpse of it before he whisked it away, but that's all I needed. I've got a photographic memory, you see. I knew from Jasper's announcement at the inn that he was aware of the stream diversion and would read the map correctly. If all this had happened ten or twenty years ago, I would have moved Patty before anyone could dig for the supposed treasure, but I've got a bad back now. I couldn't handle the digging.'

'But someone was digging,' I said. 'Someone uncovered Patty's remains.'

'I don't know who that was, but I'm not worried. With you gone and my ringtone changed, there's nothing to connect me to her death. Getting rid of the bird will just be added insurance.'

Anger flashed through me again. I couldn't stand the thought of this cruel man harming Gizmo or any other animal.

Lance gestured toward the cliff with the gun. 'Move over there.'

I knew he planned to shoot me at the edge of the cliff, so my body would fall into the ocean. That way, he wouldn't have to move me, saving his sore back.

I stood my ground. 'If you're going to shoot me, you'll have to do it here.'

'Don't test me,' he warned. 'I'll find a way to roll your body over the cliff.'

Out of the corner of my eye, I noticed movement near the top of the lighthouse, but I didn't dare look up.

Slowly, I backed toward the cliff. I was getting perilously close to the edge when the lighthouse door suddenly swung open and slammed against the exterior wall.

Lance spun around, pointing his gun toward the lighthouse and the empty doorway. In that same moment, Euclid dove down from his perch atop the lighthouse.

At the last second, Lance glanced up, but it was too late.

Euclid extended his talons and landed on Lance's head.

Lance yowled and dropped the gun as he fell to his knees.

I charged forward and snatched the weapon off the ground.

Euclid released his hold on Lance's head and beat his wings, flying up into the air where he wheeled around in a circle.

Out in the middle of the cove, the gun and cannon fire reached a crescendo.

Lance, gripping his head, let out another yell, this one a mixture of pain and fury. It was almost drowned out by the noise from the reenactment.

His eyes flashed as he glared at me and climbed to his feet.

I gripped the gun in my trembling hands, keeping it pointed at the ground. I was wondering if I could bring myself to use it when the air wavered in front of me.

Fancy materialized mid-leap as she tackled Lance to the ground, getting another yell out of him. Flossie charged around the lighthouse and joined her sister. They stood over Lance, front paws on his chest, teeth bared and growling.

Lance froze, his eyes wide.

The noise from the pirate battle covered the sound of approaching footfalls, so I nearly jumped out of my skin when Brody came running around the lighthouse, his weapon drawn.

'Flossie, Fancy, come here!' I called to the spaniels.

They saw Brody coming and backed away from their prisoner.

'Don't move!' Brody ordered Lance.

Flossie and Fancy hurried over to my side. I set the gun on the grass and then moved a few feet away from it, dropping to my knees so I could hug the dogs. They covered my face with kisses while I laughed and cried and trembled.

When I looked up, Brody had Lance in handcuffs and more uniformed officers were converging on the scene. Tessa and Callum came running behind them.

Out on the water, a final cannon fired, followed by a loud, victorious cheer.

The battle was over.

FORTY

'I can't believe I missed out on everything!' Roxy lamented several days after the terrifying events that concluded at the lighthouse.

'You didn't miss this,' I pointed out.

We'd gathered at the community center, along with at least thirty other townsfolk. The police, while excavating the site where Patty's remains were found, had unearthed a metal box about ten feet away from the skeleton. The box and its contents had since been declared to have nothing to do with Patty's murder, and so they had been released to the town. Now, the mayor of Twilight Cove, Latoya Harris, was about to open the box while those of us in the audience watched. Although the police knew what was inside, none of the rest of us did.

While some people were still hoping the box contained pirate treasure, many had given up on that hope. Flynn, who'd never believed that the map led to real pirate loot, stood near the front of the crowd, his arms crossed over his chest.

'That box is not from the eighteenth century,' he grumbled. 'It's probably not more than a hundred years old.'

I wasn't an expert on metal boxes or when they first came into use, but it certainly didn't look like a quintessential pirate treasure chest.

'It's probably just a time capsule,' Roxy said, sounding almost as unimpressed as Flynn.

'Time capsules are cool,' Tessa told her.

Roxy squished her lips to one side, clearly disagreeing, but she said nothing.

Mayor Harris asked for quiet and a hush fell over the crowd. Then, wearing cotton gloves, she opened the box.

Everyone in the audience inched closer to the table and the people in the back rows craned their necks to see better.

One by one, Mayor Harris removed items from the box, naming them as she did so. The first item, a newspaper, dated the contents to April 1953. It was a copy of the local paper, the *Twilight Cove Gazette*, which was still in business.

'See,' Roxy whispered. 'Just a time capsule.'

Tessa nudged the teen with her elbow. 'Time capsules are cool,' she repeated, also in a whisper, before turning her attention back to the open box.

The other items in the box included a one-dollar bill, a program from the play the local high school had put on that year, a packet of Hot Tamales candy, a yo-yo and – finally – a piece of paper that had seen better days.

'Unfortunately, the items sustained some damage,' Mayor Harris said. 'The box rusted and some liquid seeped inside over time. However, I think I can make out the writing.'

With the aid of a magnifying glass, Mayor Harris studied the writing on the stained paper before reading it aloud.

Dear person of the future,
I hope you had fun searching for this treasure. It might not be

pirate gold, but it's a slice of 1953. I hope life in the future is as exciting as I imagine it to be.

Sincerely,

Gideon Adams, age fifteen.

'That's my grandad!' Rayelle exclaimed from somewhere in the crowd. She worked her way closer to the table so she could get a look at the note. 'And that's the same kind of paper the map was drawn on.' She shook her head in disbelief. 'The map was made by my grandad, on vintage paper. No wonder I found it in the inn's attic. He died four years ago. I never heard him mention the map or the time capsule.'

She looked as though she didn't know whether to laugh or cry, and maybe that's exactly how she felt. I'd heard from Catherine that Rayelle had started counseling to help her deal with the guilt she felt over Jasper's death. I hoped that would, in time, bring her a sense of peace.

Some people gathered closer around the table for a better look at the objects found in the time capsule. I had Flossie and Fancy with me, and I could feel them growing restless at my side, so I decided to leave the community center. Tessa, Callum and Roxy accompanied me.

Outside, the sun shone down from a brilliant blue sky, but there was a cooler touch to the air these days. It was the last day of August, and fall was right around the corner.

Our small group gathered in the shade cast by a stately maple tree that grew on the lawn outside the community center. Flossie and Fancy sniffed around the base of the tree as the rest of us chatted.

'I get that Lance Earley killed Jasper because he wanted to destroy the map so no one would find Patty's remains,' Roxy said.

'And because Jasper had already studied the map,' Tessa chimed in.

'But why did that writer break into all those houses?' Roxy asked.

She'd arrived home from visiting her father just the day before. I'd given her a condensed version of the events she'd missed as we headed into the community center, but I hadn't had a chance to explain everything.

'Ajax was worried that Jasper might have made a copy of the

map,' I said, sharing information I'd learned from Brody and Chief Stratton in the days since Lance's arrest.

It turned out that Giles had told the truth about his late-night visit to Jasper's house. He simply wanted to peek in the window at Jasper's antiques, but he found the kitchen window smashed and hightailed it out of there. Giles had told the police that he did dig for the treasure – before selling the map to Jasper – but he didn't know about the stream diversion, so his search was fruitless.

As for Ajax, when the police found red mud caked on his hiking boots – after I'd passed on that clue to Brody – the writer confessed to the break-ins.

'Ajax broke into Rayelle's studio too,' Tessa added. 'He was staying at the Twilight Inn and overheard Rayelle talking to her mother about the fact that she'd found the map and made a copy before selling it.'

'He wanted all copies of the map destroyed,' I said.

'Because of his upcoming book,' Callum added. He and I had already talked over the recent events several times. 'Ajax was worried that the map might turn out to be real, thereby disproving his claim that Dead Eye Dawson never made it this far north. But then – just in case the map was real – he decided to look for the treasure, with Flynn's help. Flynn knew about the stream diversion and led them to the right spot. When they found a human skull instead of treasure, they freaked out and took off.'

'All those guys are bananas,' Roxy muttered.

Nobody disagreed with her.

I wished that Jasper had kept the map a secret until after he'd dug for the treasure, but wishing for such things was pointless. There was no changing the past. According to Aunt Olivia, Lance was right about Jasper knowing about the stream diversion. We figured he was probably planning to dig at a time when Dean wasn't home. Unfortunately, his argument with Flynn had led him to share his news with the town earlier than intended, giving Lance the opportunity to kill him and steal the map.

Jackie from the Moonstruck Diner came out of the community center and spotted us beneath the tree. She walked over to join us.

'Georgie, I'm so glad you're OK,' she said.

The entire town had probably heard about my almost-deadly encounter with Lance by now.

After I thanked Jackie, Tessa asked her, 'How's Dean doing these days?'

Sadness clouded Jackie's face. 'It's been hard on him, finding out what happened to Patty and knowing she was buried there on his land all those years.' Tears welled in her eyes and she took a second to compose herself. 'Lance always had a terrible temper and a jealous streak. That's partly why I divorced him, but I never imagined he was a killer.' She managed a sad smile. 'I've been checking in on Dean every day. I'm heading over there right now, in fact.'

'Please tell him we're keeping him in our thoughts,' I requested.

Jackie rested a hand on my arm. 'Thank you. I'll do that.'

She left us then and climbed into a car parked nearby.

I hoped Dean would be all right in time. He'd turned out to be the good guy Tessa and Olivia believed him to be. Thanks to my aunt, I now knew that he'd inherited a substantial sum of money from his parents many years ago. That inheritance, rather than pirate treasure, had allowed him to build his dream home, which was big enough to host his siblings and his many cousins, nieces and nephews.

'OK,' Roxy said to me, picking up our conversation again, 'but how did anyone know that Lance had kidnapped you?'

I smiled at the spaniels. 'That's thanks to Flossie and Fancy.'

Flossie wagged her tail and Fancy let out an 'a-woo'.

'Georgie texted me to tell me that she knew Lance was the killer and she thought he knew that she'd figured it out,' Tessa explained. 'As soon as I got that text, I found Brody. Then Flossie and Fancy found us in the crowd and seemed desperate for us to follow them. They took off along Ocean Drive, heading south. Brody and I jumped in his cruiser and drove after them. We picked them up from the side of the road and they barked like crazy when we reached the turnoff to the lighthouse.' She gave Flossie and Fancy each an affectionate pat on the head. 'They knew where to go.'

I knew that Euclid had played a big part in saving me too, but I didn't mention that. I thought it would sound too far-fetched to anyone but me and the dogs.

After the police had taken Lance away from the lighthouse, I'd worried that Brody might have seen Fancy camouflage herself, or witnessed the lighthouse door swinging open – probably with Flossie staring at it – but he never gave any indication that he'd noticed anything of the sort. The more time that passed, the more certain I felt that the spaniels' secret was still safe.

More people began spilling out of the community center. I didn't feel like hanging around in case I got peppered with questions about my terrifying and too-fresh experience. So, with my beloved dogs and my friends around me, I headed back home to the farm.

FORTY-ONE

That evening, Callum and I walked the dogs through the woods and down to the secluded beach I now thought of as ours. While Flossie and Fancy splashed around in the shallows, Callum and I strolled slowly along the shoreline, my arm around his waist and his resting across my shoulders.

A comforting sense of contentment had settled over me. Jasper's killer was behind bars and I could tell by looking into my aunt's eyes that Lance's arrest was helping her deal with her friend's death. Gizmo had gone to his new home the day before, and though it was hard to say goodbye to the bird, my heart swelled with happiness for him. Dean's niece had turned out to be a perfect match for the African grey parrot and the two of them had fallen in love immediately.

As for Stardust, she was now officially a permanent member of my family. Cindy had removed the posters in her shop and the kitten now wore a pink collar with a heart-shaped tag with her name and my phone number engraved on it. At the moment, Star was hanging out with Aunt Olivia while Callum and I spent time with Flossie and Fancy.

'Javi must be happy,' I said as we left prints in the sand with our bare feet.

Callum's friend had hit home runs in back-to-back games that week.

'I talked to him last night,' Callum said. 'He's feeling good.'

I knew that had lifted a weight off Callum's shoulders. I liked how much he cared for his young friend.

Flossie and Fancy charged past us, water spraying up as they galloped through the breaking waves.

'And,' he added as we smiled at the spaniels' antics, 'I talked to my parents last night too.'

'They're coming soon?' I asked.

'Probably in mid-September.'

'I'm looking forward to meeting them. Really.'

Callum gave me a squeeze. 'They're going to love you.'

I hoped that was true. I was already a bit nervous because I really wanted to make a good impression on his family, but I'd meant it sincerely when I said I was looking forward to meeting his parents. I wanted to know more about this man who was claiming more and more of my heart each day.

We paused and faced the water, watching as the sun sank toward the horizon. The sea breeze ruffled my hair, and I tucked it behind my ear before leaning into Callum's side. I felt safe in his arms, and that was something I truly treasured, especially since that eventful last day of the pirate festival.

I glanced up at Callum and caught him watching me with a slight smile on his face and an unreadable expression in his eyes.

'What?' I asked, wondering what he could be thinking.

'You're full of surprises.'

I almost looked over my shoulder to see if there was someone else he might be addressing. 'I can't say anyone's ever said that to me before. Are you sure you've got the right person?'

Callum laughed and slid his arm away from my shoulders so he could face me and rest his hands on my upper arms. He looked right into my eyes and the intensity of his gaze sent pleasant chills dancing over my skin.

'I'm absolutely sure,' he said.

My heart decided to perform an acrobatic routine in my chest and it took me a moment to find enough breath to speak. 'How have I surprised you?'

He held up his left wrist so I could see the bracelet I'd made for him. 'I thought the beads were in a random design. I probably should have known better.'

I smiled. 'You figured it out?'

'I learned a bit of Morse code way back when I was a Boy Scout. I had to look it up online to decipher the message, but I got there.' The setting sun cast streaks of orange and pink across the western sky, and golden light danced in Callum's green eyes. 'It's the best coded message I've ever received.'

I'd arranged the beads so the black ones made a pattern of dots and dashes between the white ones. They spelled out, 'I really like

you too,' a response to the words he'd said to me back in June when
we'd shared our first kiss.

'I'm betting it's the only coded message you've ever received,'
I said.

He laughed. 'True. Then I should say it's the best message of
any kind that I've received.'

'Really?' I couldn't help sounding dubious.

His face became serious as he touched a hand to my cheek.
'Really, Georgie.'

I stared into his mesmerizing eyes for a moment before averting
my gaze. I traced a finger along his collarbone, staring at that point
instead of into his eyes.

'I could add more to the message.' I hesitated before I continued.
'It's a little scary for me, but I think I'm really falling for you.'

My heart threatened to stop beating in the wake of those words.

'Georgie.'

Callum waited until I found the courage to meet his eyes again.
The depth of emotion I saw in them nearly made my knees weak.

'You don't need to be scared of falling.' He tucked a stray lock
of hair behind my ear. 'I played major league baseball. I'm really
good at catching.' He kissed the top of my head. 'You can trust me
on that.'

I slipped my arms around him and rested my cheek against his
chest.

'I do,' I said with sincerity that reached as deep as the ocean. 'I
really, really do.'

In the shallows, the dogs stopped splashing about.

Fancy tipped her head back and bayed.

But it wasn't a mournful sound. It was a happy one, full of hope.

ACKNOWLEDGMENTS

I t has taken a team of dedicated individuals to bring the Magical Menagerie mysteries to life, and I'm truly grateful to each and every one. Special thanks to my agent, Jessica Faust, and my editor, Victoria Britton, for believing in this series and helping me to shape this story into the book it has become. Thanks also to Jody Holford for always being willing to read my early drafts and for being such a fan of Georgie and Callum. Thank you to Mary Karayel and the entire Severn House team, my review crew, my readers and everyone in the online book community who helps to spread the word about cozy mysteries.